I0606589

She'd suspected something wasn't right with this man, but now she was sure of it...

It had been dark and she had been half awake when they arrived the previous evening, so she hadn't seen anything of Armando's ranch. She was amazed at the lush pastures bordering the long driveway. The large herd of cattle grazing in the pasture, the long white horse barns off in the distance, and the beautiful Arabian horses lazily milling around the large paddock in front of the barns took her breath away.

She had no idea that Armando owned such a ranch, but she should have guessed from the posh furnishing of his home.

"What beautiful horses," she said, still looking out the limo window on her side.

"Yes, they are. I ride before breakfast. Please, let me know if you would like to join me." She could hear the smile in his voice as he continued, "I would enjoy your company very much."

"Where are we meeting this man?" Darcey asked, ignoring his invitation to ride and getting back to business.

"We will go to a mutual friend's home," he said. "Someone he trusts to be discreet."

They're adding another person? What hell happened to 'no one was to know about our meeting'? she fumed inwardly. Darcey was beginning to wonder, just what was going on. She didn't like the damn rules changing in the middle of the game and was going to tell Armando just how she felt about it. She turned and leaned forward to look him in the eye. "Hold it right there, buster," she bristled. "I thought just the three of us, you, me, and this mystery guy were the only ones to know about this meeting," she said emphatically. "What's with this new guy? I want to know just what's going on!" she demanded, and then her jaw dropped in fear.

"What is the matter, Darcey?" He reached for her hand. "You look like you have seen a ghost."

When Darcey Callahan tumbles for Brad Daniels, it starts her on a dark and perilous journey that quickly turns into her worst nightmare. Believing Brad has gone missing—while investigating a sabotage attempt of his top-secret project in Peru—Darcey dashes off to find him, setting in motion a series of events beyond her control. Awakening from a near-deadly car crash, she finds herself with no memory and a prisoner in the dangerous world of human trafficking, murders, and espionage. Held captive in Morocco until she can be "sold," she doesn't know whether to trust the stranger who has come to rescue her. Is he really willing to help her, or is this a nightmare from which she may never wake up?

KUDOS for *Inescapable ~ The Beginning*

"The story is well-thought out. It has a solid plot, with plenty of twists and turns, edge-of-your-seat tension, and intriguing characters. Darcey is utterly charming, and you can't help but root for her. I can't wait for the sequel." *~ Taylor Jones, The Review Team of Taylor Jones and Regan Murphy*

"*Inescapable: The Beginning* by Madge H. Gressley contains several different elements: some action, intrigue, suspense, and romance. I was instantly charmed by Darcey's character, and was engrossed in the book from the beginning to the end. The book had a fast pace, but it wasn't a whirlwind of activity. The plot and the characters had depth and were well thought out; and I didn't find the story line predictable…I also found that Darcey's reactions to the traumatic events that she suffered were realistic. Darcey's personality changes a bit after the injury and the drugs, but who she is at her core remained the same…Gressley has managed to combine the elements of suspense, intrigue, and romance to create a balanced and interesting story. I am really looking forward to reading more about Darcey and Brad in the next book." *~ Charity Rowell-Stansbury, On My Kindle Book Reviews*

"*Inescapable, The Beginning* is fast paced, intriguing, and exciting. Gressley's characters are well-developed and realistic. I found the plot not only solid, but thought-provoking and intense, almost too realistic. I couldn't put it down." *~ Regan Murphy, The Review Team of Taylor Jones and Regan Murphy*

INESCAPABLE

The Beginning

MADGE H. GRESSLEY

A Black Opal Books Publication

Fate works its strange mystic hold over us, weaving the threads of our lives together in an intricate-patterned tapestry of inescapable destinies.

PREFACE

The Crash

Five Weeks in the Future: Lima, Peru:

W atch Out!" Darcey screamed.

The limo had just entered the middle of an intersection, when Darcey caught sight of a huge, black SUV bearing down on them. She only had time to turn and look out of the window behind Armando before the SUV had broadsided them. It hit the limo in front of the back door panel on the passenger side. The impact threw Armando into Darcey, propelling her over and crushing her against the back door on the driver's side. She could feel the armrest cutting into her side.

A white-hot pain shot through her shoulder as her head slammed into the window.

The limo spun madly—tires screeched, metal crunched, glass shattered—and then it was flying through air. The vehicle rolled over repeatedly in slow motion, while Darcey and Armando tumbled over each other inside like laundry in a dryer. The limo finally came to rest on its side shuddering, and then silence, except for the rotation whir from one of the limo's wheels as it slowly wound down to a standstill.

Bright bursts of light flashed behind Darcey's eyes. She heard Armando utter several loud expletives in Spanish, and then something heavy hit her leg. She could feel a warm sticky substance sliding down her forehead.

Something hard poked Darcey in the back and it hurt like hell. A white-hot pain hit her as she tried to shift her position to call for Armando. She scrunched her eyes in pain as tears ran down her cheeks, then she screamed.

Catching her breath as the pain subsided, she tried again to reach out to Armando. "Armando! Armando!" she called as loud as she could, but she was sure it wasn't much above a whisper. "Are you okay?" She bit her lip as she tried to move to get a better look at Armando. The pain was excruciating.

She heard nothing but a small moan.

At least he's alive she thought, relieved.

She didn't think she had any broken bones, but she hurt everywhere. The inside of her head was pounding, her shoulder felt as if it were on fire, and her legs were pinned in a painful position by something heavy. Darcey attempted to move to see what was holding her legs immobile, but an explosion of pain shot through her body—darkness.

CHAPTER 1

Persona non grata

Five weeks previously: Dallas, Texas:

The day dawned bright, clear, and comfortably warm, giving no hint of the dark storm clouds brewing on the horizon just a mere five weeks in the future.

It was Sunday. Just like all the others Sundays, Darcey and Brad had spent together riding at the Bellington Stables. Except today, for some reason the owner and old university buddy of Brad's, Mike Bellington, had decided to join them. Darcey was annoyed with his constant nervous chatter, mostly about nothing, interrupting what was supposed to have been her and Brad's quiet time away from a week of their stress-filled jobs. At least it was for her. Brad had never completely shared with her exactly what his job was. He had just said it was classified, but she would know all about it in due time—not totally satisfying to a gal with a wicked curiosity.

It was going on two o'clock when they returned to the stable, where they left the horses in the capable hands of the attendant, and followed Mike into the Stable's new Tack Room Deli and Coffee Shop, one of the topics Mike had incessantly droned on about.

Shortly after a second round of beers had been placed on the table, Darcey noticed a woman silhouetted against the

open door. She briefly surveyed the room then began walking with purpose across the floor toward their table. Brad
and Mike were deep in a friendly argument over the latest
soccer scores and hadn't noticed her.

Darcey scrutinized the woman as she approached. She
was maybe five foot six or seven and had a slim build. The
baggy shirt and prairie skirt that hung to the floor were not
at all flattering. However, her dark mahogany-colored hair,
tied at the nape of her neck with a black ribbon, flowed in
graceful waves halfway to her waist. Her skin had a slight
dusty-rose color to it, and the long, black lashes that circled
her dark eyes were curiously strange and exotic. Darcey had
never seen eyes like that on anyone.

As she approached the table, Darcey noticed she seemed
to glide rather than actually having a rhythm to her footsteps. Darcey couldn't be sure because the woman's feet
were not visible beneath the prairie skirt.

When the woman got closer, Darcey could see she had a
slight smile on her face as she looked from Brad to Mike,
but, when she noticed Darcey, the smile vanished, replaced
with a quick downturn of her mouth.

Darcey couldn't quite put her finger on the vibes this
woman was generating, but they weren't good.

Be careful of this one, her inner voice cautioned.

Mike saw her before Brad and jumped up as she approached. Brad turned, a frown forming on his face when he
saw the woman.

"Lilly, glad you're here. The office phoned to say you
would be coming." Mike nervously pulled out a chair for
her as he looked at Brad and shrugged. "Sorry, I should
have told you. I guess it just slipped my mind."

"Well, no harm done." Brad's eyes bored into Mike's.
"She's here now."

Mike gave a half-hearted smile as he made introductions.
"Lilly, I'd like you to meet Darcey Callahan, and you know
Brad, of course. Darcey is his lady love," Mike said, cring-

ing inside and wondered why he had thought it necessary to say that.

Lilly had always made him extremely nervous. She reminded him of a cobra ready to strike at the slightest movement. He, Brad, and their university research team had been on the verge of completing a ground-breaking engineering feat when the Ocean Research for Consolidated Alliances Corporation "ORCA" had made them an "offer they couldn't refuse" and bought their Bio Dome, Ecosphere, and Filtration Systems plans.

Mike and Brad were the primaries in the development of the dome and filtration system and ORCA had hired them as project managers.

According to ORCA officials, this project was to be an experimental, secret project requiring both men to sign confidential, non-disclosure agreements. The project was estimated to take upward of five years for completion.

That's where they had met Lilly. She had been promoted to Brad's assistant after the person who originally held the position had died under mysterious circumstances. Mike had his suspicions about what had really happened, but then his father had died and he had to return to Dallas to help his mother run the stables. He still received a healthy stipend as part of ORCA's buyout of his part of the project.

Darcey smiled back, cautiously. *Something's not right here,* she decided, looking from Mike to Lilly and then to Brad, who was glowering at Mike.

"Hello," Lilly said in accented English. She smiled tightly, as her eyes did a quick up and down assessment of Darcey, then her face went blank as Mike held the chair for her to sit down.

Instantly, Darcey felt a cold chill and goose bumps form on her arms.

Lilly sat down, adjusting her skirt, then folded her hands neatly in her lap. Darcey thought she seemed rather odd and noticed that Lilly kept her eyes trained on her folded hands, her face giving away nothing.

Darcey shivered again.

Looking pointedly at Brad, Mike hesitated. "Lilly came in on the morning flight from Lima. The Dallas office sent her here, since they couldn't reach you on your cell. She'll be flying back this afternoon, so she needs to talk to you—now." Mike emphasized the "now," looking anxiously at Brad. "Lilly works with Brad," Mike said, as a sidebar, to Darcey and swallowed.

Darcey could see this Lilly person was really making Mike jumpy. He looked on the verge of a panic attack.

Maybe Lilly was the reason Mike suddenly decided to join us today. Maybe he was supposed to tell Brad about her but couldn't figure out how. That would explain all the stupid babbling he did on the ride. Annoyed, she tried to analyze the puzzling situation.

As far as Darcey knew, Mike owned the riding stables, and he and Brad had gone to the university together. Since Brad had acted like the relationship was no big deal, she hadn't inquired further.

Maybe I should have, she worried.

"What brings you here?" Brad frowned, as his gaze shifted from Mike to Lilly. "Is everything all right with the project?"

A rhetorical question. She wouldn't be here if there wasn't something wrong with the project, Brad thought as he studied Lilly.

Lilly, her eyes still looking down at her hands, seemed exasperated as she looked up at Brad. Her expression quickly smoothed, concealing her emotions. "No. Everything is not right," she stated flatly, answering the question that did not need an answer.

Her presence was all that was needed to convey the importance of the problem connected to the project. Lilly raked her eyes over Darcey again before dropping them back to her lap.

Brad reached over and put his hand on Darcey's arm.

"Excuse us for a little bit, babe. I have to talk to Lilly. I won't be long." He gave her arm a gentle squeeze as he stood up.

This gal is definitely not a people person, Darcey thought shivering inwardly. *She certainly doesn't like me, and the feeling is mutual.*

"That's fine," Darcey said, smiling up at Brad. "I'll be right here. Take your time." She turned and looked directly at Lilly.

Mike gave Brad an uneasy look and stood up. "I've got horses to look after," he said clearing his throat. "See you guys later. Darcey. Brad." Touching his Stetson and inclining his head toward them, he nodded. "Lilly."

Lilly gave a slight nod of her head as she rose from her chair, her eyes hard as she glared at Darcey again.

Darcey stared back. *Geez, lady, what'd I do to you?*

Brad and Lilly followed Mike out the door. She could see them standing, just outside the window. Lilly looked extremely upset about something. She placed her hand on Brad's arm in a pleading gesture. He stood there, nodding his head every so often, his jaw tight. Apparently, Lilly wasn't giving him the opportunity to get a word in edgewise.

Darcey shivered again remembering how she had needled Brad about the project. That had been as close to an argument they had ever come. He had paced the room, frustrated at her, and finally exclaimed, "Don't you think I would tell you if I could? My hands are tied. I can't."

She let the subject drop after that, but, it still rankled her that he wouldn't trust her enough to tell her about it.

After five minutes or so, Brad turned on his heel, leaving Lilly standing alone, glaring after him. He pushed the door hard as he entered, his face livid. Darcey could feel his anger. Glowering, Brad sat down, grabbed his beer, and took a big gulp.

Darcey placed her hand on his arm. "Is everything all right?" she asked softly. She could feel the tension in his arm.

Setting the beer down and taking Darcey's hand in his, he kissed her palm—driving her crazy as it always did—shooting white-hot heat through her veins.

"No, but it's nothing for you to worry your pretty little head about," he said, his brows coming together. "Let's go."

Darcey barely had time to recover from the heat wave that coursed through her, before he entwined his fingers with hers and practically dragged her out the door.

On the silent, hour-long drive back to Dallas, the late afternoon sun faded into twilight. Darcey, not wanting to invade Brad's thoughts, snuggled up next to him. He put his arm around her. A feeling of complete happiness enveloped her. Knowing she was safe in Brad's arms, she dozed off.

❡❡❡

Darcey was half awake and coming out of the most exquisite dream, when they pulled into the parking lot of their favorite bistro for a late supper.

Brad leaned over and placed a soft kiss on her lips, and was pleasantly surprised by her instant response of complete abandonment. Pulling her onto his lap, Brad deepened the kiss, parting her lips. Darcey's heart raced and heat roared through her body as their tongues danced.

"Ummmm—if you keep that up we may have to skip dinner," Brad breathed heavily into her hair. "Of course, I wouldn't mind that at all." He chuckled. Pulling back, he placed a teasing kiss on her nose.

Darcey made a pouty face and reluctantly slid off his lap. "Yeah, I think you're probably right, but I'm starving. Let's go," she said with a laugh, not waiting for him to come around and open her door.

As soon as they were seated at their favorite table, Brad's cell vibrated in his pocket. Frowning, he looked at the caller ID. "What the hell does she want now," he mumbled under his breath as he shoved himself away from the table and walked stiffly out to the lobby to answer it.

The low hum of muffled voices, silverware and china clattering prevented Darcey from hearing his low agitated comment. She watched him disappear through the archway into the lobby. The sinking feeling in the pit of her stomach was back.

Brad had been gone close to ten minutes when the waiter stopped back by to see if they were ready to order. Darcey looked up to tell him "Not yet," when she noticed Brad coming through the archway from the lobby. He was looking down, but she could see his face was stiff, and his lips formed a straight line—he was angry. That was the same look he'd had after talking with Lilly, but it was more intense now. He looked up, saw her watching, and immediately the anger was replaced with that heart-stopping, lopsided grin of his.

Brad sat down, giving Darcey a half smile as he tried to concentrate on the menu, seemingly oblivious to everything going on around him.

"Okay, what's going on?" Darcey asked, giving him a playful jab in the arm.

"Something pertaining to the project has come up unexpectedly." Laying the menu down, he looked at her. "It's nothing for you to worry about. It will be resolved, but I will have to go back to Lima to take care of it."

Darcey felt a cold chill, and the sinking feeling in the pit of her stomach hit her again as she listened to Brad. She knew he had been going back and forth between the Dallas and Lima offices ever since they'd started dating over a year ago, but the tone when he spoke of work now gave her chills. She didn't understand it, but his voice had a foreboding ring to it, and she could see the worry he was trying to hide behind that half-hearted grin.

"I shouldn't be gone for more than a couple of weeks," he said, looking her in the eyes. "This is something I have to take care of immediately,"

Cupping her chin, he gently pulled her toward him and

kissed her. He was trying to reassure her, but she could tell he was worried—a lot.

A feeling of helplessness came over Darcey. She wanted to help but didn't know what she could do. "Tell me what I can do," she said softly, gently brushing back the dark auburn lock that perpetually fell sexily across his forehead.

"Just be here when I get back," he whispered, taking her hand and holding it to his cheek, before turning it over to kiss her palm.

Naughty thoughts raced through her head as the white-hot heat from the kiss pulsed through her veins. Brad was leaving her breathless and blushing in the middle of the restaurant. He continually left her breathless and blushing from their very first date—when she had skinned her palm from tripping on a loose stone, and he'd kissed the pain away—to now. The kiss that had been intended for comfort, had instead, ignited a burning passion in both of them and formed a connection between them that neither could explain.

Darcey's heart turned over as she watched him from under her eyelashes, during dinner. Worry lines creased his brow as he tried to make light conversation. Finally, he leaned back and ran his fingers through his hair, pulling the wayward lock back in place again.

"Sorry, I know I'm not decent company tonight," he apologized, forcing a smile that never quite reached his eyes. He had spent the last half hour while they ate in relative silence, trying to decide whether to tell Darcey why he had to go to Lima but, if just half of what Lilly had told him was true, he couldn't afford to put Darcey in danger.

She could see the worry that had been building all evening in the depths of those green eyes, and she shivered, as the feeling of dread swept over her again.

"Let's go." He signaled the waiter for the check.

CHAPTER 2

The Present and The Past

Brad was still worried about how he had left things with Darcey as he drove to the Ocean Research for Combined Alliances "ORCA" office. He didn't want her to worry, but he had seen it in her eyes. She was. He knew Darcey was as deeply in tune with his feelings as he was with hers.

Damn, he thought. *I hate this. I've never kept anything from her, except this project. Damn!* He slammed his fist on the steering wheel.

The phone call at the restaurant had been from Lilly. She was waiting in the ORCA hangar at the airport to board the plane back to Peru when she had decided to call Brad. She felt she needed to remind him of his obligation to the project and make sure he understood the enormity of the situation. She had to impress on him again just why he needed to leave immediately.

When Brad answered, Lilly hadn't waited for him to respond before she started repeating again the laundry list of things she had told him that afternoon. Things that corporate had instructed her relay to him.

Security believed someone had purposely tampered with some of the reactor's crystals. A few miss placed crystals in the binary system's control panel had triggered an alarm that shut part of the system down. It was the consensus of the technicians that the repairs could be made with no re-sulting damage provided they were done quickly.

The ensuing chaos had drawn Security away from the safe room. Upon returning, they discovered the dome's safe open and the Bio Dome and Ecosphere Air Filtration dia-grams missing. Security believed the alarm had been a ruse to provide someone the opportunity to steal the classified diagrams.

Security immediately locked the dome down and searched everyone. Armando Martinez, Assistant Mainte-nance Manager, had been caught red-handed with the pouch containing the diagrams. Security had quickly put the dia-grams under guard on a plane back to Dubai. The investiga-tion was still ongoing into the situation and Martinez had been detained pending the results of the investigation.

For over a week, the daily reports, the Operations Room technicians who routinely monitored the dome's system control panels, noted there had been slight anomalies in the readings and had reported it to ORCA's main office director Leo Jordan, affectionately known as "Topside."

Topside thought it warranted immediate attention and had authorized the ecosphere and biosphere system dia-grams be brought in from their secure location in Dubai, so the technicians could assess the situation, thus providing Armando the perfect opportunity to steal them.

However, the technicians again assured Topside that the anomalies were still occurring, and believed that something had been introduced into the system, possibly a virus. At present, the anomalies were small and infrequent, but the technicians worried it might turn into something much big-ger that might damage the filtration system that provided the oxygen to the dome.

Since the anomalies had been appearing sporadically, the technicians feared they might have to do a total shut down in order to run a complete diagnostic workup to locate the problem. If that happened, the backup system would have to be put online; something the techs really did not want to do.

The backup system did not have the capacity to keep the entire dome running. Only the first two rings of the main dome would be operational and even then that might only last a week at the most before the entire system failed.

It had been several years since that system had been online and it had only been meant to last a few months to provide oxygen and lighting to the original dome while the workers installed the main biosphere filtration system. Once the main system was operational, the technicians had decided to leave the backup in place just in case of an emergency, knowing it would provide enough time for the dome to be evacuated if it became necessary.

Topside and ORCA Corporate's concerns were that repairs to the system would cause a major delay in the completion of the dome. The whole system might have to be reprogrammed. Corporate was doing a full internal investigation, but thus far, had come up empty. Armando was the only suspect and he had pled not guilty. He said he had no idea who had asked him to get the diagrams and claimed he had been contacted by email and that the request had come from headquarters. Unfortunately, that particular email had been accidently deleted. He had no idea he had been asked to do something wrong.

In the light of all of this, it was Corporate's assessment, that Brad must return to Lima immediately, in order to personally handle the situation.

Lilly had informed him that she was still leaving that evening, but insisted that Brad leave as soon as he could get to the airport. One of ORCA's jets would be standing by.

Clearing his mind, Brad concentrated on what Lilly had told him. He was trying to avoid thinking about the reactor parts that had been tampered with. Even if the repairs were easy, it was still dangerous, and one wrong move in exchanging the crystals could cause the whole project to implode, killing everyone inside. There would be no escape—for anyone—two hundred and fifty souls lost.

That won't happen, I won't let it, he promised himself.

First, he had to take care of things at the office. Being sent to Dallas was only to have been a short stay, but when he met Darcey, he had requested to have his stay extended—indefinitely. The Lima office had approved it. Provided he was on the project site in Lima during the week, he could spend his weekends and free time in Dallas. He smiled as he remembered the first night he'd seen her…

∾∾∾

That night four beautiful women had trooped through the door at the Sweetwater, laughing and talking, maybe a little louder than they should have because they attracted the attention of everyone in the room, including Brad.

"Oops." The perky little brunette laughed, waving to the other customers who were watching them. "Looks like we'd better tone it down a bit."

They all nodded put their forefingers to their lips and in unison said, "Shhhhh!" still laughing, as they made their way toward the table where he was sitting. They came to an abrupt halt and stared as they reached it.

The tall redhead couldn't take her eyes off him and he couldn't take his off her. His heart did a complete somersault.

Well, would you look at that? he thought, his eyes appreciating every inch of her—tall and leggy with curves in all the right places; a tanned, flawless complexion; coppery, pixie-short hair; and sparkling hazel eyes.

Perfect, he thought.

Her eyes looked right into him and it was like a jolt of electricity went surging through him.

You don't have time for this, he told himself. *You go back to Lima in a couple of weeks.* He shook off the stupor he had let himself fall into and stood up.

"Excuse me, but I believe you are sitting at our table," the perky little brunette said.

"Ladies." He touched the brim of my Stetson. "My mistake. If you'll excuse me, the table is all yours."

He watched as the redhead blushed and his heart did a cartwheel. Everything else in the room disappeared. The only thing he was conscious of was that this beautiful, tall redhead with sparkling hazel eyes and a body to die for was looking directly at him. It was as if she was seeing right into his soul.

He vaguely remembered pulling out a chair and holding it for her.

It was the perky little brunette who finally spoke up and asked him to join them. He watched as she made eyes at the redhead and wondered what that was all about.

"Don't mind if I do," he said as he reached over, pulled a chair from the next table, and sat down—right next to the redhead.

She smelled heavenly. He had no idea what kind of expression he had on his face, but the girls were looking from one to the other with raised eyebrows when he glanced in their direction.

He felt like an awkward schoolboy and tried not to stare at her. He hoped he wasn't drooling, but this was the most exquisite woman he'd seen in ages—maybe ever. Thankfully she seemed as equally mesmerized by him as he was by her.

He mentally shook himself. *You don't have time for this*, he told himself again. *Get a grip, Brad, you leave in two weeks—remember?*

He gazed into her eyes again and realized it didn't matter if he was leaving in two weeks. He would have those two weeks to get to know her. Besides, she wouldn't be the first of his many short-lived romances, to end in only two weeks, he rationalized.

He leaned over and introduced himself to her. "I'm Brad Daniels, Director of Operations for the ORCA Corporation, stationed here in Dallas. So nice to meet you, and your lovely group of ladies," he said, pulling his eyes away from the redhead long enough to look around the table, his eyes ending back on her. "Who are all of you?"

The perky brunette cleared her throat and started the introductions. "This is Donna Jorgensen, Ashley Turner, Darcey Callahan, and I'm Marti Campbell," she said, pointing to each one of the women individually.

"My pleasure, ladies." He touched his Stetson again. "I presume y'all come here regularly since you have this table reserved," he teased, his eyes focused on the redhead, Darcey. "I wondered why everyone was looking at me when I sat down here. Now I know why." He grinned a lopsided grin. She was blushing and the room faded away again.

"At least once a week," Donna answered, jolting him back to reality. Her eyes narrowed as she scrutinized him. "This is the first time we've seen you here, though."

"Yes, I'm here for a few weeks on business from our Lima office. This is the first time I've had to relax and unwind since arriving," he explained, glancing around the table again, his eyes returning to rest on Darcey. "I was told this was the place to be if I wanted to meet some beautiful women, and they were right!"

He turned on the Texas charm that he was noted for, but his eyes never left Darcey's face. It became increasingly hard to concentrate on what the others were saying as he found himself drowning in her sparkling hazel eyes and unblemished complexion.

"Just what does a Director of Operations do, exactly?" Ashley asked with one raised eyebrow.

She was a tall willowy blonde with clear blue eyes, and he might have been interested in her if he hadn't noticed the redhead.

Reluctantly, he transferred his gaze to her, coughed, and cleared his throat. "Well, now ma'am, if I told ya that, I'd have to kill ya," he replied with a stern expression on his face, then smiling broadly, he continued, "Seriously, though, I can't tell you exactly what I do, but it has to do with deep-water ocean research. That's all that I'm at liberty to say," he finished, looking at each of the women as he spoke. He raised his arm and signaled the waitress then asked the ladies what they would like to drink. "This rounds on me," he said, grinning. "So, what do you lovely gals do?" he inquired, his eyes shifting to Marti, who looked up at him and gave him a reserved smile.

"Well, let's see." Marti cleared her throat, giving Darcey, who glared back, a brief glance. "I am part owner with my dad in Campbell's Sporting Goods." She laughed and pulled a face, reciting, "'If sports is your thing—see Campbell's. We have it all.' That's my Dad's favorite line."

"I just might have to stop by and take a look," he said seriously. "I'm more into horses, but I do enjoy a good game of soccer now and then."

The other brunette, Donna, also shot Darcey a glance. "I'm a kindergarten teacher at Mark Twain Elementary. Love those little ones." She smiled, playing with what he thought must be a new engagement ring on her finger as she kept admiring it. "They can be such a hoot sometimes. You never know what will pop out of their little mouths," she said with a good-natured laugh as she looked back at him.

"Yes, they can. I have a niece who just turned five and she's quite a little imp," he agreed. "I sometimes have a hard time keeping up with her."

"Well, I guess it's my turn." Ashley beamed at everyone, her eyes sparkling. "I own a small boutique downtown. I specialize in high-end designer clothing and accessories. If you need something for your girlfriend, do stop in, I'm sure I can find you something that's just right for her." She cocked her head slightly to one side looking, directly at him, subtly asking the obvious question—did he have a girlfriend?

He didn't turn his head to look at Ashley's face. Darcey was looking right at him when he answered. He was completely immobilized. "I might just do that." He grinned as he gave Darcey a very thorough assessment. The room faded again.

Darcey cleared her throat. A delicate pink still tinted her cheeks. "Guess it's my turn." She endearingly pulled her lower lip between her teeth. "I'm a graphic designer," she said.

Brad could tell she was trying to keep her voice under control and stop her hands under the table from shaking. At that moment, he wanted nothing more than to caress those delicate fingers and tell her he was feeling it, too.

"I work for an advertising agency with offices in Dallas and Fort Worth." She paused to swallow.

"Which office do you work out of—Dallas or Fort Worth?" he asked, leaning forward to look her in the eye. She shook her head slightly and quickly looked down. As she did, the connection was broken.

"Neither, I work out of my home." She swallowed again. "It's more efficient. Low overhead and all." She laughed nervously, still looking down.

Then she looked up quickly, but he couldn't hold her gaze. She was blushing and quickly looked away. "Everything can be done now days electronically, so there's really no need to take up office space. However, if I'm needed in either office, I do have a work area at both locations," she finished in one breath.

"I wish my job was where I could work from home," he mused, looking out across the room remembering he really had no place to call home. "I travel all the time. It gets to be a little much sometimes. I've never really had a place I could call home," he said quietly, "not since I started this job anyway."

He looked back at her and smiled. She blushed again, and his stomach erupted with a million butterflies. He felt like an awkward schoolboy on his first date.

The band began playing and several of who he assumed were regulars at the bar, asked the other women to dance, but he noticed no one asked Darcey to dance or even looked her way. He wondered what was up with that.

Maybe his six-foot-nine, bodybuilder's frame was too intimidating, he thought smugly. He rose from his chair, extended his hand to her, and gave her that lopsided grin. "Shall we?"

She placed her hand in his. An electric shock surged all the way through his body when she touched him. Butterflies erupted in his stomach again, and he knew she felt it too. He could see it in those hazel eyes.

He pulled her into his arms and wrapped them around her, holding her possessively as if he would never let her go. They danced, oblivious to their surroundings. He had no idea what anyone was thinking. He didn't care. By now, he was beyond caring. He didn't even remember if they talked—he was lost and she felt right in his arms.

Could this be' love at first sight'? he wondered blissfully as they glided around the dance floor, his head nestled against hers. His eyes closed, her heavenly scent invading his senses. For him, time stood still.

"Last call for alcohol," someone hollered from behind the bar when the last song ended. Brad didn't know how anyone heard him over the noisy roar, but they did. They finished their drinks and got up to leave.

"It's been great meeting you. We've had a wonderful time this evening," Ashley smiled broadly at him. "We must do this again."

"Yes, lets. Does anyone need a ride home?" he asked, his eyes boring into Darcey's.

"No." Marti jumped in quickly. She smiled sweetly all the while looking at Darcey. "We came together and we go home together. It's just our pact. Thanks anyway."

He felt Darcey stiffen as she glared back at Marti.

What's up with that? he wondered.

Donna and Ashley headed toward the door. Marti followed and kept glancing over her shoulder to make sure Darcey was following. She was, with Brad right behind her.

He gently took Darcey's elbow and directed her a little ways away from the others as they turned and watched. He could see they were unhappy with her. She smiled back at them, gave them a just-a-minute sign, and turned to face him.

"Do you really have to go with them?" He grinned at her as he pulled her into his arms. "I would be happy to take you home."

His lips brushed against her hair. He closed his eyes. She felt so right in his arms. He felt her body soften against his, and he couldn't control his desire for her.

"I'm sure you would, but it's a pact we made with each other—if we come together, we go home together. Sorry, but that's how it works," she said softly.

He detected a slight intake of breath as her body responded to his.

She kept her eyes glued to his chest, refusing to look him in the eye. He sensed, like she did, that she if she looked up, they both would be lost.

"Okay, I see, it's a girl thing. I can live with that," he whispered in her ear. "Why don't we fix it so the next time, you come with me, then you can go home with me? Just give me your number, and I'll take it from there."

He pulled back and grinned, placing his finger under her chin, tilting her head up, and, in the deep pools of her eyes, he saw that their worlds had collided in an excitingly, explosive way. There would be no turning back now.

His leaving in two weeks didn't seem important anymore.

ೕ

Driving back from the ORCA office on his way to the airport, Brad was deep in thought. He had no idea what waited for him in Lima. Someone had gone to a great deal of trouble and expense, he figured, to snag an inside man to sabotage the project. Even though Armando was insisting he was innocent, he *was* the perfect choice for the job. Armando was an egotistical, self-absorbed ass, and he was greedy. Brad knew Armando would have seen it as an easy way to line his pockets.

Corporate had all kinds of security in place surrounding the dome, so that's probably why the people behind the plot sought out someone on the inside. If you can't break through the security from the outside—work it from the inside, and who better to do that than a greedy bastard with no conscience.

Unusually secretive, Corporate kept the exact location of the diagrams, worth billions of dollars, under wraps. ORCA had purchased Brad's Bio Dome design and the new high-tech, biosphere, air filtration system designed collectively by Brad's college research team. Ever since then, the diagrams had been locked in a vault at an undisclosed location. Lilly had assured him that they were now safely locked away once more.

Brad's design for the Bio Dome structure was engineered to withstand up to 16,4472.2 pounds of pressure per square inch (psi) underwater without imploding—a cutting-edge engineering feat. The dome was the first of its kind, as was the design of the filtration system, which had been engineered to be the heart of the dome. It controlled everything—air, water, lighting, atmosphere, hydroponics, heating, cooling—everything that made it like living on the earth's surface but inside the dome.

However, choosing a site for the dome had taken longer than expected. After three years of research and testing, ORCA scientists finally adopted the Peru-Chile Trench for the Bio Dome. Although the trench was a subduction zone, intensive research into the rate of movement of the Nazca Plate where the dome was to be located showed that movement had slowed to an incredible rate of less than two centimeters per year over the last three decades. Stabilization supports had been designed by ORCA engineers that would absorb the movement in the plate with no disruption to the dome.

Meanwhile, during that time, ORCA engineers had also

perfected a global positioning satellite warning system that globally monitored the movement of the Earth's plates. The system of satellites could determine in a matter of seconds any minute shift in the Earth plates that might trigger an earthquake and initiate a warning to the area where the earthquake might happen. Since its launch five years ago, the system had saved thousands of lives. Now, with the slowing of the Nazca Plate, the GPS warning system, and stabilization supports, it was decided the location on the Nazca Plate was the perfect spot.

Brad's primary concern now was that, if the damage required a major overhaul, the project might not make the completion deadline. Not making the deadline would be costly to ORCA. They were under a strict completion deadline and would be fined a million dollars for every day past that date.

On any other project, that would have been a drop in the bucket, but with the research and development of the Bio Dome, costs had run into the billions. ORCA was walking a financial tightrope until the dome was completed. That was not public knowledge, but Brad wondered if maybe that information had leaked and the attempted theft of the diagrams might have been because of it.

Whoever these guys were, they seemed hell bent on stopping the dome from being completed on time. The idea of a second insider was now a distinct possibility since it was apparent that someone on the inside had to have given Armando the codes to the safe. He made a mental note to ask Lilly to quietly check it out.

Looking at his watch, Brad saw it was three-ten in the morning. The streets were mostly deserted and the rock in his chest hurt like hell.

This was not how he had wanted his evening to go. He had caught himself repeatedly thinking that he should just take Darcey with him. She had vacation time coming, and it would only be for a week or two at the most, but each time he decided against it.

Brad feared that these mystery culprits might strike again, now that their first attempt had failed. If they found out about Darcey, they might try to use her as leverage to get the diagrams. He couldn't take that chance. They had already reached the Lima office and tapped Armando. Who else might they try to entice or even coerce?

No, it would be too dangerous to take Darcey with him. What he didn't want now was to bring her to their attention. He was the only one besides Asad Damji, the corporate head, who knew exactly where the plans were, making Darcey a prime target for kidnapping and him for blackmail. Thank goodness, the plans were safely back in the corporate office in Dubai, and Darcey would stay safely in Dallas.

Hitting speed dial, he heard Darcey's phone ring and held his breath; the answering machine picked up. Brad sighed.

"I'm leaving, now. I'll be out of reach with my cell, so don't worry if you don't hear from me for a couple of days. I wish I could tell you what's going on, but it's not safe. I'll call as soon as I can. I love you so much and miss you already."

Holding the phone to his ear until the dial tone came back on, a small part of him hoped she would have heard the phone and picked up. He could have heard her voice one last time, not just a recording. He hit the disconnect button and let the phone slip into his jacket pocket. He had never felt so alone or cold in his entire life.

CHAPTER 3

The Dome

Brad wished he could have stayed with Darcey just one more night, but Lilly had already arranged for the ORCA jet to be ready to take off when he arrived at the airport. Thomas, ORCA's Flight Director, was waiting when Brad boarded.

"Evening, Thomas," Brad said, shaking hands with him.

"Evening, *señor*. You have a message from Señor Damji to return his call," Thomas said. "We are ready for takeoff whenever you have finished your call. The pilot already has clearance."

"Thanks. I suppose you have been briefed on the situation," Brad inquired as he placed his briefcase on the seat beside him and flipped out his phone.

"Yes. Bad business," Thomas said shaking his head. "I will tell the pilot you are here and we can go after you finish your call."

Brad nodded his head, acknowledging Thomas's comment, as he waited for Asad to answer his phone.

"Yes, Asad here," he answered briskly.

"Brad here. I'm returning your call."

"I called to warn you to be cautious," Asad told Brad. "There has been an attempt to take over the ORCA board from an outside source, and I'm not sure, but I thought the two incidents might be connected. So, until I have a handle on everything, I do not want anyone but the people in the dome to know you are back. I have alerted all of the appropriate personnel that you will be meeting before you arrive at the dome."

"Thanks, Asad. I'll be careful," Brad promised.

The call finished, Brad pulled the seat belt across his body. The silver buckle made a sharp click as he shoved it into the clasp. He laid his head back and closed his eyes, listening to the plane's engines roar to life. In eight hours he'd be back in Lima, and Darcey would be thousands of miles away, but safe.

He still felt guilty about the goodbye at Darcey's apartment. It had definitely been less than satisfactory—a kiss, a hug, and a promise that he would call just hadn't cut it. Even though he had told her how much he loved her, he wanted to hold her in his arms just one more night. He wanted to feel her skin against his as they lay together, to taste her, and to feel her hands as they caressed his body.

When he was settled back in Lima, he'd ask Lilly to send flowers to Darcey. He couldn't afford to send them himself, just in case he was being watched. He didn't think so, but it didn't hurt to be cautious. Brad knew flowers would hardly makeup for him having to leave in the middle of the night, but at least she would know he loved her and, hopefully, how sorry he was.

ᐸᔆᐳ

Eight hours later the plane landed and taxied inside the ORCA hangar. The captain assured Brad no one would know he'd arrived.

Brad took the stairs two at a time down to the waiting limo. This wasn't the first confidential flight he had taken, but it might be the most important.

"Take me to the dock," he told the driver, as soon as he shut the door. "Remember—you are to tell no one you have seen me. Understood?"

The driver nodded and pulled out of the hangar.

It was a two-and-a-half-hour descent into the ocean's depths to reach the dome, and the only way to reach it was by submarine. ORCA had had several subs specially built for just for that purpose.

The sub-captain, waiting at the top of the gangway, signaled the first mate to meet the limo as soon as it stopped on the dock.

"Ready to go, sir?" the sub-captain asked as Brad walked up the gangway followed by the first mate.

Brad nodded and preceded the sub-captain and first mate down the ladder. The captain secured the hatch behind them.

"We should reach the dome around two-thirty or so," the sub-captain said, signaling the sub to dive. "Lunch will be served in the mess hall shortly. Would you like something to drink now?"

"Yes, a Scotch if you have it."

"Right away, sir. The steward will bring it to you," the captain said, handing a packet to Brad. "Miss Lilly left this for you when she surfaced yesterday."

Brad found his way to the guest quarters, where he proceeded to sit down and sort through the packet. He found the follow-up report and read Lilly's notation on the top of the first page that ORCA's security head had pulled Armando's Security One clearance that had allowed him total access to the dome.

Glancing on down through the report, he noticed that Lilly had been unclear as to why Armando had not been fired. She speculated that someone in corporate had not want him fired. She felt that was evident, as he had been left in his position as assistant to Mark Williamson, the maintenance manager. He was still able to order supplies and equipment for the dome. Lilly had made a notation that she felt this was highly unusual and dangerous.

She had also noted that she wasn't comfortable with Armando still being able to order supplies and equipment, so she had ordered all new supplies and equipment through Mark Williamson himself. She would then have everything thoroughly checked before it would be allowed into the dome. It would take up valuable time, but she felt it necessary to make sure nothing else happened.

Finally, the sub reached the dome and docked. Tired from the long flight and the decent to the dome, Brad wearily loaded his bags into one of the golf cart-like shuttles at the shuttle bay and drove the fifteen minutes to his quarters. He dropped off his bags before going in search of Lilly. He found her in the storage bay, checking off supplies and equipment from the last shipment of the day from topside.

"How's things goin'?" Brad asked, as he looked around.

There were numerous stacks of boxes and several hundred pallets filling the vast expanse of the storage bay. They were all stacked full of shrink-wrapped parts, equipment, and stock for the retail shops. He noticed that it had all been neatly inventoried and marked with the section number that each pallet belonged to.

"We have finally received the last shipment for today," she said, slipping her pencil under the clip on the clipboard. "The crystals to fix the damaged panels will be down tomorrow. Those will be installed after they are unloaded and checked in. The big problem will be determining how much damage has been done to the filtration system. I hope you are ready to tackle it." She looked at Brad. "We cannot wait much longer. The techs are certain something has been introduced into the programming, possibly a virus." Lilly rambled on as she and Brad walked out of the storage bay. "They have run the diagnostics several times. Sometimes the anomalies show up in the reports and then, in the next report, they do not. That one fact has them worried."

"Since I can't do anything until tomorrow, I'll take a preliminary look at their reports this evening," Brad advised her, as they headed for her office. "That way I'll know how best to begin tomorrow. Will you have the reports sent to my quarters, please?"

Brad and Lilly walked down the gray, tube-like corridor heading toward the central plaza area of the dome.

The main plaza and center of the dome would eventually become a small, main street shopping plaza, but right now, it was full of workers finishing up installing the electrical and plumbing hookups. The plaza area itself was circular and consisted of several cubicles around the perimeter that would eventually house the small retail shops.

There were four connecting corridors radiating out from the center of the plaza, similar to spokes on a wheel. Those corridors connected to another circular cylinder ring outside of the main area. That ring housed the corporate offices, the service and maintenance areas, the Operations Room, The Bajo el Mar Cafe; hydroponic gardens; schools; medical; and recreation area, including a bowling alley, movie theatre, and a gamer's corner for the younger set. Below that ring, was the area that housed the livestock.

Connecting corridors from the second ring radiated off to join with the third ring that would be the living quarters. From the third ring, connecting tunnels joined the four other domes with three residential rings each.

The whole complex would eventually house up to five hundred families.

Brad and Lilly walked across the plaza and entered the connecting corridor on the other side, heading for the second ring and Lilly's office.

"I will leave you here," Lilly said. "I have to log all the new parts into the computer tonight. I will be most glad when Topside sends down the palmtops, so I do not have to do double entries." She opened the door to her office and stepped inside.

Brad walked back toward the connecting corridor to the third ring, where his quarters were located, a twenty-minute walk from Lilly's office. Before he reached the connecting corridor, he stopped and talked with several of the evening maintenance workers who were heading to the Bajo El Mar Café for their evening meal.

ᘓᘓᘓ

His things put away, Brad went to the shuttle park located a few yards down the corridor from his quarters and got into the shuttle assigned to him.

In the ten minutes or so that it took to drive to the Operations Room, Brad worried about what kind of damage he would find. He prayed that the anomalies the techs had been finding wouldn't trigger something in the system that would cause it to backup into the reactor. If that happened, it would cause the dome to implode. Then everyone in the dome would be doomed.

Brad had a cursory knowledge of the workings of the filtration system, but no idea how the computer-programming end of it worked. He could design and build a structure to withstand thousands of pounds of pressure five miles underwater, but he had no idea how to write a computer program.

Using his ID card, Brad entered the Operations Room. It was empty now as the techs would be on their evening break. The low steady hum told him, for now, everything was running smoothly and that was a relief.

The filtration system was on the level below, so he swiftly descended the stairs. A quick glance at the control board all green lights indicated everything seemed to be operating efficiently.

Brad noticed that most of the covers on the lower panels of the binary system connections had been left open. He had been told that a couple of the crystals had been removed and replaced with the wrong ones.

This must be the damage Armando is accused of doing, he surmised. *This certainly would have caused the system to shut down and the alarm to sound,* he thought examining the surrounding crystals.

In the forty-eight hours that the main binary system had been off line, the secondary system had been employed and seemed to be handling the situation. However, had all five of the dome structures been fully inhabited, this would have been a serious problem. The secondary system could not have handled it for any length of time.

"Whoever had instructed Armando on what crystals to switch out, must have known the exact ones to use that would not cause serious damage at this point. Armando wouldn't know a crystal from his ass unless someone told him the difference. I'll check the schematics to be sure no permanent damage has been done," he grumbled to himself, moving on to the operating panels.

The operating panels housed the electronic program digital files that controlled the ecosystem for the entire dome. Computer operated, they maintained accurate levels and operated at maximum capacity. According to the report, it was here that the technicians had found the anomalies.

Brad went to the computer and ran a cursory diagnostic, then compared it to the previous six reports the techs had generated. The oxygen levels were slightly elevated, but not enough to be noticed by the mass population. There were also small anomalies in the other files as well, none of which would be noticeable unless specifically looked for.

By this time, he could hear the techs returning from their dinner break. He gathered up the printouts of the diagnostic reports and headed up stairs to discuss the information with them.

"Hey, guys," Brad said, reaching the top step.

"Hey, yourself," Joe Talbot, head technician greeted him. "'Bout time you got back. We've had some real excitement around here."

"Yeah, so I've heard," Brad said, placing the printouts on one of the desks. "I've just run another diagnostic, and I'm concerned about this."

Pointing to the atmospheric levels for the hydroponic area, Brad motioned for them to come look at the printout.

"These are totally out of balance," Brad noted, "and since no one will be working in that area until shortly before the completion date, it would never have been noticed until it was too late."

Over the hour or so, Brad discussed his findings with the techs, noting their concerns and suggestions on how to handle the problem.

"Now, the main priority is going to be securing the hydroponic gardens section since it is vital to the survival of the dome's residents," Brad told them. "Nothing against you guys, but I may have to call in an expert with specific knowledge about viruses. However, I'm going to wait until I've had a chance to look at the files once I get the codes from IT topside and have you run a total system diagnostic."

"I think you're right about getting and expert to check about a virus," Joe said. "Paul and I have been concerned about that since the anomalies started showing up. We reported this to IT topside, but they have been reluctant to authorize us to go any further. Said we had to talk to Javier Montego, whoever that is."

"Yeah, glad you're here to set 'em straight," Paul chimed in. "We can't seem to get anything past that Javier Montego guy to talk with someone who has the authority to give us the codes."

"Why didn't you just ask Lilly? She's in charge when I'm away. She has the authority to request the codes," Brad questioned, wondering just why they hadn't asked her.

"We did," Joe replied, "'n she said we needed to call IT topside for permission."

"I'm sorry. I'll check into it," Brad said, puzzled at this turn of events. "Okay." He picked up the printouts. "I'm hitting the sack. It's been a long day. I'll see you all in the morning."

"Nite, boss," Joe and Paul said in unison.

He hated this. "It's going to be longer than anticipated before I can call Darcey," he grumbled to himself, heading for his shuttle. "I'll swing by Lilly's office again to find out just what's going on."

Jumping in the shuttle, he drove back to Lilly's office. She was just pulling her door shut when he stopped.

"Hey, got a minute?" he asked.

"Yes. What can I do for you?" she asked, wondering what else he could possibly want. She had already had the reports delivered to his quarters, and she was late for her dinner.

"I need to know what's up with you not giving the guys in Operations the codes to check out the files," Brad demanded.

"Well, they never specifically asked me to get the codes. They only wanted to know who to contact up top," she said misrepresenting the facts as anger boiled up inside her. "I directed them to the IT office since they were not actually sure if anything was wrong with the files. I thought it best to let IT authorize the codes." She looked Brad directly in the eye, never flinching.

Bastards, she thought.

"Yes, I can understand that, but now we are sure there is something wrong in some of the files. So, from now on, if they request anything pertaining to Operations, you are authorized to get it for them," Brad said, smiling at Lilly. She briefly returned the smile as she readjusted the strap of her shoulder bag.

"Now, I need a special favor," he said, with a sideways sheepish grin. "Would you call the Dallas office and ask them to discretely order some flowers for Darcey? No one is supposed to know I'm here yet, or I would do it."

"Yes, it would be my pleasure," she said smiling sweetly but had a strangle hold on her bag's strap. "I will call them in the morning. Do you have anything special in mind?" she asked sweetly, irritated that he would want to send flowers to *that* woman. It pissed her off that he was still dating *her*. Why couldn't he see what was right in front of him? she wondered, then, switched her thoughts to the flowers. *Flowers are a waste of money. They just have to be thrown out in a couple of days. Yes, definitely, a waste of money, but it's his money.*

"Yes, I want a dozen roses with white daisies. Make them lavender roses," Brad told Lilly, thinking maybe he should make it two-dozen, but decided that might be too much. "On the card, just have them put 'I love and miss you very much. Call you soon.' Sign it 'Brad.' Bill it to the Dallas office; I will take care of it."

He watched as Lilly pulled a small notepad and a pen from her purse and wrote down what he had said.

She half smiled at him. "Yes, I think I have it. I will take care of this in the morning."

If I think of it, that is.

"Is there anything else I can do for you?"

"No. Thanks. I'm swinging by the Bajo for some coffee. Can I drop you somewhere?" he asked.

"Yes, if it will not be too much trouble. I would like to go there as well. I was just on my way there when you stopped," she said, honey dripping from each word.

Men are such fools.

"Sure thing. Hop on in."

Stopping at The Bajo, Brad grabbed some sandwiches and a pot of coffee to take to his quarters, and then waved goodbye to Lilly, on his way out the door. It had been an arduous day and he was ready to hit the sack.

Brad put the sandwiches on the counter along with the pot of coffee. He poured a half a cup and wolfed down a sandwich and realized that even the strong coffee wouldn't keep him awake long enough to go over all of the reports.

Instead of trying to muck through the reports with half a brain tonight, he decided to take a hot shower, set the alarm for five, and read over the reports in the morning. That sounded like a much better plan. No one would be in the office topside until eight in order to get the codes anyway.

Kicking off his shoes in the living room, Brad headed to the bedroom, wishing he could have called Darcey after he had landed, but there wasn't a secure line available at the airport, and, in all of the commotion, he had forgotten to put his secure cell on the charger.

He knew she would be worried, but he was sending flowers and she would understand how much he loved and missed her when she got them. He must remember to ask Lilly when the new phones that worked in the dome would be available.

Brad's head had barely hit his pillow before he was fast asleep.

A vision of Darcey drifted into his dreams…

∽∾∽

She was beautiful, but she floated just beyond his reach. Brad struggled hard, reaching for her. But, for some reason, he couldn't touch her. Frustration urged him on. She smiled teasingly as she reached out to him—drifted away—floated in again, inky black. Fear gripped his heart. He couldn't see her. His heart beat faster.

Now, she was lying on a black surface. Strange hands held her. She reached out to him, called to him. Her image faded.

Fear gripped him again. Her image returned, but her face metamorphosed until it was no longer Darcey, but something sinister.

Still reaching for her, he was running and running and running…heart pounding trying to catch her…falling…a black abyss just out of range. He grabbed for her hand. She pulled it away. He was falling and falling and falling…

∽∾∽

Brad bolted upright sweating and breathing hard. He looked at the glowing green digital numbers on his clock— it was three twenty-nine. His breathing slowed, but the nightmare still raced through his mind. It must have been the worry of leaving her and the stress over the mess here that triggered the dream.

He threw off the sweat-soaked sheet and lay back, closing his eyes. He saw Darcey in his mind's eye, slender tanned body with graceful curves, pixie-short, copper hair, and hazel eyes—beautiful. Brad held that image until he was once more lost in sleep.

❧❧❧

The alarm blared. Brad rolled over, slapped the off button, and groaned. He was sure he had done nothing but toss and turn once he'd finally dozed off again after the nightmare. He sat up on the side of the bed and stretched his arms up over his head, reaching for the ceiling. It felt good to stretch the muscles in his back. They had been tied in knots after that dream about Darcey.

Grabbing his robe, he shrugged into it and picked up the reports on his way to the kitchen. While the coffee brewed, Brad read over the reports he'd spread out on the kitchen bar.

So far, this looks straightforward, he thought. Once he had the codes to get into the files, he was hoping he would quickly be able to see what needed to be done. This was not his field, but he did know enough to call in an expert.

He began to surmise that someone from corporate had to have taken down the firewalls on the ORCA servers so they could be accessed from the outside to target the filtration system.

No one, except a person in authority within the corporation, would have had knowledge of the security measures that had been put in place to protect the dome.

He remembered the call from Asad at the airport in Dallas before he took off for Lima. Asad had warned him to be cautious, and Brad began to wonder who he could trust to find out what was really going on. Asad said he wanted things to appear normal so he would be keeping everything internal and under wraps.

Lilly and Asad were the only ones he was sure of, but Lilly was rarely up top and Asad was in Dubai. If it was someone in the Lima office, the culprit might become suspicious if Lilly started spending more than her usual time there. As soon as he checked things out, Brad would call Asad to quietly send in his security people.

Picking up the reports from the bar, Brad drove his shuttle to the Bajo for some breakfast. It was still early and all the tables were empty, except for one with three men he didn't recognize.

Must be some of the new workers HR has hired over the past few months to help speed up the work, he thought.

Helping himself to a big mug of coffee from the beverage station, he picked up some eggs, bacon, and toast from the food line. He then chose a table close to the men and walked over to it. Brad noticed them watching him as he placed his tray on the table. He could tell they were curious about him, so he walked over, held out his hand, and introduced himself. "Hi, guys, I'm Brad Daniels, the project manager. Don't believe I've met you." He shook their hands as they introduced themselves to him.

"Mark Donavon, glad to meet you." Mark was dark complicated and the stockiest of the three.

"Jim Thomas, glad to meet you." Jim had carrot-orange hair and was the shortest of the three.

"Chad Michaels, glad to meet you, too." Chad was almost as tall as Brad. He had a python tattooed up his right arm.

"How long have you guys been here?" Brad asked, looking from one to the other.

Chad shrugged. "We came on board with the new electrician's crew. We're working on the wiring and hook-ups for the shopping area. I guess it's been about two months, maybe three. Sometimes it's difficult to keep track of time down here," he said with a laugh.

"Yes, it is. But, it's not as bad as it was in the beginning; before the simulated day and night lighting was installed. That has made all the difference. Just set the clock in your quarters to the dome's main clock, then program your room lighting to sync with the clock in your quarters and you should be okay."

"Nice meeting you guys," he said and turned back to his table to eat his breakfast before it got any colder. He inhaled his food, eager to get started on figuring out the mystery that had become a major problem.

☙❧

The Operations Room day shift was not due to come on until seven and the night shift was busy finishing up their reports. So, Brad decided to email IT topside himself to ask for the codes he required. Lilly had already informed them that someone from the dome would need the codes this morning. She intentionally did not mention Brad by name as he had requested.

Much to his surprise, he received a prompt reply to his email. Someone was actually in the Lima office this early in the morning. He asked that the codes be sent to the Joe Talbot's computer. Several minutes later, an email with the codes popped up in Joe's inbox.

Brad quickly printed out the codes, logged in, and keyed them into the computer. He opened the program and began running a mid-level security diagnostic scan on each of the individual files. It would take an hour or so for the scans to be completed.

By the time the scans were finished, the day shift was already at work, and Brad was reading the reports generated by the scans.

This was not going to be the easy fix he'd initially assumed it would be last night. The scans had discovered a virus in the filtration system, affecting all of the files within the system, which he knew was beyond his capabilities to correct. He also knew, because of the attempted sabotage, that an expert from the outside who was not involved with ORCA or familiar with the present situation would be necessary. It was no reflection on the present tech's capabilities to correct the situation, but Brad decided it would be safer if it were someone not associated with ORCA.

Since Asad wanted everything to appear normal, Brad had to follow the standard procedure when requesting a new hire, but he hesitated to call corporate. If there were someone at corporate who was behind this, that person could send in "an expert" who could possibly do more damage.

He called Lilly to get her thoughts about bypassing corporate for the expert. She thought it was a good idea and within a couple of hours, she had someone in mind who would do the job. She would call him and then arrange his security clearance.

ozcro

It took two days to track down the guy Lilly had told Brad about and then another week to secure his clearance and get him down to the dome.

Lilly was at the sub bay when it docked. Her eyes narrowed as she watched him walk down the gangway. He wasn't exactly the computer geek looking type she had expected, but Javier had been positive that he was the one to hire.

Lilly smiled and shook his hand. "You must be Señor Horton," she said. "Nice to meet you. If you will follow me, *por favor*, I will take you to meet Señor Daniels."

She turned and walked out of the sub bay to her waiting shuttle leaving the man to follow her. The twenty-minute ride to Brad's office was accomplished in silence.

Lilly followed Ty into Brad's office. "Brad, this is Señor Ty Horton, he will handle the job," Lilly said without emotion.

"Man, that was some ride," Ty said, striding forward to shake Brad's hand. "Blew my mind when I found out where the job was."

Brad shook Ty's hand and invited him to take a seat. Gathering up the printouts on his desk, he gave them to Ty.

"Don't mean to sound like I'm rushing you, but I am rushing you. We are on a tight completion schedule. Time is of the essence. As you can see, this report has flagged a virus, in every one of the files running the filtration system. Each one of those files runs a particular part of the dome's ecosystem. How long will it take to fix?" Brad explained, practically in one breath.

He watched Ty as he paged through the printouts. Ty didn't look like a geek with his snakeskin cowboy boots, faded Wranglers, and a blue chambray shirt that left no doubt that there was a rock-hard six pack under it. His Stetson had to have been years old. Sweat stains showed above the snakeskin hatband, the sides were rolled up, and the front bent down, casting a shadow across his face. Ty looked more like a rodeo cowboy than a computer geek. Brad sure hoped Lilly was right about this guy.

"Won't know 'til I've studied all the reports," Ty said, still flipping through the pages. "Give me an hour or so to see how far this virus has worked itself through the files. Where's the office you want me to use? I'd like to get this started." He looked up at Brad.

"Lilly will show you to the office and get you logged into the system," Brad said. "I will be here if you need me."

Ty followed Lilly back into the corridor and a short ways down to the office that would be his.

Closing the door to his office, Brad slumped down in his chair and closed his eyes. He let his mind drift to Darcey. He wondered if she was still upset about how he left. He hoped the flowers had somehow made up for part of it. He wished he could contact her, but he couldn't take a chance at least not for a couple of more days. Maybe, by then, he would know how severe this virus really was. Asad was sending a security team he could trust from corporate to investigate.

∽∾∽∾

Two hours later, Ty gave a short knock on Brad's door and walked in. Brad jerked awake, not realizing he had drifted off to sleep.

"Sorry, 'bout that, but you need to see this right now," Ty said, spreading out the reports on Brad's desk. "Each file has a separate virus designed to cause specific damage, but ya see this code right here?" he asked, pointing at a line of numbers, letters, symbols, and words in the code. Brad nodded. "Well, that's found in each of the viruses," Ty explained. "It looks like it's a trigger to cause a cascade, wiping out all the files at once. And it will if the individual viruses can't be neutralized in the order they were uploaded into the system," Ty said, exasperated. He took his hat off and ran his hand through his hair. "I've never seen anything quite like this."

"How do you suggest we handle this?" Brad asked, staring at the report.

Designing the dome with all of its complexities and then building it, five miles beneath the surface of the Pacific Ocean, had been a snap for him, but he was completely lost when it came to computers. He knew just enough to know he didn't know enough.

"This is gonna take more than just me to figure this one out. I've got three other guys who I'd recommend to come 'n help me. With them, we should be able to figure this out in a couple weeks," he said, with conviction, knowing with his guys here, they could solve the problem.

There was a reason they were known as "the best geeks in the business." For the last three years, they had worked together, and there hadn't been any problem, they couldn't solve.

"Well, contact them and let's get this thing done. Give Lilly their information and I'll have her get security clearances for them." Brad picked up the phone and called Lilly, telling her to expect Ty with the information for his other men and to start the security clearance process immediately.

"When you get your guys here, can you make it quicker than two weeks? Like I said, we're on a tight deadline, but we need the hydroponic system up and running for at least three weeks before the grand opening. We need to have time to make sure things are going to work. Is that going to be doable?" Brad asked as he hung up the phone.

Ty gave Brad a Texas-sized, reassuring grin. "You get my guys here 'n we can make it happen."

Ty stopped by Lilly's office and gave her the information on his guys. He had already notified them and they were ready to be here at a day's notice.

Lilly said it would take at least a week, to get clearance for them, but it would save time if they flew down to Lima now, ORCA would house them until their approvals came through.

Ty thanked her and walked down to Brad's office to let him know he had done the preliminary work up and would be ready to get to work when his guys arrived. He was sure that they could clean out the virus, and maybe without having to even use the backup system Lilly had told him about when she first called him.

"That sounds like you're right on top of things, Ty. Let's hope Lilly can get their clearances quickly," Brad stood up motioning at the door. "How about some coffee? My pot's broken. I've been trying to get a new one, but supply doesn't seem to think a coffee pot is a top priority." Brad laughed.

They took Brad's shuttle to the Bajo, passing several workers on the way. Work had been progressing quickly on the dome over the last month.

Completion of the retail section was almost finished. Some shops were already stocking inventory in anticipation of the grand opening of the dome. The living quarters in the main dome had been completed first in order to house the families of the workers who would be finishing off the other four residential domes.

The schools would be completed in another week and ready for students the week after the opening. The medical section had been the very first thing up and running in case of accidents or injuries.

The safety of the workers and other employees was the top priority with ORCA.

"Looks like you guys are gonna meet your deadline," Ty commented. "The main street area is lookin' real good. I saw there's even gonna be a cinema. Just like home, 'cept your five miles under the ocean." He chuckled.

"Yes, when this is complete, we will be able to support five hundred families. There will be schools, entertainment including live theatre, nightlife, restaurants, retail shops, business services, farming—it will be just like living on the surface. That's why the filtration system is so important. Besides the reactor that powers the dome, the biosphere filtration system is the heart of the dome. It will run the simulated lighting, water, the heating and cooling for the living quarters, the atmosphere for the entire dome, including the hydroponic farming and gardening area, as well as the main shopping area and parks," Brad told Ty, walking into the Bajo and making their way to the beverage station. "Maybe you'll like it well enough to sign on permanently. We're still filling the slots in the tech division."

"Ya know that's not a bad idea. What's it pay?" Ty asked. "I've been freelancin' for the last three or four years, so havin' somethin' permanent might be a good change," he said, adding cream and sugar to his coffee. *This job offer is looking mighty tempting* he thought. *I suppose I could get used to living down here if the pay is right.*

Brad laughed and slapped Ty on the back. "Well, when this is over, go see Lilly and tell her to hire you. If she gives you any grief, come see me."

ℰℐℰℐ

A week later Lilly stopped Brad in the corridor and handed him the clearance forms for Ty's other guys.

"They are already topside, just tell them their clearances are here. They will have to sign the nondisclosure forms before they come down," she said.

"Thanks! I'll give them a call and tell Ty his guys will be here in three hours," Brad said over his shoulder, walking on down the corridor toward his office. "Ty, Brad here. Your guys should be down in about three hours. Make sure housekeeping has their quarters ready. They will not be going up top till this thing is over." Brad hung up, glad they were here, but still nervous about the job.

What will happen if they can't fix the virus? The project is too close to completion to start over at this point. I have worked too hard on it to see it come apart now.

ℰℐℰℐ

Ty put the receiver down, looked through the extension list for housekeeping, and informed them his guys would be here shortly. He asked that they make sure their living quarters were in order.

Ty opened the folder with the stack of printouts he'd been going over the past weeks, trying to figure out the order in which the viruses had been introduced. He was sure of all except the hydroponics system. That one was a bugger.

Maybe Matt can figure it out.

Matt was the programming specialist of his crew. Ty was sure Matt could write a program to fix almost anything.

Three hours later, Ty heard loud, boisterous laughing coming down the corridor. It could only be his three partners in crime. He chuckled.

The four of them had been a team going on three years,

ever since they had worked a government job in Saudi Arabia. They had been known as the boys from Texas.

"Hey! What took y'all so long?" Ty hollered at the men.

Backslaps and handshakes were made all around.

"You're lookin' good, you old dog." Matt grinned at Ty. "I see ya couldn't get along without us, huh?"

"Sure thing, man! Y'all wanna put your stuff away before we get started?" Ty asked. "I'll show ya to the living quarters. I think they're all ready for ya now."

"Say, this is some place," Matt said. "How'd ya land this gig?"

"Don't know," Ty said, shaking his head. "Gotta call outta the blue, said they needed an expert in viruses 'n I was available, so I took it. You know the rest."

"Come on, let's get you settled in, and I'll see ya back in my office," Ty said as he jumped out of the shuttle.

He left them the shuttle and directions to his office. It took him fifteen minutes to walk back to his office. He swung by Brad's office to let him know his guys had arrived.

"When they're settled, I'll show them the printouts an' bring them up to speed. I'll have a progress report for you in the mornin'," Ty told Brad. "Come on over an' meet the guys when they get here."

Brad leaned back in his chair, locked his fingers behind his head, and stared at the ceiling. He was missing Darcey. His promise to call her in a couple of days had turned into three weeks. He hoped the roses had somehow helped take away some of her worries. There would be plenty of groveling for forgiveness and much penitence to do when he returned to Dallas. But he deserved every bit of it, and he knew it.

With the new tech guys on board and with the security guys Asad had sent, Brad hoped things would be under control and he would be able to call her by the end of the week.

Ty knocked on the doorframe, jolting Brad back to the present. He motioned to Brad to follow him. "The guys are here, come meet them."

"Guys, this is Brad Daniels, the project manager. He's the big Kahuna around here and this—" Ty swung his arm around indicating the dome. "—is his baby. Brad, I'd like you to meet my guys—Matt Wilkins, Steve 'Hot Dog' Nelson, and Scott Taylor." Ty beamed at Brad, his arms circling the shoulders of Matt and Hot Dog. "We're the boys from Texas and the best damn techs money can buy."

"Glad to meet you guys." Brad smiled shaking each one's hand. "I hope you're ready to tackle our problem. It isn't going to be easy to get rid of the virus from what Ty has told me. So, I'm glad you're here," he said, looking at Ty. "Ty can show you where the break room and Bajo el Mar Cafe are. I'll leave you guys to it."

Brad walked back to his office and found his message light flashing. Lilly had news that Armando had been asking questions about him. So far, no one, not even corporate aside from Asad, knew he was in Peru, let alone that he was in the dome. Brad called Lilly and told her to make sure it stayed that way. He didn't know who was behind the whole thing, but it had to be someone higher up the food chain than Armando.

Lilly might be right, he thought. *Someone from corporate, or maybe one of the investors has to be behind the sabotage.*

Lilly told him she would keep looking.

CHAPTER 4

The Boys from Texas

Ty, Scott, and Hot Dog spent the next two days pouring over the printouts from the diagnostics. They were trying to pinpoint the order in which the viruses had been introduced, while Matt worked on putting together a program he was calling Code Blue—a superbug killer.

"It's ready," Matt announced, walking into the workroom, waving the printout of Code Blue.

"This will not only tell us when the bugs were introduced, but will kill all the code it finds related to the bugs in the order they were entered. There is also a subroutine that will shred all of the bug code the scan finds."

"Wouldn't this mean puttin' the backup system online?" Ty asked, tapping his pencil on the table. "I'd have to clear it with Brad."

"No, there's no need to go offline for this," Matt said, pushing the old printouts off the table and spreading out the Code Blue printout. "We can switch up to safe mode, which will freeze the virus while we run Code Blue, and it won't interfere with the standard operation of the system or the dome's daily routine."

"That just might work," Scott said, seriously, getting up to pour a cup of coffee.

"Whatcha mean 'that just might work'?" Matt laughed, wadding up a piece of the old print out, and throwing it at him. "Have you *ever* known any of my programs not to work?"

"No, that's why we keep ya 'round." Ty laughed, tossing his pencil at Scott.

Scott ducked both missiles, laughing. "Okay, okay. Sorry I mentioned it." Still laughing, he picked up the paper wad and pencil and tossed them back on the table.

"I've written an algorithm that lets Code Blue run on all the systems simultaneously," Matt pointed out. "Ty, have you checked with Brad about the backup files. How long will it take them to get brought down here?"

"I'll check with him and update him on what we're plannin' on doin' with this new program," Ty said, standing up and stretching. "I'm ready for some chow. How about the rest of you?"

"I'm in," Hot Dog said, who was already halfway out the door. "Last man pays." He laughed, making a dash for the shuttle. Matt and Scott took off after Hot Dog, racing to the shuttle. Ty watched them go, shaking his head, as walked to Brad's office.

"Hey, big guy." Ty grinned after he knocked on the doorframe. "We've got a new program we're gonna try out this afternoon and wanna let ya know about it. Also, how long will it take to get the backup files down here, just in case they're needed after we clear out the virus?"

"It will take about two and half hours, but there won't be another sub until tomorrow. You might want to put off running the program until then if you think you will need the backups," Brad said, leaning back in his chair. "What's this new program you're going to try?"

"It's a superbug killer program that Matt wrote. He's calling it Code Blue. It will scan the whole system all at once," Ty said, leaning against the doorframe, his arms folded across his chest. "It should only take two, maybe three hours to run the whole system. But could take longer, dependin' on the problems it finds."

"Sounds like you guys are making progress. That's good

news. We can use some right about now." Brad smiled, but it didn't reach his eyes. "The first sub is scheduled to arrive at seven in the morning. If you want them to come down on that sub, let me know and I'll have Lilly call IT topside and have the files sent down in the morning."

"That works for me. I'll tell the guys we're a go for the mornin'," Ty said. "Now I'm headin' for some chow. Ya comin'?"

"Naw, I've still got paperwork to finish," Brad said, picking up his pen again. "Later."

Brad watched Ty saunter down the corridor and let his mind wander.

He would be glad when this was over. He had worked too hard these past five years on the project to let some damn asshole like Armando screw it up. He and Mike would have worked the project together if Mike's dad hadn't died.

ORCA bought out Mike's part of the project when he went back to Dallas to help his mom run their family's stables. Lilly had been promoted to Brad's assistant when Mike left. Mike had confided to Brad that he'd never cared much for Lilly. Said she sometimes gave him the creeps— too quiet and organized for his tastes. He felt something lurked just under that placid facade she showed the world.

Brad missed Mike.

The program the guys had come up with had to work. Time was running out and, if it didn't work, well, they were out of options.

Once they had the virus taken care of, he would have Asad's security people issue an arrest warrant for Armando. Then he would find out who was behind the whole thing. He was sure Lilly was right—someone from corporate or one of the investors, was dead set on delaying the completion. He even got the same vibe from Asad, although he'd never said it out loud.

Now, until he knew who was behind this and had them arrested, Brad couldn't take any chance on contacting

Darcey. These people seemed to have eyes and ears everywhere and, for all he knew, there could be one of them in the dome right now. Asad's security people were almost through vetting everyone and, so far, everyone had passed.

CHAPTER 5

Nightmares

Friday morning, four weeks and five days after Brad left for Peru:

It was close to two in the morning when Darcey finished the last preliminary layout for her new client. She had to meet the client on site along with her boss later in the afternoon to go over them.

Yawning, she pulled on her sweat pants and reached for her tee shirt. The framed photo of Brad sitting on her dresser stared back at her when she poked her head out of the neck hole of the tee shirt.

"Why haven't you called?" she yelled at the photo, pulling the tee shirt the rest of the way on.

It had been four weeks and five days since Brad left.

"You've got two more days to call. If you don't, I'm gonna find you and give you a piece of my mind," she yelled again. She shook her finger at the photo. "You'll be sorry."

Darcey picked up the small throw pillow from her bed and flung it at the photo, knocking it over. The framed photo fell on the carpet with a soft thud.

Shit! she thought as she picked up the photo and set it back on the dresser.

Crawling into bed, she turned off the bedside lamp and

pulled the sheet up under chin. She was still pissed off as she drifted off to sleep…

☙❧❧

Can't see. My arms are extended. Brad's barely visible. It's so dark. My side—burning. You can't stop, she told herself. *Pick up your feet. Run faster!* "Brad wait!" she screamed.

Her heart was pounding. *It hurts. Blood pounding in my ears. Can't run anymore. Can't breathe. It hurts. You can't stop,* she reminded herself. *Find Brad. They're coming. I hear the sound. They're coming closer, louder.* She turned in a circle. *It's so dark. I can't see them. I can't see Brad. But I hear them.* Panic. *They are almost here. Run faster!*

Fear. The pain in her side—burning, piercing. *Can't breathe—hurts so bad, can't stop.* She forced herself on.

Terror. *My feet, lead weights. My legs, numb. Run faster! They're almost here. It's so dark. I hear them—*

☙❧❧

Darcey's body constricted and she bolted upright in bed. A short scream had escaped her lips before she realized she was awake and in her own bed.

She pulled the sweaty, tangled sheet from around her legs and lay back down. Her breathing slowly returned to normal. Another terrifying night, just like all the other nights that had plagued her for the past five weeks.

I should get up, she thought as she stared into the inky blackness of her room, her arm across her forehead.

Slowly the sun began to filter through the mini blinds but Darcey was still worrying. *Where are these crazy dreams coming from? Am I going crazy?*

She racked her brain for something to make sense as to why she kept having the same nightmare night after night.

Am I stressing too much over Brad not calling? Is that what's causing these nightmares? I guess these past almost five weeks have been taking a toll on me.

Her best friend Marti Campbell was absolutely sure of it. That's why Darcey hadn't told her about the dreams. It would be just one more thing for Marti to worry about, and she'd been trying to be so optimistic for Darcey.

Darcey could tell Marti was worried that she would shut down like she did the summer before she met Brad. Marti had attempted to warn her that the guy she was dating was no good, but Darcey was so infatuated with him, she couldn't see it until it was too late.

Darcey hated herself because she had let him make such a fool of her. So much so, that she had shut everyone out, including Marti.

Finally, after all of Marti's coaxing and pleading didn't work, she put her foot down, and yelled at Darcey. "Get over yourself!"

That got Darcey's attention. Marti made her realize that it wasn't her fault the stupid guy left, but it was her fault that she was acting like a damn idiot about it.

Darcey knew this was different, though. Brad was different. She was different. She had no doubts that they belonged together. Because of their connection, it made her next decision an easy one. If she didn't hear from Brad in the next two days, she was going to go find him.

Darcey had told Marti yesterday and she'd practically had a cow.

"What the heck are you thinking?" Marti exclaimed. "He said he would call, and you know he will. He's never missed calling you, when he's away—not ever. Just hold your horses. He'll call," Marti scolded, standing with her hands on her hips making her point.

Well, if he doesn't call, I'm going, Darcey told herself emphatically. *Marti will just have to live with it. No, on second thought* she supposed, *that wouldn't be fair to Marti.*

Darcey knew Marti wanted nothing but the best for her,

and sometimes, she'd not been very tolerant of Marti's good intentions.

But, this time she's wrong. I wish Marti would just accept the fact that, if I don't hear from him by Sunday, I am going to find Brad.

Darcey had already talked with Brad's office, and they'd told her everything they knew; so now, she would go to the Lima office.

Darcey supposed she could just call and save herself a lot of time and expense, but she wanted to talk to someone face to face. She knew people could tell you any damn thing they wanted to over the phone. But this time she wanted to see their faces.

My mind is made up! I need to find Brad. Besides, my track record's good. I can't remember any time I've ever let reason get in the way of something I wanted to do, and things have always worked out just fine, she rationalized to herself.

Well, there's a first time for everything, an inner voice cautioned her.

The phone rang, jolting Darcey back to the present. She cleared her head and saw it was Marti. She debated about answering but figured she'd better. Marti would be banging on her front door, in exactly twenty minutes, to make sure she hadn't done something "really dumb and stupid," as Marti put it.

Sighing, Darcey punched the button, just before the answering machine picked up.

"Hey, Marti! What's up?" Darcey really didn't feel like talking. But, since she was her true BFF, she couldn't hurt Marti by shutting her out. Especially since Marti had made it her prime mission these past four weeks, to check on Darcey daily—sometimes twice a day.

Darcey sighed. She loved Marti to pieces and appreciated her concern, but really? Darcey felt guilty not telling her she had already made plans to go Peru. But she knew if she did, Marti would throw another hissy fit. Marti would do her best to try and talk Darcey out of it, or worse—she would insist on coming. But this was something Darcey had to do alone.

"Nothing. Just making sure you're all right." The sunshine resonated in Marti's voice. "You know I'm a worrier." She laughed. "Look—" Marti put on her no-nonsense voice. "I know it's been almost five weeks, but he's going to call. You've got to remember that. He told you this was a high priority job, so maybe he can't contact anyone on the outside, just yet. Give it a few more days. You'll see. He. Will. Call," she said, enunciating each word with force.

Marti was as worried as Darcey. It wasn't like Brad to neglect Darcey in any way. From that first night they'd met, he had hardly let her out of his sight when he was here on weekends. He spoiled her completely.

So much so, Marti mused, that she was even a little jealous. Sending her flowers for no reason, other than to say he loved her, or missed her. Always buying her something, just because he thought it looked like her. And the way he looked at her, when she wasn't looking, you could see it in his eyes—he was deeply and completely in love with her.

"You're probably right." Darcey sighed, running her finger across the page of her open planner and stopped on Sunday's date and what she had written there.

"Let's go for coffee. We can have some 'girl talk.' You'll feel better. I can be there in twenty minutes," Marti said, hopefully.

She knew just how hardheaded Darcey could be when she set her mind to something, so redirecting her was almost impossible, but she kept trying. She wasn't going to let her best friend fall to pieces again if she could help it.

"Thanks, but no, I can't. I've got a new job that's due in a couple of weeks. I have to run through the prelims with the boss and the client at two. I'll take a rain check."

Hoping she didn't sound like she was putting Marti off, Darcey said bye and hung up. She would be back from Peru in plenty of time to meet this job's deadline, she assured herself.

👁️‍🗨️

Friday evening, four weeks and five days since Brad let for Peru:

Plopping down on the sofa and kicking off her sandals, Darcey slouched against the back, propping her feet up on the coffee table. A luxury, she denied everyone else except Brad.

It had been a long, exhausting afternoon. Her boss and the contractor disagreed on the implementation of the design and Darcey had been caught in the middle.

She heaved a sigh and let herself slide down, sideways until her head rested on one of the throw pillows. She hugged the other one to her chest and stretched out on the sofa. Her eyelids slid down, and she drifted, remembering the Monday morning after Brad left…

👁️‍🗨️

It had been a little after six a.m. when she finally gave up trying to go back to sleep, and crawled out of bed. She was exhausted from the crazy dream that bordered on a nightmare—of Brad disappearing in a black void, her running and running, and someone or something chasing her.

She couldn't remember all of it. She didn't want to remember *any* of it. She didn't have any idea what would have triggered the dreams. Shivering as she padded to the bathroom, she looked in the mirror.

"Eeesh." She squinted, trying to focus on the face in the mirror. The face that reflected back showed all the signs of the nightmarish night she'd just spent.

Her short, copper-colored hair pointed in all directions, and the bags under her eyes, weren't bags—they were trunks! Damn, she had raccoon eyes. She'd forgotten to remove her makeup before going to bed. To put it bluntly, she looked like a wild woman.

She freshened up, and maybe she didn't look much better, but she felt better. However, the dream of last night still haunted her.

She shuffled into the kitchen, picked up the coffee pot, glanced over at Brad and her matching mugs, sitting side-by-side on the counter, and sighed again.

As she watched the cold water inching its way up the inside of the pot, the flashing red light on the answering machine caught her eye. A call must have come in after she went to bed. She set the pot down and punched the play button. The machine whirred to life, delivering its message. The velvet tones, of the voice I knew so well, resonated from the answering machine.

That's not fair, she thought. She didn't even get to say a proper goodbye, and last night—a brief kiss and hug in the car—what was that?

He could have waited and left this morning. They could have had one more night together.

What's the big rush anyway, she asked herself, just a little pissed off about the whole situation. Maybe, she could catch him on his cell. She picked up her phone and punched in his number.

She needed to say goodbye; needed to hear his voice. It was necessary. The phone rang and rang and rang. She decided to go see for herself. Even though she wouldn't—couldn't—admit it, she knew deep down it was going to be a wasted trip. Still, she had to try something—anything.

She ran to the bedroom, pulling off her PJs as she went. Yanking open the dresser drawer, she dug around, found a clean pair of Wranglers, and grabbed her yellow country blouse from the closet. Slamming her feet into a pair of sandals, she grabbed her purse and car keys off the hook by the door. She drove with her hands shaking, the five miles to Brad's condo.

The note, on the super's door, indicated he would be on the third floor, She finally found him repairing a leaky faucet. He was useless. He didn't know anything except Brad had paid his rent for next month. She turned and walked down the hall to the elevator. Her hand still shaking, She pushed the "DOWN" button and waited.

She didn't remember the elevator ride, walking back to her car, getting in, or how long she sat, with her mind idling in neutral.

She shook her head and pressed her fingers to her temples, trying to suppress the slowly forming headache.

This is stupid, she told herself. *Call some place where you can get some answers.*

She pulled her phone out and called his office. No, Brad was not there. He left for the Lima office last night. No, they did not know what time he had landed. No, they didn't have a phone number for him other than the Lima office number and his cell. Yes, they would be glad to call there and see when he landed. Yes, she would hold while they called. No, the Lima office had not heard from Brad, and no, they did not know if he had arrived. They were extremely sorry they could not be more helpful. She thanked them and let out a big long sigh.

Shit! Looks like I'm just going to have to wait till he calls, she thought, frustrated. *Good grief. He's only been gone a few hours, and already you're pushing the panic button.*

She exhaled a ragged breath and decided to go home. She had jobs waiting.

CHAPTER 6

Remembering

Rubbing her forehead, Darcey closed her eyes. The headache, the result of another nightmarish night, had been dancing around the edges of her skull all morning. It was just waiting, for the drum and bugle corps to make an appearance and send it into a full-blown migraine.

She shook out a couple of tablets, migraine strength, from the Tylenol bottle, popped them in her mouth, and washed them down with the last of the coffee in her mug.

Ugh! Cold! She wrinkled her nose as the cold liquid slid down her throat.

The only thing Darcey hated worse, she supposed, than cold coffee, was being out of her favorite snack—Pop-Tarts. She pulled her sole box of strawberry Pop-Tarts from the cupboard and unwrapped the last one.

Perfect timing. I'll hit the store when I get back, she thought, taking a healthy bite of the tart.

She jotted Pop-Tarts on the memo pad then filled her mug with hot coffee and strolled over to the kitchen table. Pulling out Brad's chair, she sat down and drew up her left leg, resting the heel on the chair seat.

Reaching for her planner, she pulled it toward her and thumbed to tomorrow's date where, in bold red ink, she had written *10 a.m. AA #2012*. A wave of excitement and anticipation hit her—butterflies and goose bumps—all at the same time.

Tomorrow will be five weeks to the day that Brad left for Lima, she thought, staring at the date.

She had decided to not tell Marti she was leaving for Peru in the morning. It had been a tough decision. She and Marti had been friends since grade school and shared practically everything, but Darcey knew Marti would just try to talk her out of going and then get upset because she couldn't.

No, I won't put her through that, she rationalized. *I've already made up my mind. I'm going. The subject is closed.*

Darcey had to know what had happened to Brad. Trying to make sense of it, she brooded again, on how things had gone since the first week, after Brad left…

✍✍✍

The day after Brad had left in the middle of the night for Peru, a dozen lavender roses mixed with white daisies had arrived with a card expressing his love and that he missed her—but no phone call.

After the first full week since he'd left and he still hadn't called, she'd started to worry—a little.

Marti reassured her that he was probably just tied up with the job and not to worry. He would call.

"When has he ever missed calling you?" she reminded Darcey.

The roses withered and died.

Then, when he hadn't contacted her by the second week, little twinges of panic, began to nibble away at Darcey.

Hadn't he said he would only be gone a couple of weeks? Hadn't he promised he would call in a couple of days? How can he not know how worried I'd be?

Marti still tried to bolster Darcey's spirits. Darcey could see she was afraid of being shut out like last time. But this was different. Brad wasn't some fly-by-night playboy, just out for a good time. He was serious about their relationship, and that made it all the harder to understand, why he hadn't called.

By the third week, she was in full-blown panic mode. *Surely, he knows how worried I am. Yes, he would know, and he would move heaven and earth to contact me to let me know he's all right, if he could.*

If he could. Those words echoed in her mind, igniting that sinking feeling in her stomach, that told her something was definitely wrong.

Had his plane crashed? Had he been in an accident? He hadn't explicitly told her what this job was, so she had no idea how dangerous it might be.

If it had to do with the ocean, he could have drowned, or been eaten by a shark. All kinds of crazy scenarios ran through her head—none of them good.

And, then the nightmares—night after night. She hadn't had a good night's sleep for the past two weeks—

♊

The coffee pot's auto shutoff beeped, interrupting Darcey's thoughts. She poured the last of it in her mug, sighed, popped the last of the Pop-Tart in her mouth, and turned to stare out the window, resting her chin on her knee.

No matter how many times Darcey admonished herself, she couldn't keep from obsessing over the fact that Brad had not called.

Not a single word, not a phone call, no email, not even a text—nothing. Just that lovely bunch of lavender roses that had arrived the day after he left. It made no sense.

She knew she was making a pest of herself, calling twice a week to see if there was any news. The Dallas office had nothing new to tell her, and they still had no information on when, or if, he had landed, and after contacting the Lima office again, they couldn't help either. It was as if Brad had literally fallen off the face of the earth.

She knew he was out there…somewhere. She just didn't know where. The message he left on his way to the airport said he would call as soon as he could, but not to worry, if it was a couple of days before she heard from him.

Well, it's been four weeks, six days and ten hours since he left, and I still haven't heard from him. I know something is wrong, I feel it.

She set her foot back on the floor and stood up.

Darcey slowly walked over to the sink and poured the rest of the cold coffee down the drain, rinsed the mug, and turned it upside down on the counter next to Brad's. Drying her hands on a the towel, she stared across the room at the music box Brad had surprised her with, remembering the last Saturday they had spent together here...

ϰϰϰ

When he came by the Saturday morning before that fateful Sunday, she was finishing dressing. She heard him let himself in through the front door. Hearing the door shut, she called, "I'm in here."

He moved softly up behind her and wrapped his arms around her, pulling her tightly against his hard body, that fit hers so perfectly, heat pulsing through her veins.

"Ummm, you shouldn't leave your door unlocked. You never know who might walk in," he breathed in her ear, kissing it softly. He moved to her neck and that sensitive spot just below her ear, and she heard him inhale deeply. He loved the smell of her skin after a shower.

"Ummm, you smell heavenly. Good enough to eat."

Slowly, he proceeded kissing his way down her neck, sending her heart into overdrive. Reaching her shoulder, he raised his head and turned her around, brushing his lips across hers. It was heaven!

She kissed him back, their lips moving in sync. Running her tongue across his lower lip, she gently bit it. Brad groaned softly and deepened the kiss, pulling her closer into his arms and against that body she craved. Her body melted into his, as they fell onto her bed.

Her fingers wound themselves in his hair, pulling him closer. Gently, he pulled her arms from around his neck and held them above her head.

"Don't move," he breathed.

She grabbed the edge of the headboard to keep her arms from flying back around his neck.

He gently moved to his side and slowly slid his hand under her shirt. Watching her he pushed it up, revealing her breasts. He kissed the tops of her breasts that pushed up above her bra then lightly traced their contours with his tongue. Rolling her over on top of him, his hand quickly unhooked her bra and pulled it from between them. He tossed it on the floor and buried his face in the valley between her breasts.

"You are so beautiful," he whispered, kissing first one, and then the other, their tight little buds, growing harder with each kiss, smiling as she caught her breath. "Your skin is like velvet to the touch." He slid his hands down her back then across her buttocks and back up her sides. "Ummmm flawless."

Goose bumps and butterflies exploded. It was increasingly harder to breathe as her passion grew. She pushed his head away so she could reclaim his lips. She trailed kisses down his neck to his chest, savoring every inch of him. Winding her fingers through his, she pulled his arms up over his head. Unwinding her fingers, she traced, in feather-light motions, all the way down from his wrists to his shoulders and onto his chest, watching as passion smoldered in his emerald-green eyes as her hips gently moved against him.

Groaning, he rolled over, taking her with him. Straddling her, he propped himself up on his arms, all the while watching her, as he pulled his mouth into that sweet, tantalizing lop-sided grin. Rising to his knees, he slowly pulled off his sweater. His eyes, never leaving hers. She appreciated every inch of his hard muscled body, as her hands reached up to caress his chest, loving the feel of the texture of his skin beneath her fingers as they slid down his body.

Slipping his fingers under the waistband of her shorts, he backed off the end of the bed and, in one swift move, her shorts were on the floor. She quickly threw her shirt off, as he left his khakis on the floor beside her shorts. A flash of light, a supernova of passion exploded, and then time stood still.

They lay in each other's arms, peacefully and blissfully content.

Sometime later, after breakfast, she picked up their plates, put them in the dishwasher, refilled their mugs, and sat back down at the table.

"Here." He handed her a small, white box tied with a gold ribbon.

"What's this?" she asked, pulling on the bow.

"Just a little something I picked up, that reminded me of you."

The ribbon fell to the floor, as she opened the box. Inside was a beautiful, gold filigree music box. She turned the key, winding it up, and the little tinkling sounds of "This Guy's In Love with You," played in the air.

Reaching over, he picked up her hand and kissed her palm, sending a wave of heat through her body. She couldn't think of a thing to say. She was too busy trying to remember how to breathe…

⟡⟡⟡

This was getting her nowhere. She sniffed and wiped away the tear that had slipped down her cheek. Tossing the towel on the counter, she sat down at the computer.

Darcey wanted to do another quick search on the Internet again. Until this past week, she had never researched the corporation Brad worked for. But since he'd left and hadn't called, she wanted to know more about the organization, thinking maybe it would give her a clue to why he hadn't called.

She couldn't believe there wasn't more listed about the company, Ocean Research for Combined Alliances Corporation "ORCA," but there wasn't. ORCA was a multi-billion dollar business, specializing in oceanic research and development, based in Dubai, United Arab Emirates. It had offices in Dallas, Texas, USA, London, England, Madrid, Spain, Cairo, Egypt, and Lima, Peru.

The last thing on the screen, before she opened her emails, was the information on deep-water ocean research. Did Brad's project have something to do with ocean research? She could only guess. He had never given her any of the details, only that it was highly classified.

Logically, Darcey knew the thing to do was just wait till he called.

There will, more than likely, be an excellent explanation for it all, she figured. *But, shoot, when have I ever put logic or reason first in the things I do? Well, not since I was thirteen.*

Once Darcey had made a decision it was, Damn the torpedoes. Full speed ahead.

Right now, her gut was telling her she needed to go full speed ahead to find Brad. Finding Brad outweighed everything else. There was something pushing her to go. She knew it had to be Brad.

Darcey put on another pot of coffee and sat down to read her emails from work. Most were about the new job she had been given yesterday.

She sighed.

CHAPTER 7

Non Truths

Darcey glanced at the clock—six twenty-two a.m. She was almost packed, but she still had to call Marti. She had lingered over her morning coffee, working up enough nerve to make the call.

Yesterday, Darcey had called the Dallas office for the last time to get the information she needed concerning the Lima office and who she should contact once she arrived. They had given her the name, Armando Martinez, and told her they would arrange for him to pick her up at the airport. She jotted his name down in her address book, along with his phone number, just in case.

Finally, after her fourth cup of coffee, Darcey thought she had pumped herself up enough to call Marti to give her the news that she was leaving, without actually telling her *where* she was going.

Marti had been Darcey's rock, making certain she didn't go bonkers and do something stupid. Darcey was sure that Mari would consider her plans to fly to Peru incredibly dumb and stupid.

No, I'm not telling Marti where I'm going, just that I am going, she repeated again to herself waiting for Marti to answer.

"Hey, Darcey," Marti answered her phone. "How's it going, girlfriend?"

"Sorry, I know it's early, but I just wanted to let you know I have to go out to the site for this new job I picked up," Darcey fibbed. *Well, I am going to the job site, just not yet,* she thought, crossing her fingers. "Should be three or four days at the most. I leave this morning. I'll call you when I get back."

Darcey hoped Marti wouldn't ask for specifics or, worse, to come along, because, if she did, Darcey would have to lie to her. Fibbing was bad enough, but an outright lie, she couldn't do.

What do you think you're doing now? A fib is the same as a lie, her inner voice reminded her.

Darcey pushed that thought to the back of her mind and turned her attention to what Marti was saying.

"Wish I could go with you, but Dad needs me to help at the trade show this week." Marti sighed. Regret was clear in her voice.

"Me, too." Darcey replied, hoping Marti couldn't hear the relief in her voice. "I'll call when I get back. Later!"

Darcey tossed her phone onto the bed, feeling like a weight had been lifted from her, and finished packing. She was only taking what would fit in her carry-on. If she needed anything more, she had her credit cards.

Glancing at the clock, Darcey saw she had three hours before she needed to be at the airport. Giving her ticket confirmation and passport a final check, she shoved them into her shoulder bag.

Darcey's stomach tied itself in a knot and her mouth turned to cotton every time she thought about what she was getting ready to do. Regardless, she was determined to find out what had happened to Brad. She was nervous because this was a huge step, even for her, but she'd made the decision—she was going to Peru.

Zipping up her carry-on, Darcey gave her apartment one last look to double check that everything was okay before locking the door. She pulled the door shut, her hand shaking, as she turned the key in the lock. A strange, almost creepy feeling washed over her, and she shuddered. She felt like it might just be the last time she ever saw her apartment.

Shake it off, she told herself. *It's just your imagination and nerves.* But, something told her intuition that maybe it wasn't just nerves.

Darcey pushed the thought away as she methodically went through the motions of loading the car. She put the key in the ignition, turned the key forward, and started the engine.

She needed the order of those actions to keep herself from flying into a thousand pieces. Darcey had never been so nervous about anything in her entire life. Not even submitting the dissertation for her Master of Fine Arts Degree to Professor Johnson compared to this. She had a death grip on the steering wheel as she pulled out into traffic and headed for the airport.

This is it. I'm really doing this. She took a deep breath, and tried to swallow. *If I had any sense, I'd turn around right now and go home! I hope I'm not going to regret this.*

Traffic was light, giving Darcey time to rethink what she was doing.

No. She shook her head. *I really don't want to do that. The less I dwell on this, possibly stupid, trip I am embarking on, the better. And yes, I know going off on my own, and not telling anyone my plans is actually dumb. But, I have to— no, I need to find Brad.*

Darcey put an end to the argument with herself and decided it would be more prudent to keep her eyes on the road. It would be better to think about what she would do when she finally got to Peru. She hadn't given that much thought yet, because she didn't know exactly what to expect once she was there.

After she had booked a round-trip ticket to Lima, Darcey had called and made reservations at the Sheraton Lima Hotel, for three nights. That should give her enough time to sort things out and find Brad, she had decided.

Darcey also decided against renting a car, because everywhere she wanted to go, she would just take a taxi. She wasn't going to risk driving and getting lost. Besides, she could also ask that Martinez guy the Dallas office had told her about.

Darcey saw the exit sign that said: *Dallas Fort Worth International Airport—2 miles*. She signaled and moved over into the far right lane, so she wouldn't get caught in the middle lane and miss the exit.

Rush hour traffic was beginning to build, even though it was still early. Taking the airport exit, she followed the signs to the Long-Term Parking lot. The airport bus was just leaving as she pulled in.

Damn, I'll have at least a ten-minute wait until the next bus arrives, she grumbled to herself, annoyed at this delay in getting to the terminal. Darcey was ready to get going and she didn't like these little "life moments" popping up and delaying her. However, the long-term lot was mostly empty, and she found a place to park close to the pickup spot.

Locking the car door, Darcey checked her ticket confirmation and passport again. A small wave of panic swept over her, and her stomach moved up to her throat, but she pushed it back down. She couldn't hurl—not now, not here.

The airport bus pulled into the lot and stopped at the pickup spot where she was waiting. The door opened, a couple got off, and she got on.

The driver asked which terminal Darcey wanted. She told him International.

Bile still churned in Darcey's stomach. She was glad now she hadn't eaten any breakfast. She was positive it would have been all over the bus floor, right about now.

The bus stopped in the international terminal. Darcey grabbed her carry-on, slipped the strap of her bag on her shoulder, and hesitantly stepped out onto the sidewalk. She was so nervous that she forgot to thank the driver.

She stood staring at the auto-open doors swishing back

and forth as people streamed through them heading for destinations unknown, but she knew hers—Lima, Peru.

She tried to swallow but her mouth had gone dry.

I must be out of my mind, she thought as her sweaty palm pulled up the handle of her carry-on. *Too late now, my mind's made up. It's Damn the torpedoes. Full speed ahead. I don't back down.*

Inhaling the pungent odors that hung heavy in the air outside the busy terminal, she pulled herself up straight and walked through the auto-open doors, heading for the check-in area. Her heart was beating out a fandango, while her other sweaty hand tightly clutched the strap of her shoulder bag.

The attendant at the American Airlines counter smiled pleasantly as Darcey approached. She handed him her ticket confirmation and passport. He checked the computer, made a notation on the ticket, and gave it and her passport back. Then, wishing her a pleasant flight, he instructed Darcey to proceed through the security checkpoint to the waiting area for Gate 32.

Anticipation built as Darcey headed off in the direction the American Airline attendant had indicated. It was quickly squashed as she saw the long line waiting at the security checkpoint.

Another delay, she groused inwardly.

Glancing around, curious at who might be some of her fellow passengers for the next several hours, Darcey saw they were a diverse mix of nationalities. The family in line, in front of her, looked to be of Mexican descent.

They had two, beautiful dark-eyed girls, maybe, three and five. Darcey thought the little girls were well behaved for that age. She smiled at both, and they smiled back, ducking behind their mother's legs. The mother turned, also smiled, and said something in Spanish that Darcey couldn't understand.

"Sorry, I don't speak Spanish." Darcey held out her hands, palms up, and shrugged.

"Oh, sorry. I just wanted to make sure they are not bothering you," the woman replied in perfect English.

"Oh, no, they're fine," Darcey assured her. "You have two very lovely daughters. What are their names?"

"This one is Maria, and the little one is Rosa." The woman beamed as she gently pulled them from behind her. "Maria will be six tomorrow and Rosa is three."

"Glad to meet you. And happy birthday, Maria." Darcey bent over slightly and extended her hand to the little girls. They giggled and shook her hand.

Loud voices caused everyone to turn, and look at a disturbance around the metal detector. A burly man was yelling at a TSA agent but Darcey couldn't hear what was being said. It was loud, whatever it was.

Airport security arrived on the scene and had to physically subdue the man before they took him away in handcuffs. Maria and Rosa stared wide-eyed at the spectacle.

Darcey followed the Mexican family through the metal detector, smiled at the stone-faced TSA agent, grabbed her stuff out of one of the tubs, and slipped her flats on in mid-stride as she walked toward the waiting area.

Checking the departure board, she saw her flight was on time. More butterflies erupted. The sooner she got in the air, the better. Darcey didn't do hurry-up-and-wait very well.

Stopping in one of the airport stores, she bought a couple of magazines, a book, and a couple of candy bars. She checked the departure board again. American Airlines 2012 was scheduled to depart in thirty minutes.

Seating in the waiting area for Gate 32 was at a premium, so she stood, surveying the people, as she waited to board. They all seemed preoccupied with their own thoughts.

She noticed the little Mexican family that had been in line with her would be on her flight, too. Maria and Rosa shyly waved to her. Smiling, Darcey waved back.

The knot in Darcey's stomach was building and tightening. An American Airlines attendant announced that flight

2012 to Lima, Peru, was now boarding. Passengers with children were to board first. The little Mexican family collected their bags and walked through the boarding gate's door.

Boarding went smoothly, as the passengers filed through the gate, down the ramp, and onto the plane. Darcey shuffled past several passengers before she found her seat, thankfully noticing she had the window seat.

She tossed her shoulder bag on the seat before lifting up her carry-on to put it in the overhead compartment. Grimacing and puffing, she struggled to wedge it into the cramped space. Finally, with the carry-on snug in the overhead, she sat down and stuffed her shoulder bag under the seat in front of her. Heaving a sigh, Darcey pulled the seat belt across her lap and shoved the buckled into its lock with a click.

Darcey heard giggling and looked up to see, Maria and Rosa, displaying impish grins as they watched over the top of the seat in front of her. They apparently had been watching Darcey struggle with the carry-on and seemed to have found her facial expressions quite amusing.

"Hi, girls." Darcey smiled at them. They giggled and ducked their heads as Mama told them to leave the nice lady alone and turn around and sit down.

The dull hum of the engines increased, as the plane started backing away from the loading area, headed for the runway. Clicking on the intercom, the flight attendant's voice was barely audible over the constant hum of the engines and the passengers' conversations.

First in English, then in Spanish, the flight attendant gave the safety instructions.

Humpf! Darcey grumbled to herself. *A lot a good that will do. There probably wouldn't be any survivors to follow all of those stupid instructions, even if you could remember them.*

She tuned out the flight attendant, like most of the other passengers seemed to be doing as they chatted with their fellow passengers or had their noses buried in some type of reading material.

Darcey turned and watched out the window, as the busy airport vehicles went about their business. Watching the goings-on took Darcey's mind off of things for a few minutes.

The plane had taxied for several minutes before it came to a stop, waiting its turn to takeoff.

Come on; get this plane in the air, Darcey pleaded silently.

Finally, the plane moved forward onto the main runway. The roar of the engines increased as the plane accelerated, pushing Darcey back in her seat. Her ears popped, her stomach turned over, and her heart rate accelerated like a race car heading for the finish line as the plane barreled down the runway and lifted into the air.

A roar and a rumble under Darcey's feet indicated the landing gear had come up. She squeezed her eyes shut.

Finally.

Darcey's cheeks puffed out as she exhaled, making her realize she had been holding her breath practically the whole time while the plane took off. She tried to swallow, but her mouth was full of cotton. Then, looking down, she saw she had been gripping the right armrest so tight that her fingers were cramping and the knuckles were white. Her left hand was balled into a fist so tight that her fingernails had left impressions on her palm.

Geez Louise, that was stupid. This is not my first flight. No, but it is my first flight out of the country. Somehow, that thought just added to her tension.

No, what is *stupid was me not telling anyone where I'm going,* her inner voice scolded.

CHAPTER 8

Unwanted Attention

The flight was mostly uneventful, except for a late-boarding passenger. The new addition was a *very* chatty businessman from El Salvador, who had plopped down in the vacant seat next to Darcey.

He had a swarthy complexion, high cheekbones, short-cropped black hair, and piercing brown eyes that gave her a creepy, repulsive feeling. He reminded her of a cockroach.

He introduced himself as Carlos Santiago and proceeded to inform Darcey—she wasn't sure why—that he was meeting his wife in Lima for a much needed vacation. Darcey wondered what kind of a woman could, or even would, be married to him.

He said he was looking forward to two weeks of doing nothing but sightseeing. Darcey agreed, that sounded nice. And, for the most part, she answered his questions as much as possible, with only one-syllable responses. She was trying hard not to be rude, but hoped she was getting her—*leave me alone*—message across to him that she wasn't interested carrying on a conversation.

He either didn't take the hint or chose to ignore it, because he continued to inquire about Darcey's trip to Lima. The man proceeded to grill her about what she intended to see in Lima. Did she have plans to visit the surrounding cities? How long was she staying? On and on and so on.

She was getting annoyed and thought his behavior was borderline rude and definitely too damn nosy. Biting her tongue, she replied with a non-committal answer—she hadn't decided yet, and was meeting friends.

He had smiled, and said he hoped she had a good time. As he opened his mouth to ask another question, Darcey turned and looked out the window. She moved so her back was half-turned to him hoping he would take the hint—she didn't want to talk.

Carlos studied the girl for several minutes after she turned away, making it obvious she did not wish to continue their conversation.

Maybe, he had overdone it with all of the questions, he pondered. *Maybe, just a little too over anxious?*

Ever since he spied her on his way down the aisle, he knew he had to have this one. He only had eight hours before they reached Lima to find out where she was staying and devise a plan to snatch her.

It was just his luck he thought smugly that he was able to book a seat on this flight and that the seat next to her was unoccupied. He had had a dry spell these past couple of months and his funds were running lower than he liked. Maybe his luck was changing. He smiled to himself. There was just a short window of opportunity at this point. He needed to take advantage of it.

She had introduced herself as Darcey Callahan from Dallas, Texas. *An American, oh yes, she would do nicely*, he had thought. *Señor Vargas will be very pleased with this one.*

A little-wicked smile played around his mouth. *She's the right height at about five foot nine, reddish brown hair, although it's too short, but it can grow out. Hazel eyes bordering on green, smooth tanned skin, and a body to die for. Yes, this one could bring a king's ransom.*

Settling back in his seat, he smiled and opened the newspaper he had picked up at the airport. Carlos was feeling *very good* about himself.

Ignoring Carlos, Darcey pulled one of the magazines from her bag in an attempt to find something to take her mind off of everything. She tried to concentrate on the articles, but it was useless. She was too keyed up to concentrate on anything.

Maria and Rosa diverted her thoughts briefly while she had played peek-a-boo between the seats with them until their mother decided they needed to rest.

Since the magazines couldn't hold her attention, she picked up the book she'd purchased at the airport—James Patterson's *12th of Never*. Reading the synopsis, it sounded like it was going to be a real thriller. She turned to page one hoping this new diversion would work.

"I see you like Patterson," Carlos observed, invading Darcey's space, again.

Damn! She clenched her teeth and didn't acknowledge him.

"I've read some of his books. They are superb. I have not read that one, however," he persisted.

Darcey saw him smile out of the corner of her eye. It was a cold smile. It gave her chills.

Shit!

Darcey inhaled, before she replied. "Well, I just started it, but it promises to live up to expectations," she answered, not moving her eyes from the page, hoping that was enough to shut him up.

If he keeps this up, she thought, *I'm just going to be rude, and tell him to shut the hell up. I don't like doing that, but desperate times call for desperate measures, and this is one of those damn times.*

He picked up his paper again. Darcey guessed she must have gotten through to him.

She reread the words on the page. They didn't make sense and it couldn't keep her mind off of Brad, anyway.

Frustrated, she stuffed the book back in her bag along with the magazines and stared out the window, not really seeing the billowing white clouds racing by below her. She closed her eyes and let her mind drift off. A vision of her parents took form and then tragedy struck…

ⲟⲟⲟ

At thirteen, her life took a ninety-degree turn in the wrong direction when her parents were killed in a head-on collision, on their way home from Abilene. Her secure, happy life was wiped out in the blink of an eye. If it hadn't been for her dad's family, she would have been put in the system, and who knew what she would have become, or where she would have wound up. But, thankfully they took her in, although begrudgingly.

Next to having to endure their pity was the fact that none of them really wanted her on a permanent basis. She was bounced around from one relative to another. Looking back now, she guessed she couldn't really blame them. She was thirteen and more rebellious than they were prepared to deal with. She was angry with her parents for leaving her, and she hated her dad's family for pitying her.

After only three months, her dad's sister, Maggie, said she was too much of a handful. So from Aunt Maggie's, they moved her in with Uncle Mark and Aunt Darlene. That lasted about a week. They had no children and had absolutely no idea how to deal with a teenager, least of all Darcey.

Finally, at a family pow-wow, her dad's brother, Jack, told Uncle Mark, he would take her. That evening, he picked her up, along with what little belongings she possessed, and took her home with him.

Uncle Jack was two years younger than her dad and had never been married—probably never would be, either. He enjoyed living the free life, too much. She had been instructed never to call him uncle. He said it was bad for his reputation.

She loved Jack. He didn't pity her. He helped her to stand on her own two feet and gave her the will and desire to move forward—to not be angry with her parents for leaving. He helped her to be her own person and fend for herself.

They got along great. He wasn't too strict and she wasn't too much of a brat—most of the time.

◌◦◌

Darcey vaguely heard a voice off in the distance asking her something, but she was still half asleep and took no notice. She drifted off again.

Carlos cautiously watched her out of the corner of his eye, trying to work out some plan to get her alone.

She is so beautiful, he thought. *She is such a prize. Vargas will pay top dollar for this one.*

The flight attendant interrupted his train of thought with the menu cards for the in-flight meal.

Carlos gently tapped Darcey on the arm. "Would you like something to eat?"

"Ummm…sure, what are we having?" Darcey asked, still groggy, rubbing her eyes, realizing she must have dozed off. For a brief moment, she forgot where she was.

"Looks like we can choose between rosemary chicken and chip crusted halibut," he said, reading, from the menu card in his hand.

Neither sounded particularly appetizing to Darcey. "I'll do the chicken."

She wasn't sure she could keep it down, but needed to eat something since she hadn't eaten anything since early morning.

Sometime later, a flight attendant came with the food cart. Carlos smiled a creepy little smile, as he passed Darcey's plate to her. She let him place it on the fold-down table. She didn't want to take the chance she might touch his hand. The chicken was dry. Darcey ate a few bites, shoved it aside, and asked for a cup of coffee.

"You did not eat much. Are you feeling all right?" Carlos asked, a little later after the flight attendant had picked up the dirty plates.

For a moment, Darcey thought he was going to reach over and pat her hand. "Yes, I'm all right." she replied, taking a drink of her coffee. It was lukewarm now. *Ugh! Nothing worse than lukewarm coffee, unless it's cold coffee or this stupid jerk sitting beside me,* she grumbled inwardly, setting the cup back down.

Carlos looked at his watch. They would be landing soon. He only had two hours left to get her to commit to his plan—sharing a taxi with him. The plan wasn't great, but it would have to do on such short notice.

While she had been asleep, he had sent a text to Quin Alverez, his job manager, to have him find out where she had hotel reservations. Quin sent a text back that she was staying at the Sheraton downtown and that he had made Carlos a reservation there, as well.

This one looked like an easy catch, but you couldn't always be sure. Something still could go wrong..

He liked finding unexpected jewels for Señor Vargas, whose operation was quite different from the others in the business—cleaner, more reputable—if there were such a thing in this business. Not that it mattered to him. As long as he got paid, his world was right side up.

Carlos understood that Vargas did not hold with cruelty, violence, deviant behavior, or prostitution, where it concerned the women he rescued. At the beginning that was one of the reasons, Vargas had expanded his holdings to include this business, as disgusting as he said he found it.

At first, his intentions had only been to rescue, what he called lost jewels from the clutches of men who profited by buying and selling women for the sex and slave trades.

It then became Vargas's mission to see that those men, who had committed such atrocities and those who provided the women to them, were eliminated—permanently. Vargas had no qualms about removing such vermin.

Vargas's elite squad of enforcers was swift and efficient. They left no doubt that those who continued to deal in the trade within the realm of Vargas's influence, would be dealt with swiftly and permanently.

During those first few years, he kept only the women who did not wish to return to their families after being rescued. Those who stayed, he lavished them with the finer things in life—clothes and jewels—but, now they were his property to with as he saw fit.

As the years went by, Vargas had gotten caught up in the thrill, intrigue, and the dangerous side of the human trafficking world. Before he realized it, he was also dealing in women. In his mind, he was giving them a better life—they wanted for nothing—except freedom.

Soon, rescuing women did not offer the adrenaline rush it once had. The desire to feel that rush again drove him to start collecting his own women. He hired finders such as Carlos and gave them particular criteria for what he required.

Then, with the addition of these new women, his collection grew to such proportions that he was forced to liquidate some of his jewels.

Being a businessman, Vargas was not opposed to increasing his capital worth, and he created his Bel Ami Gala in order to reduce his collection. For the Bel Ami Galas, Vargas would accept nothing that was not the most beautiful in every way.

Only exclusively invited guests came to the Gala. They were thoroughly background checked and vetted, and then, only those who passed the inspection were allowed in.

Even after his jewels were purchased, Vargas used his enforcers to keep an eye on all of them. If it were discovered that any of the women had been physically or emotionally damaged after they were purchased, Vargas would employee his enforcers to reclaim the women. He would then punish the purchaser by blackballing them from any future Galas or permanently eliminating them, depending on the severity of the violation, and at Vargas's discretion.

Carlos had escaped Vargas's wrath for the past six years by adhering to Vargas's stringent set of rules, and he had faired *very well*.

What pleased Carlos most was the fact that Vargas always paid top dollar. His only requirement, besides the beauty, was proof of perfection, whenever possible. During his time working with Vargas, Carlos had never presented him with damaged jewels. This one looked to be one of the best, if not *the* best, he had ever attempted to deliver. Of course, one could never be sure these days if they were still virginal. However, with this one he had a feeling, Vargas would take her, even if she were not.

Carlos had two hours left. He was going to have to be careful here, not to scare her off.

"Will your friends be picking you up?" he inquired casually, not looking at her.

"I'm not sure. Most likely they will," Darcey answered, eyeing him suspiciously.

Shit, now what? she fumed inwardly.

"What hotel are you going to? Maybe we could share a taxi." He smiled and turned to look at her.

He could tell by her expression, he presumed too much. He should have worked up to it. However, the damage was done.

Work with what you have, he thought.

"Thank you, but no. I'll just wait and see if my friends are there."

The question had caught Darcey off guard and she eyed Carlos cautiously.

Bad vibes are swirling around this guy, she thought. *There's just something, not quite right about him. He creeps me out.*

"My wife, made reservations for us, at the Sheraton downtown," Carlos persisted, smiling again.

He could see that did not please her at all, but he kept smiling.

"If your hotel is along the way, I would be happy to share a ride—that is, if your friends are not waiting, of course. The ride in from the airport to the hotel can be quite expensive. I would be happy to share the cost."

Oh, shit! She gritted her teeth. "Thank you very much," Darcey said, regaining her composure. "But I'm sure my friends will be there to pick me up." *He just won't freaking give up,* she thought, turning to stare out the window.

I will have to be more careful, Carlos cautioned himself. *She is getting suspicious again. I must try not to press so hard, but it is so exciting, to be on the hunt and your prey just inches away.*

Adrenaline surged through his veins, he turned to smile at her, but she had turned toward the window again. Mentally Carlos was licking his chops over this delicious find.

The pilot announced they would be landing in a few minutes. The weather was ninety and sunny.

"Thank you for flying American Airlines. Please enjoy your stay in Lima."

The pilot had turned on the *Fasten Seat Belt* sign.

Darcey's stomach tightened, and her palms began to sweat. She tried to swallow, but her mouth had gone all Sahara Desert on her.

The landing gear growled, whirring as it dropped and locked in place, with a thud. The noise, of the wheels locking into place accentuated the rapid beating of Darcey's heart. She could hear the blood pulsing in her ears.

The wheels hit the runway with a sharp screech. It was like a sharp knife and it cut across her nerves. The palms of her hands were sweating and her stomach tied itself in a knot again.

Darcey squeezed her eyes shut tight and inhaled then exhaled slowly.

Time to go.

⌘

Carlos had gathered his things and stood waiting for Darcey. She hesitated then picked up her bag, stood up, and reached for her carry-on in the overhead compartment. Carlos beat her to it. Wiggling it out, he sat it on the floor. Darcey raised the handle and gripped it tightly. Her knuckles turned white.

She stood waiting for the passengers clogging the narrow aisle to thin out, before moving. She could just barely see Maria and Rosa over the line of passengers as they turned and waved before they disappeared out the plane's door.

Carlos had been quietly watching her.

She's delaying, he thought. *At least, she is staying where I can keep an eye on her.*

Quin had warned him that it would be difficult at this point, to grab her quietly. Apparently, she did have friends picking her up, but Quin didn't know if it would be at the airport or the hotel. He thought it would be best to bide their time for now.

Darcey! Pull yourself together, she admonished herself.

As anxious as she had been to get here, now that she was here, nervousness overwhelmed her, and her feet seemed to be glued to the floor of the plane. She hadn't lost her determination to find Brad. In fact, she was more determined than ever.

However, all of the things she had avoided thinking about, and had pushed to the back of her mind, came rushing out at her.

The dam broke—*she was alone*—nobody knew she was here in a strange country, with people she didn't know. The one thing she just realized was that she hadn't completely thought through how she was actually going to find Brad. Or, worse, what she would do if she couldn't? She didn't have a clue. Just like always, she had leaped before she looked.

Yeah, that's me—Damn the torpedoes. Full speed ahead, she chided herself. She knew she wasn't a quitter, and she didn't back down, no matter what. Inhaling deeply, and with great physical effort, Darcey made her feet move.

I can do this.

CHAPTER 9

New Complications

Carlos led the way through the doors to the Customs area. Their passports checked and stamped, Carlos looked for the doors leading to the outside. He turned to motion for Darcey to follow, but realized she had already moved off in the opposite direction. She was heading for a small group of people, clustered just outside the Customs area. They were holding signs with the names of the passengers they were to pick up.

"¡*Maldito*!" he cursed, under his breath, as he spotted an old acquaintance holding a sign with Darcey's name in big bold letters. *Now what is Armando doing here*, he wondered.

He hadn't seen Armando in over two years. Actually, since Armando had kicked him off the ranch in spite of his stepmother saying he had nothing to do with the disappearance of two women from the house day staff. Remembering, Carlos chuckled to himself.

What's his connection to this woman? he wondered. *It does not matter. I will have Quin check it out and make a new plan. What's one more day*, he reasoned. *I'm not on any time schedule.*

∽∾∽

Her passport stamped, Darcey proceeded out into the

main lobby area. Looking around, she saw a small group of people, standing a short distance from Customs. All of them were holding signs, with different names printed on them. That's when her eyes fell on a very handsome gentleman, holding a sign with her name on it.

He must be Armando Martinez, the Dallas office would have told him I would be arriving today, she thought.

Darcey turned and found Carlos right behind her, so close she almost ran into him.

"Oh, sorry," she said, stopping abruptly. "My friends are here, so thank you for your consideration. It was nice meeting you."

The words stuck in Darcey's throat. If she could have, she would have coughed them up and spit them on his Gucci loafers.

Something flashed in his eyes, but Darcey didn't have time to analyze it before it was gone, and he smiled, wishing her well, also.

Carlos looked past her as she turned and walked in the direction of Armando. "*¡Mierda*!" he said under his breath, his jaw tightened as he turned and marched angrily away, shoving several people out of his way as he headed for the outside doors.

A big, broad smile spread across Armando's face, as he watched the woman walking toward him.

She is much prettier than the emailed photo the Dallas office sent, he mused. *It did not do her justice.*

Looking past her, he thought he had caught a glimpse of a man who looked like Carlos but immediately dismissed it. Carlos would not dare to show his face in Lima again.

"Bienvenido," Armando said. "You must be Señorita Callahan. I am Armando Martinez at your service." He gave a slight bow and a smile that bordered on a leer.

"Yes, I'm Darcey Callahan." She gave a sideways smile, not knowing exactly what to make of his expression. "So pleased to meet you." Darcey extended her hand and he took it raising it to his lips.

Just a brush across the back of her hand, but it sent a chill up her arm. A feeling of foreboding swept over her and chilled her to the core.

¡Dios mío! But she is beautiful, Armando kept his face neutral.

"I have a car waiting," he said, taking the handle of Darcey's carry-on waiting for Darcey to go ahead of him.

Darcey assessed Armando out of the corner of her eye as they started toward the outside doors. He was at least as tall as Brad and his olive skin covered a well-muscled body that was evident even under his well-cut navy suit jacket. He gave off vibes of someone who was very self-assured and confident. Someone whose decisions you didn't question. However, there was something else she couldn't put her finger on. It was that something else that worried her.

They walked through the auto-open doors into the sounds of the bustling airport, diesel fumes, mixed with people odors, honking horns, people chatter, and the heat. All of it hit Darcey head-on.

Idling at the curb was a black stretch limo. The chauffeur opened the door for Darcey as Armando popped the trunk and put her carry-on in.

Darcey got in and sat down, fresh cigarette smoke and leather lingered in the cold air inside the limo. Armando smiled as he slid into the seat beside her. The limo's engine purred into action and they merged into traffic.

"So, tell me, did you have a good flight?" he asked, looking genuinely interested.

Darcey smiled at him. "It was uneventful, but thank you for asking." She didn't see any reason to mention Carlos since he had gone on his way and she probably would never see him again. "When will we be going to the ORCA office? I'm anxious to find out anything I can about Brad. I suppose the Dallas office told you the reason for my visit?"

Darcey figured she might as well jump in with both feet and get things going, the sooner the better.

"Yes, but we cannot go today. The person we need to

speak with will be out of town until tomorrow," Armando said, without looking at her. "I'm sorry to say we have not heard anything from Señor Daniels since he left Dallas. The gentleman you will meet with tomorrow will have the information you require."

"Does this person have a name?" Darcey noticed he hadn't mentioned the name of the person who 'had all the answers. An alarm bell jingled a small warning.

"Ah—er—I'd rather not say at present if you do not mind," he stammered. "It is most imperative that he remains anonymous at present. He is helping only if his name is not mentioned. That is why we will be meeting him tomorrow, away from the ORCA office. It would be very inconvenient for him if the company knew he was meeting with you about this. It is an extremely classified project, and he is in a very sensitive position. You understand. "

Darcey's head snapped around in Armando's direction. Another alarm bell joined the first—louder now.

"Whoa—wait a minute. What's going on here? What do you mean, '*very* inconvenient' if he talks to me?" She bristled. "Is there something going on here you would like to tell me about? I understand the job being classified, but don't you think this is a little ridiculous, secret meetings and all?"

Darcey was beginning to get some *danger*-type vibes. Her stomach sank to her feet and her heart was on the verge of stopping while panic set in as the third alarm bell sounded in her head.

What had gone wrong? Her plan had been straightforward—find Brad, make sure he was all right, give him what for for not calling, go home. Simple. Right? Now, it looked like it was turning into much more than she'd bargained for.

Oh, crap!

"I am afraid it is not that simple." Armando looked at her, watching the blood drain from her face. "I guess Señor Daniels did not give you any details, did he?"

"No, he just said he'd been called back to take care of

something to do with his project," Darcey replied, short of breath. "He did say it was classified, though, but he's not called me like he said he would, to let me know everything is okay."

Darcey was beginning to get nervous wondering just what kind of project Brad really was working on.

A fine time to think about that now, girl, her inner voice chided.

She sat there, absently winding and unwinding the leather strap of her shoulder bag in her hand, her mind refused to move forward.

Armando covertly looked at her and wondered what possessed her to come all the way to Peru just to look for a man only because he had not called her.

Most women, he assumed, would have cried, or cursed the man, working him out of their system then gone on with their own lives. Not run off to some foreign country, trying to find the guy. Women—he had given up trying to understand them long ago.

He cleared his throat. "Like I said, this is an extremely classified project, so I cannot really go into details. Suffice it to say that if Señor Daniels has not called you, he is probably somewhere he is unable to."

He was watching her with interest. Did she believe him? No one knew where Daniels was, not even the Lima office if he could believe his friend. He had made inquiries on his own when he had been told she was coming, but to no avail. He had even gone so far as to call Lilly.

"I am sure my corporate friend will have more information for you when we meet with him tomorrow. Do not concern yourself, por favor. I am sure he is perfectly safe." Armando reached over and patted her hand. "My corporate friend may be able to get him to a place where he can call you." He could see touching her had been a mistake as she immediately jerked her hand away.

Darcey sat there, fuming. *Where did he come off thinking he could do that?*

She glared at him and she thought he had gotten the message. He moved slightly away from her.

"Excuse, *por favor*," he said, inclining his head.

She inclined her head with a tight-lipped smile.

He cleared his throat again. "I must caution you this project is not public knowledge at present," he said, quietly looking at the closed privacy window to the front of the limo. "That is why we must proceed with caution. As the assistant to the maintenance manager, I do know a little about the project. However, no one knows everything except Señor Daniels and the head of ORCA, of course."

Then Darcey remembered that the Sunday Brad left, the Dallas office had sent a woman from Peru out to Mike's to find Brad. She thought Mike said her name was Lilly something or other. Darcey remembered thinking the woman was a little strange, but dismissed it and had never thought of her till now.

"About five weeks ago—" She turned and looked at Armando. "—right before Brad came back here. We were at our friend's riding stables when the Dallas office sent a woman named Lilly with a message for Brad. She was from the Lima office. I thought she was a little odd. I didn't think any more about her until now. Does she have anything to do with the project?" Darcey asked, wondering how that Lilly person fit in this strange turn of events.

"Yes, she does, but I am not sure what or how much," he acknowledged. "She is rarely in the office, so I have not had a chance to find out exactly how she is connected with the project," he said confidentially, lying about what he knew about Lilly.

Armando had frustrated himself trying to find out about Lilly for the last two months ever since Javier Montego, his corporate friend, had cautioned him to steer clear of her. That should be easy, he had thought at the time, since he had seen her only once in the entire time he had been employed at ORCA.

Knowing how women liked to gossip, Armando had

turned on the charm and acquainted himself with several of the office's female clerical personnel. It had been easy to persuade them talk about Lilly. Apparently, she spent all of her time in the dome, but no one knew exactly what she did there, other than that she was Daniel's executive assistant.

Armando had always suspected Lilly had had a hand in his security clearance being cancelled after he was caught with the filtration diagrams, and it was only thanks to Javier that he had not been fired. He was definitely grateful for that.

The limo pulled up in front of the hotel and Armando collected Darcey's carry-on from the trunk. The reservations clerk checked her in and gave her the key to the room 404.

Thanking Armando, Darcey told him she would like to go and rest a while. He said he would pick her up at eight for dinner. Darcey smiled at him as she stepped into the elevator.

Armando watched her, as she walked to the elevator, speculating about Brad, who he knew was never one to make any permanent commitments. In fact, he couldn't remember Brad ever dating a woman for more than a month, and he certainly would not have mentioned anything about the project to any of them. However, this one, he had told her he was working on a classified project, just, not what it was.

This one has to be something special, he mused, inclining his head and smiling as the elevator doors closed.

☙❧

Getting off the elevator on the fourth floor, Darcey walked down the hall to her room. She was pleasantly surprised at the spaciousness of it. The windows across one wall overlooked the swimming pool and she could see dozens of sun-worshipers lounging by the pool or splashing in the sparkling blue water. It looked so inviting, but she hadn't packed a swimsuit, since lounging by the pool or swimming had not been on her radar when packing. She was here to find Brad.

She tossed her carry-on on the bed. It bounced once and tipped over on its side. Righting it, she unzipped it and laid out clean underwear. She felt dusty and gritty and a good hot shower sounded heavenly.

The phone was ringing as Darcey stepped out of the shower. Grabbing a towel, she wrapped it around her and went to answer it.

"Hello, Señorita Callahan," Carlos said. "This is Carlos Santiago. We sat next to each other on the plane." He didn't wait for her to answer. "My wife and I would like to invite you to dinner with us this evening. Please do not say no, I've told my wife all about you and she is very excited to meet you."

Oh, shit! "Ahem, ah—er—hi, Carlos," Darcey stammered, and a whole bank of alarm bells started going off. Her body went cold. "This is unexpected, but I'm sorry, I already have dinner plans. Please give my apologies to your wife."

Ah, this is not good. I will try another tactic, Carlos decided. "Oh, such a disappointment. We were so looking forward to having you join us." Wheedling, he attempted to make her feel guilty about turning the invitation down.

"I am truly sorry, and I really do appreciate you inviting me, but I'm afraid I already have plans for this evening," Darcey said, trying to sound sorry, but she really wasn't.

"Well, perhaps we can arrange something for tomorrow. I will call," he said and hung up before she could respond. Darcey stood there, her mouth open, staring at the receiver.

He ground his teeth in frustration. Now, he would have to come up with another plan. He would call Quin and see what could be arranged on a moment's notice. Quin was good at that sort of thing.

First, he would have him find out why Armando picked

her up and what his connection to her was. That could be a problem.

∽∾∽

Now that was weird, Darcey thought. Her alarm bells were still sounding as she replaced the receiver. *This is not good.*

She had completely forgotten he had told her he was staying at the Sheraton.

I will ask Armando if he will arrange for me to move to another hotel. I can't stay here.

Darcey glanced at her watch. It was seven-thirty. That gave her a half an hour to get ready. She slipped on her little black dress, added her silver pendant and earrings, pulled on her strappy heels, and picked up her lace shawl. Darcey was ready to go with two minutes to spare, just enough time to take the elevator down.

As Darcey reached for the doorknob, there was a light tap on the door. Her hand froze in midair; her body went cold. She swallowed and peeked through the peephole to see who it was, fearing it was Carlos. It wasn't, it was Armando. She gave a sigh of relief and opened the door.

"Well, this is a pleasant surprise." She smiled up at Armando. "I thought we were meeting in the lobby."

"When I invite a lady out, I expect to collect her at her door, not have her meet me in the lobby," he said, softly. He smiled, offering her his arm. "You look lovely this evening."

"Thank you," she said, trying not to blush as she pulled the door shut behind her.

Darcey didn't look up, but she took Armando's arm and they headed for the elevator. He seemed to be on his best behavior after that little lack of judgment in the limo.

They rode down in a comfortable silence. The elevator doors slid open and Armando stepped aside, letting Darcey step out first. She took two steps and hesitated. Across the lobby, at the consigner's desk, was Carlos and a woman she guessed was his wife.

They hadn't seen her so she turned, and quickly ducked behind a large bank of potted palms. Darcey motioned to Armando to follow. He raised his eyebrows, questioning her behavior, as he walked over to where she stood peeking between the palm fronds.

"What is wrong? You are white as a sheet," he asked.

"That man over there, at the consigner's desk—" Her mouth was dry as she pointed at the desk. "—he was on my flight, and he sat next to me. I can't explain it, but he gives me the creeps, you know, there's something strange about him." Her voice a hoarse whisper. "He said he was Carlos Santiago, a businessman from El Salvador, meeting his wife here for a vacation. But he was way too nosey about why I was coming to Lima. You know, what was I was doing, where was I going, did I know anyone here. You know, stuff like that. Then he wanted me to share a taxi to the hotel. I'm just so glad you were there. Then tonight, just before you came up, he called inviting me to dinner with his wife," Darcey said, in a breathless, hoarse whisper. "Can you get me booked at another hotel, please?" she pleaded.

"Why, of course, if that is what you wish." Eyeing her with concern, he started to put his arm around her shoulders and quickly decided against it, considering her earlier reaction to his just having touched her hand in the limo. "We can arrange for that right now if you like."

"Yes, please," she whispered.

They both peeked through the palm fronds, watching Carlos and the woman walk out through the hotel front doors. They waited until the doorman haled a taxi for them and they drove off before leaving the sanctuary of the palms.

Armando had watched Carlos at the desk. *Now, just what is he doing back in Lima,* he wondered? He would ask Javier, to find out what he was doing here.

Armando walked with Darcey over to the reservation desk. He spoke to the clerk in Spanish. The clerk looked at Darcey several times and finally smiled.

"We'll take care of it, *señor*." The clerk smiled broadly, as Armando slid some money under the newspaper that was lying on the counter. Armando offered Darcey his arm once more and they headed out the front door.

"What was that all about," Darcey asked, a little frustrated that he had spoken in Spanish. *I should have paid more attention in my Spanish class in high school. Even high school Spanish would have helped here,* she groused inwardly.

"I was arranging for your move to other accommodations," Armando said, smoothly carefully avoiding disclosing the location of her new accommodations. "The clerk will take care of collecting your things from your room and having them delivered to the new location. We will not be coming back here, so you should not have to run the risk of running into to this Santiago person again."

She sighed. "Thank you." It sounded like a perfect plan to Darcey. She felt immediately relieved.

Armando decided he wouldn't tell her until dinner was over, that he had arranged to have her things taken to his home. Besides, if Carlos was up to his old tricks and had decided Darcey would fit the bill for whomever he was working with now, then he would continue to stalk her. More than likely, he would find her if she moved to any hotel in the city.

She would be safer from Carlos if Armando kept her someplace where he could keep a personal eye on her. *Of course, I wouldn't mind if it got a lot more personal,* he thought smugly. *She seems a little cold, but then, I do love a challenge.*

Leaving the hotel, they drove through the city to a lovely restaurant several miles away. The maître d' smiled broadly as they walked in. Apparently, Armando was well known at this restaurant. Their table was already prepared. The maître d' motioned for them to follow him. Armando seated Darcey and asked for the wine list. Bowing slightly, the maître d' hurried away, Darcey presumed, to retrieve the wine list. Instead, their waiter instantly appeared with it.

It was a leisurely dinner and conversation was light, neither of them wanting to discuss the reason Darcey had come to Lima in a public place.

When she finished her coffee, Armando asked for the check. They walked out of the restaurant and the limo was waiting for them. Armando spoke to the chauffeur in Spanish as they merged into traffic.

"What hotel did you book me in?" Darcey asked, realizing that Armando had not mentioned it since they had left the Sheraton.

"You will not be going to another hotel. I have made arrangements for you to come to my home." Armando took her hand. "I feel you would be safer where I can keep an eye on you, personally. I have asked a friend of mine to check out this Carlos Santiago person. He may be a legitimate business man, but I would like to be sure, and I am more comfortable with you staying under my roof until we know."

"*No!*" Darcey almost shouted, jerking her hand away. "I do not want to do that. I'll be perfectly safe in another hotel. He won't know where to find me."

Darcey couldn't believe what he was proposing. How could he presume such a thing? He was a perfect stranger and she couldn't accept staying in his home.

"Not to worry." He took her hand again and squeezed it. "It will be all perfectly proper. My housekeeper will be there all the time. You have nothing to worry about," he said, patronizingly.

Darcey jerked her hand back and glared at him. She couldn't believe what was happening. "I do not want to inconvenience you. I want to go to a hotel," she said, forcefully, still trying to be polite.

"It is all arranged, my dear Darcey." He reached for her

hand again but thought better of it. She was already upset, no use in pushing it. "There is no use in arguing, the Lima office has already approved for you to stay at my home," he lied. The office did not even know she was here yet. "You will be perfectly safe, and it will be my pleasure to have you as a guest in my home."

Darcey didn't like the idea of staying at his home, and she didn't like how he was taking too much for granted, but at this point what was she going to do? *Jump out of the car?*

She was too tired to argue, and it wouldn't have done any good, anyway. She could see the arrangements had already been settled and that was the end of it. Besides, the Lima office had approved of the plans.

Hadn't they?

പ്രോ

Darcey didn't know how long they'd been driving. It seemed like an hour but was probably shorter or longer— time had no meaning. She was exhausted. The day had taken its toll on her and she wanted nothing more than to put her head on a pillow and sleep.

She let her head fall back on the headrest, and then sometime later, she felt Armando put his arm around her and gently pull her head to his shoulder.

I shouldn't let him do that, she thought through the haze of sleep.

The thought drifted through her mind, but she was too tired to protest.

"We are here, Darcey." Armando sat her up. "Here let me help you out."

The door opened and he gently pulled her out of the car. Still fuzzy from her nap, she swayed. He put his arm around her waist to steady her. He left it there as he walked her up the front stairs.

Darcey was vaguely aware of Armando's arm around her

waist as they climbed the stairs, too tired to figure out why it was there.

The smell of freshly mown hay and horses drifted gently on the cool night air. Darcey inhaled the fresh clean smell, guessing they were in the country, somewhere. It was too dark to see even though the moon was out. They reached the top of the stairs as the front door opened. Light from the inside flooded the porch. Darcey squinted, trying to make out the figure silhouetted in the doorway.

"Oh, my dear *niña*, you must be exhausted. I have your room all ready."

She reached out, put her arm around Darcey's shoulders, and guided her into the house.

This must be the housekeeper.

"Señorita Darcey, this is Maria Gomez, my housekeeper. She has been with my family for over thirty years. She will take excellent care of you." Armando leered after her as Maria led her up the stairs.

"Come, *niña*, right this way." Maria smiled, and gently guided Darcey up the massive staircase that sat squarely in the middle of the foyer.

Darcey looked back at Armando, still standing at the bottom of the stairs. "Night," she managed through a yawn.

"I will see you in the morning. *Buenas noches*." Armando inclined his head slightly, a sideways grin playing at the corners of his mouth. *Yes, I will see you in the morning, maybe sooner,* he thought eagerly.

Darcey followed Maria down a large hallway. She stopped and opened the door to the room and motioned her to enter, then followed her in. Darcey's carry-on sat on a bench at the foot of the bed. It appeared Maria had unpacked her things and put them away.

"I would have laid out your night clothes, but I did not see any," Maria apologized.

"That's okay, I usually wear my sweatpants and a tee shirt," she said, slightly embarrassed.

"Well, we cannot have that. I will see that you have

some proper night wear," Maria said, as a matter of fact.

"Oh no, that's not necessary. What I have is perfectly fine," Darcey said. "Please don't bother."

Maria hesitated. "Well, if you are sure."

"Yes, I'm sure," Darcey replied, stifling a yawn.

"Well, then, I will leave you to it. Breakfast is at eight. I will see that you have a wake-up call," Maria said, as she looked around the room once more. *"Buenas noches."*

"Good night," Darcey said as Maria closed the door.

Darcey started to look for her sweatpants and tee. There were several pairs of double doors covering one whole wall. The first pair of doors was a closet, with her clothes hung neatly on hangers, but no sweatpants or tee. The next pair of doors—more closet space, but was empty. Behind the next pair of doors—a built-in armoire, with numerous shelves and drawers, but still no sweatpants or tee. The last pair of doors opened onto a full-length, three-way mirror and cubby-holes for shoes.

Turning around frowning, she saw her carry-on. She walked over and unzipped it. There, on the bottom, lay her sweatpants and tee. Apparently, they weren't good enough to put in the armoire. She smiled to herself.

Darcey was too tired to think about it anymore. She hung her dress in the closet, put her shoes in one of the cubby-holes. Then, pulled on her sweatpants and tee.

Stifling a yawn, she plopped down on the comfiest mattress she'd ever felt. Her head had barely hit the pillow before she was off to dreamland.

⋐⋑

Armando watched Darcey from the media room as she slept. She was perfect in every way. He would bide his time, getting to know her better, gaining her trust, he plotted.

If he played his cards right, he would be the one to step in and comfort her when they didn't find Daniels. He just had to make sure Daniels was never found, but first he had to find out what had happened to him. He would ask Javier when they met tomorrow. He was closer to the situation, and if Armando got up the nerve, maybe call Lilly.

Turning off the monitor, he grumbled to himself. It was too bad he had been caught with those plans and his security one clearance canceled. However, the bright spot in all of this was that the board had believed him when he insisted he was innocent. They let him keep his job thanks to Javier, who had pleaded his case before the board.

The board had no idea that Javier was paying him over twenty million dollars to stop the project and get the Bio Dome plans—anyway necessary.

"It was not my fault that I got caught," he groused out loud.

Armando had chosen a plan that had required the least amount of physical effort on his part, and that was to switch out some of the connector crystals on the reactor. Nothing dangerous of course, he could not put his own life at risk. He would do just enough to trigger an alarm and create a distraction, while he lifted the dome stuff from the safe.

Easy enough, he had thought. Javier had given him the combination, but, unfortunately, had not bothered to make sure he knew how to work it.

It definitely was not his fault, and he was not going to take the blame that it had taken longer to open the damn safe than planned, which had left him no time to make his escape.

Had I gotten the plans, he whined to himself, *this would all be water under the bridge, and I would be enjoying my-self somewhere on the French Riviera.*

He slammed the media room door on his way out.

❡❡❡

Sometime during the night, something woke Darcey. She wasn't sure what it was. She listened for several minutes but didn't hear anything.

The moon shone through the windows, casting eerie shadows across the room. She couldn't see anything, but she had the distinct feeling someone was watching her. She reached over and switched on the lamp on the bedside table. It cast a soft glow over the room. Everything looked the same as when she'd gone to bed. She fluffed her pillow and switched off the light. It wasn't until sometime later when she finally went back to sleep.

⁂

Darcey awoke to a gentle tap, tap on her door.

"Come in," she yawned, rubbing her eyes.

"*Buenos días, señorita*. I am Juanita. Breakfast is in one hour," she said, giving a slight curtsey and smiling sweetly at Darcey. "Is there anything I can help you with?"

"No, I'm okay. Thank you," Darcey told her.

Juanita smiled again and left the room.

Darcey rolled over and stretched, surveying the room. She had been too tired last night to notice much about it except the closet.

The morning light flooded through the floor-to-ceiling windows showing off the beauty of the room. The walls were a rich cream color, hung with gorgeous tapestries and beautiful paintings. The polished wood floor was partially covered with lovely antique carpets. The floor-to-ceiling windows overlooked a stunning garden. She made a mental note to explore that before she left. The bed was king sized and was flanked on either side by matching bedside tables and lamps.

Looking at the time, Darcey jumped up and headed for the bathroom. She had to hurry if she didn't want to be late for breakfast.

"Oh, my, gosh," she exclaimed, standing in the bathroom doorway. "I could fit my living room in this bathroom."

A large, round, marble tub filled the far corner of the

room. Behind the tub sat several huge palms, planted in graceful stone, three-foot high pots. On the opposite wall, a glassed-in shower. Huge fluffy towels hung on racks and baskets filled with soaps and lotions sat on the counter top.

Darcey took a quick shower. Maybe she would take a leisurely soak in the tub tonight. She quickly dressed and slipped on her sandals. Giving herself a once over in the three-way mirror, she decided that she looked presentable and headed downstairs.

ぐめぐめ

Armando enjoyed his morning coffee, watching Darcey shower and dress, from his chair in the media room. He was glad he had decided to put in the surveillance system last year after the attempted break-in. But, adding cameras in the bedrooms and baths had been a stroke of genius. As soon as she left the room, he headed for the stairway to wait for her.

Stepping out in the hall, Darcey was amazed at how large it was. She saw the stairs and headed in that direction.

Waiting for her, at the bottom, was Armando. She started to think it was a pleasant surprise, but remembered yesterday about his attempts to get friendly—too friendly for her liking. She smiled anyway, just to be polite.

"*Buenos días*, Darcey. We are having breakfast on the patio this morning, so I thought it would be better for me to escort you rather than letting you try to find your way on your first day here." He smiled and gave a slight bow.

He reached his hand out for her to take. She placed her hand on his as she stepped down the last three steps.

He took her hand and pulled her arm through his as they walked down the hall.

Whoa, wait a minute here. I think you're getting just a little too familiar and taking too much for granted, buster.

She unwound her arm as easily as she could, trying not

to offend him. He just smiled and let her arm go. They walked out onto the patio where a table had been set for two. He pulled out a chair for her to sit down.

"What a lovely garden," Darcey said, looking for a neutral subject to break the awkward silence that followed the arm thing. "Is this the one I can see from my room?"

"Yes, it is." Armando smiled. "You must take time to explore it. Ah, here comes Maria with our breakfast. Would you like coffee?"

"Yes, please." Darcey held her cup for him to fill with dark rich coffee. "When do we meet with this mystery man?" she asked, looking directly at him.

"It will be later this afternoon. He will call when he is ready. In the meantime, please, feel to look around and make yourself at home. If you have any questions, Maria or Juanita will be glad to answer them. I will be gone this morning but will be back in plenty of time for the meeting."

Maria placed plates full of steaming scrambled eggs, ham, cheese, fresh fruit, and a basket of fresh rolls on the table. Darcey didn't realize how hungry she was until the delicious smell of the ham invaded her nose. The food was delicious and she probably ate more than she should.

If I don't watch it, I'll be putting on pounds and that will mean I'll have to do an extra day at the gym when I get home.

Armando excused himself saying he would see her that afternoon.

During the hour drive to the ORCA office, Armando sorted and sectioned his morning in his mind in the order of priority.

The first priority was to contact Javier. He had connections that could find out what Carlos was doing back in Lima, precisely how Darcey fit into his plans.

Next, the parts and equipment requisitions he had been shuffling from one side of his desk to the other for the past week and a half probably should be worked on today—if he found the time.

Since he had lost his security one clearance, the only option left to him to try and cripple the project was with the orders that went through his office. For any request from the dome he would conveniently misplace or accidently on purpose order the wrong part. He held up orders until he had no choice, but to get it right.

Time was of the essence for the project. ORCA wanted it completed within five months. If he could delay the project by even just a week, it would cost ORCA a substantial fee every day past the set completion date.

He knew he was doing his job on this end, but had no way now of knowing if Javier was holding up his end of the bargain—finding someone to hack into ORCA's servers and plant a virus in the dome's filtration system files.

Javier had said that once that had been done, it would be just a matter of hours before the whole system was corrupted and it would take weeks to correct if it were even possible. But, there had been no news good or bad from the dome in over four weeks.

∽∾∽∾

Darcey finished her cup of coffee and decided to explore the garden. It was small, but beautiful, and full of colorful blossoms. A large tree, its branches heavy with foliage, stretched out, shading several stone benches at the far end of the garden. She thought that looked like the perfect place to read the book she had bought to read on the plane, but hadn't been able to focus on.

When she went to retrieve the book, she noticed the room had been tidied. Her sweatpants and tee shirt were now neatly folded in the armoire.

Back downstairs she went in search of Maria and found her putting away the dishes from breakfast in the kitchen pantry. She turned and smiled as Darcey entered. "How may I help you, *señorita*?" she asked, wiping her hands on a towel.

"I was wondering if it would be possible to have a container of coffee and a cup to take with me out to the garden?" Darcey asked, smiling.

"Yes, that would be possible. I will prepare it. Juanita will bring it to you," Maria said, closing the cupboard door. Darcey thanked her and headed to the garden.

By the time the sun was overhead, Darcey was only on page 89. After rereading the last several pages, she still didn't know what she had read, finally gave up, and laid the book on the bench.

Her mind kept drifting to Brad and this unknown man who had all the answers. She sure hoped that was true, but she had doubts. That foreboding feeling was back and she couldn't shake.

Thoughts of Armando also crept in as well. She didn't know what to think about him. On the surface, he seemed *exceedingly* kind, except he was trying too hard at being friendly and taking too much for granted. She was beginning to feel that something else lurked under the surface.

You'd better be careful with this one. Her inner voice poked her with a warning she knew she needed to heed. Even though it was hot out, Darcey's body turned cold and she shivered.

She walked up the patio steps as Armando stepped out through the patio doors.

"*Buenas tardes*," he said, greeting her warmly. "I hope you have had a pleasant morning."

"Yes, thank you." She held up her book, "I've been reading."

"Ah yes, James Patterson." He took the book in his hand. "I find his books, shall we say—interesting," he said, handing it back to her by the corner. "My friend has called to say that this Carlos Santiago is just a businessman, after all. Your worry was for nothing, but I am glad you were worried because it has allowed me to welcome you into my home."

Armando conveniently left out the part about Santiago

trafficking in women—mainly white women. Yes, he was a businessman; the kind Armando had always suspected Carlos was, so, as long as Darcey was with him, she would be safe.

Darcey heaved a sigh of relief. "I am so relieved and thank you, for finding that out and, please, thank your friend for me, too." *Maybe I was just paranoid about the whole thing,* she thought. But, she had that feeling in the pit of her stomach, that something was still not right.

From somewhere inside the house, the phone rang. Armando excused himself and went to answer it. Darcey entered the house and was half way up the stairs when Armando called to her.

"Darcey that was the call we have been waiting for. He is ready to meet. How soon can you be ready to go?" he asked.

"I just have to freshen up a bit and I'll be ready. Give me about ten minutes," she said, continuing her climb.

"Excellent, I will meet you here in ten minutes."

CHAPTER 10

The Meeting

The limo and chauffeur were waiting in the driveway as Armando and Darcey walked down the front stairs. It had been dark and she had been half awake when they arrived the previous evening, so she hadn't seen anything of Armando's ranch. She was amazed at the lush pastures bordering the long driveway. The large herd of cattle grazing in the pasture, the long white horse barns off in the distance, and the beautiful Arabian horses lazily milling around the large paddock in front of the barns took her breath away.

She had no idea that Armando owned such a ranch, but she should have guessed from the posh furnishing of his home.

"What beautiful horses," she said, still looking out the limo window on her side.

"Yes, they are. I ride before breakfast. Please, let me know if you would like to join me." She could hear the smile in his voice as he continued, "I would enjoy your company very much."

"Where are we meeting this man?" Darcey asked, ignoring his invitation to ride and getting back to business.

"We will go to a mutual friend's home," he said. "Someone he trusts to be discreet."

They're adding another person? What hell happened to

'no one was to know about our meeting'? she fumed inwardly.

Darcey was beginning to wonder, just what was going on. She didn't like the damn rules changing in the middle of the game and was going to tell Armando just how she felt about it. She turned and leaned forward to look him in the eye.

"Hold it right there, buster," she bristled. "I thought just the three of us, you, me, and this mystery guy were the only ones to know about this meeting," she said emphatically. "What's with this new guy? I want to know just what's going on!" she demanded, and then her jaw dropped in fear.

"What is the matter, Darcey?" He reached for her hand. "You look like you have seen a ghost."

"*Watch out!*" she screamed.

∾∾∾

Armando came to with the smell of gasoline assaulting his nostrils and the shrieking of metal rubbing on metal putting his teeth on edge as the wind blew through the battered limousine. Slowly reaching up he gingerly touched the side of his head discovering a large bump had formed there. When he pulled his hand away, it was covered in blood. His stomach churned and he closed his eyes drawing a painful, ragged breath. There did not seem to be a place on his body that did not hurt. Slowly he moved his left arm to see what time it was, but his watch face was smashed leaving bits of the crystal embedded in his wrist. He had no way of knowing just how long he had been out, but at least he was alive. Inhaling a jagged breath, he tried to move his leg but he couldn't. Resting his throbbing head on the edge of the seat, he closed his eyes.

Just seconds later, his eyes flew open as it hit him that Darcey was not in the limo. His first thought was that she had been thrown clear of the vehicle. But then, he saw her seatbelt strap had been cut. A piece of bloody material from her jacket was caught on a piece of twisted metal and fluttered in the breeze.

Then how the hell did she get out? Someone would had to have taken her, but who? Why? In spite of the pain, his mind was moving at lightning speed. *How am I going to explain this?*

Of course, no one but Javier and the person at the Dallas office, who had sent her photo and arrival information, even knew she was in Peru right now. The Lima office was not expecting her until tomorrow. Nevertheless, this was still a complication he had not anticipated, and he had no idea how he was going to explain it all.

The accident would have to be reported and he would have to explain how it had happened, followed by the mounds of forms that had to be filled out.

Maybe I can just not mention that Darcey had been a passenger. I can count on my driver to back me up, he reasoned.

The idea of, not mentioning Darcey definitely appealed to him much more than coming up with a plausible explanation why Darcey had been with him and he had not told the office she was here. The less he had to explain to the authorities and ORCA, the better he liked it.

Armando tried to pull himself into an upright position so he could see if his driver was all right. Grimacing in pain he peered through what was left of the security window between the front and back seats.

Armando saw him on the floorboard, crumpled against the front seat, his head, and shoulders resting on the shattered passenger door window beneath him, breathing, but unconscious. The sirens were wailing in the distance and getting louder as they moved closer. Armando leaned his head back and closed his eyes.

"Are you all right, sir," an officer peered over the side, through the broken window, and into the limo. "Stay still and we will have you out in just a minute." The officer backed away from the limo and said something that Armando couldn't hear.

"You will be just fine, sir," one of the paramedics said, checking Armando's eyes with a small, high beam flashlight. "We will be transporting you to the hospital for a complete check over. It does not appear that you have any serious injuries. However, your driver was not so lucky. He has a broken leg and possible broken ribs from impacting the steering wheel."

The paramedic talked to Armando as they loaded him into the ambulance. Armando raised his head, looking back at the wreck through the open back doors of the ambulance. He could see one of the officers sorting through the wreckage. He stood up holding Darcey's bag. He opened it and rummaged through its contents, pulling out a wallet. Armando dropped his head back on the gurney and gave a low groan.

¡Mierda! No way out of it now—there will be lots of questions, and I do not have any answers to give that will not implicate me further he whined to himself.

He saw the officer heading over to him.

"*Señor*, can you tell me about this," the officer asked, holding up Darcey's wallet. "I see it belongs to a Darcey Callahan of Dallas, Texas, in the United States. Was she in the car with you?" he asked, looking at Armando with narrowed eyes.

There was no wiggle room left for Armando, and judging by the look on the officer's face, it was about to get more complicated. He was hurting too much to think of a way to weasel out of the situation.

"Yes. We were on our way to a meeting when a vehicle came out of nowhere and broadsided us," he said. "I have no idea what has happened to her. She was gone when I came to." His voice quivered, his hands balling into nervous fists under the blanket the paramedic had covered him with.

"Do you know where she was staying? We will need to check her things," the officer inquired as he dropped

Darcey's wallet and bag into a plastic evidence bag and sealed it.

"Yes, she is my house guest. My housekeeper will be glad to show you her room." Armando closed his eyes and gave the officer his address.

This is going to be a nightmare he thought. *Why me?*

Armando could see he had no choice now but to sign the form a second officer had thrust at him, reporting her as a missing person. There would be endless paperwork to fill out, and insurance people to contact and ORCA would find out she had been here and he had not told them.

Just one more black mark to go in my file along with the attempted theft and the damage to the dome, he thought wearily.

Then he decided that what appeared in his file would be irrelevant because, as soon as he could get the paperwork done, he was going. Where, he did not know, just as long as it was far away from here. He had already banked five million of the twenty promised by Javier, and figured that was enough get him far away from Peru and keep him in the lifestyle he had grown accustomed to—at least for a while.

Javier, too, would find out that she was missing and of course, would blame him. Javier had indicated he had plans for her, although he had not been specific, only mentioning in passing that the Dallas office had told the Lima office she would not be arriving until tomorrow. Thus, he had assumed was the reason for the rushed secret meeting today. Javier had strongly cautioned him to let no one know she was here.

Arriving at the hospital, Armando had been jostled from the gurney to the narrow, hard bed in the Emergency Room. He lay shivering, in spited of being covered with a blanket, staring at the ceiling noticing how dirty and fly specked the tiles were, and wondered just how long they had been there.

Probably since the hospital was built, he guessed.

The hospital smells assailed his sensitive nostrils, almost to the point of nausea, reminding him why he did not like hospitals. He shivered and pulled the blanket up, covering his nose.

Armando had been poked, prodded, listened to, blood drawn, and hooked to an EKG machine, and then, had been to X-ray. Now he was waiting to be wheeled in for an MRI.

He thought that was a little over the top, considering the doctor had checked him over and had already confirmed nothing serious was wrong. However, they still wanted to keep him overnight for observation, just to be on the safe side, he had assured Armando.

Armando guessed the real reason was that the doctor just wanted to rack up the charges since ORCA's insurance would be paying the bill and, from the look of the place, it could use the extra cash.

Staying overnight was not what Armando wanted to hear, but under the circumstances staying the night in the hospital might be a better choice than going home and facing Javier, who he knew would be waiting for him.

How was he going to explain Darcey's disappearance? Did it even matter if he *had* an explanation? He knew, sure as hell, he would be blamed for it even though it was not his fault.

∽∾∽

It was well after midnight before the hospital sounds died down and Armando drifted off. Through a half-awake haze, he thought he heard the nurse come in the room. A cold hand clamped down on his mouth jerking him wide-awake.

"Hello, Armando." The cold voice sent chills down his spine. "We have been waiting for you to come home but you did not, so we have come to get you."

The hand was removed and Armando tried to focus on the face of the intruder. Panic overtook him as he tried to struggle, grabbing the intruder's arm. The man was too strong and picked his hand off like it was a feather. He slapped Armando across the face. Armando would have hollered for help if he could. His mouth felt as though it had been stuffed with cotton balls. He could not even swallow.

"Now, find your clothes and get dressed," the intruder said in low, threating tones. "We have a car waiting."

Armando swung his legs over the side of the bed and sat up. Fear and nausea taking hold, he started to shake non-stop.

The intruder slapped him across the face again. "Get a hold of yourself!" the intruder growled, through clenched teeth. "Now, get up and get dressed or I will do it for you. I do not think you want that."

His hands trembling, Armando managed to pull on his slacks, button his shirt, and shove his sockless feet in to his loafers.

The intruder checked the hallway. Seeing it was clear, he grabbed Armando's arm and pushed him out the door. There was something hard poking Armando in the back as they moved swiftly down the hallway. He had no doubt it was a gun.

They met no one on the way down to the first floor. The automatic doors slid silently open as they approached. Armando could see the shiny black car waiting on the driveway outside, and began to shake again.

The intruder pushed the gun harder in to Armando's back. "Move!" he commanded.

The door of the car swung open and he was roughly shoved inside. Armando could not see who was in the car. The overhead lights did not come on, but he was sure that Javier was the other passenger. "Well, Armando it seems you have gotten yourself into a bit of a bind," Javier said, quietly. "What are we going to do with you?"

"I—I—it wasn't my fault," Armando, stammered. "We—w—we—were b—br—broadsided. I have no idea who t—to—took her or w—why," he babbled, shaking uncontrollably.

The intruder with the gun slapped Armando across the face again. "Get a hold of yourself!" he commanded.

"Now, that is enough, Marcos," Javier said, laying his hand on Marcos's arm. "We do not want Armando here thinking we are violent people, now do we?"

Armando closed his eyes. He could hear the veiled threat in his voice.

What were they going to do to him? Why had he even listened to Javier? Why had he agreed to their deal? His mind raced as he realized that that was one question he could honestly answer—*money.*

Now it was too late. He had made a deal with the devil called the Eastern Alliance. There was no turning back. Now, in just a matter of minutes, the easy money that he had coveted with all of his soul had lost its allure. He just wanted to get out of this with his life.

It was unbelievable how fast one's perspective changes with a gun poking you in the ribs, he realized.

"Armando! Look at me!" Javier shook Armando's arm. "Do you know who took her?"

"N—n—no," Armando stammered. "I did not even see the car coming. She was gone when I came to."

"I see." Javier paused, his eyes narrowing. "Does this have anything to do with this Carlos Santiago you asked me to look into?"

"Maybe—she met him on the plane and was afraid of him. She asked me to move her to another hotel." Armando immediately regretted mentioning that she had requested to be moved to another hotel.

"And did you?" Javier asked.

He sensed Javier already knew the answer to that so it would have been useless to not mention her request.

"No, I took her to my home. I thought it would be safer for her there." Armando closed his eyes waiting for the other shoe to fall.

"You thought? You did not think!" Javier growled, at him. "You should have contacted me as soon as you knew

Santiago was in play. We would have put the plan into action right then. Now, she is out of our reach, and we have lost our leverage."

Javier took a cigarette from his gold cigarette case. Annoyed, he tapped it on the case planning his next move. Marcos pulled out his lighter and lit Javier's cigarette.

"You will only report her as a missing person. There is no need for me to be involved in this." Javier blew smoke in Armando's face. "Understand?"

"Y—ye—yes," Armando replied, coughing. "What should I tell the police when they come back asking more questions?"

"What did I just tell you?" Javier took another drag on the cigarette. "You just report her as a missing person. Someone kidnapped her. You do not know who or why. Do you think you can handle that?"

Javier leaned back in the seat and took another pull on his cigarette. His big disappoint was the leverage he thought he had had in the palm of his hand. Then in a flash, it had all evaporated into thin air because of Armando. Acid built in his stomach as he fumed over the situation.

Javier frowned as he remembered how elated he had been when his friend in the Dallas office called to let him know that Daniels's woman would be coming to Peru. He had his plan all laid out. It was simple—Armando would bring her to the mock meeting today, there they would take her and hold her for ransom. The ransom payment would be the diagrams for the dome and the air filtration system.

Damn Armando! He will pay for this. Javier ground his teeth, thinking about it. *On the bright side,* he reasoned, *all is not lost. I still have my 'ace-in-the-hole' yet in play—the computer virus.*

Javier was banking on the virus to bring the dome to a swift and final halt. Still, it concerned him that he had heard nothing from the dome about anything unusual happening there. He should have heard something from Lilly by now, but had not.

The car was slowing down, and Armando could see they were almost to the gate of his ranch. The car briefly slowed and then picked up speed as Marcos opened the door and shoved Armando out.

Armando hit the pavement with his shoulder and rolled into the ditch beside the driveway. When he climbed out of the ditch, stagnant water dripped from his clothes. The smell gagged him as he plopped down on the grass to pour the water out of his shoes. He estimated it was a quarter of a mile up to the house from the front gate. He thought about calling and having someone come pick him up, but he remembered his phone was on the bedside table at the hospital.

Standing up, he walked over to the entrance gates and gave them a hard shake. They were locked, just like he had instructed the staff to do at night, and he could not climb over them either. They were too high and there was no hand or footholds, per his design. The walls surrounding the ranch were ten feet high and constructed with glass shards embedded in the stones and mortar, all per his design to keep intruders out. But who would have ever imagined he would be the one locked out and trying to get in?

No choice left but to walk the half-mile around to the service entrance. There was an intercom there he could use to wake up some of the staff to let him in. He would get an intercom installed at the front gate tomorrow.

Finally reaching the service entrance, wheezing, he leaned on the buzzer.

"Yes, yes, what is it you want?" came the angry voice of Maria.

"Maria! It is Armando!" he shouted at her. "Let me in. Now!"

He heard the click of the gate unlocking and pushed it open. Maria was standing in the doorway waiting for him. "*Señor*! What has happened to you?" She looked him up and down, concern in her eyes.

Furiously, he pushed past her through the door. "Draw

me a bath and get me some clean clothes. And burn these," he commanded, pulling off his shoes and flinging them across the room as he headed for the stairway.

"*Sí, señor*, right away."

Maria scurried away up the stairs. She had reached his room just seconds before he walked through the door.

"Maria, is the bath ready, yet?" he shouted, at her.

"*Sí*, it will need just a few more minutes for the tub to fill," she said, pulling out his pajamas and laying them on the bed. "It's ready, *señor*," she said, motioning to the open bathroom door.

Armando threw his dripping clothes at her as he marched into the bathroom—naked. "Burn those!"

"*Sí, señor*."

Maria closed the bedroom door and hurried downstairs. She picked up the wet shoes and carried everything to the ranch's outside incinerator.

CHAPTER 11

Armando's Disgrace

What Armando dreaded most about this morning, he decided, was going to the office and having to report that Darcey had arrived in Peru looking for Brad and had now been kidnapped, and that he was responsible as well for, not notifying the office that she was here.

He took his time dressing and then only picked at his breakfast. The acid in his stomach churned every time he thought about what was waiting for him. The longer he put off leaving, the better he liked it. Of course, he would eventually have to face the reality that she had been kidnapped while under his protection, and that he *was* responsible.

The drive to the office seemed shorter than usual, even though he had driven under the speed limit all the way to the office. Pulling into the parking garage, he found his usual space was taken.

"*¡Maldito!*" he cursed.

Swinging around to the next row, he found a spot and parked. The walk to the elevator was much longer, and he grumbled all the way to the elevator doors.

This morning was starting out just great, he thought sarcastically. *I wonder what else can happen.* He savagely punched at the floor button panel as the doors closed.

Taking the back way into his office, avoiding as many people as possible, he slipped through his office door and shut it. Thank goodness, his secretary was not at her post, he thought until he saw she had already placed a stack of messages for his attention on his desk.

Sorting through them, he tossed the ones that could be taken care of later into a jumbled pile on the side of his desk. But, there were two, he could not avoid. One was to call Javier and the other to call Lilly. Javier he would call last, he decided, wanting to put it off as long as possible. He picked up the phone and punched in Lilly's extension number.

"Lilly here. How may I help you?"

Her voice grated on his ear. He knew he was not going to like this. "Armando here. I have a message to call you," he said, trying to sound unconcerned.

"Yes, Armando," she said. "It has come to my attention that you know about a woman from Texas who has come here looking for Señor Daniels. What can you tell me about this, and why you did not notify the office that she had arrived?"

She already knew all about it from Javier's call she had received earlier, but she needed Armando to confirm it before she told Brad that his stupid girlfriend had gotten herself kidnapped—not that she cared.

"Ah—yes—well—umm—she arrived two days ago looking for Brad," Armando stammered, the words sticking in his throat. "She said she was worried that something had happened to him. Besides, I did not know I was supposed to notify the office since I had received an email directing me to pick her up at the airport. I assumed the office already knew when she was arriving since the email came from the director's office. That's about all I know."

He closed his eyes, he knew that sounded lame, but it was partly the truth. A migraine was making its way to its usual spot in the middle of his forehead.

"I see, and what was she doing with you yesterday when you had an accident? More importantly, what has happened to her?"

Lilly knew she had caught him in a half-truth and was sure, now, he knew every detail of what happened. It was just a matter of getting him to tell it to her, so she could figure out just how much she wanted to relay to Brad.

"Well…you see, I do not know exactly what happened to her. Yes, she was with me. We were on our way to the office when the accident occurred, but she was gone when I came to."

¡Mierda! he thought. *She knows. How could she find out so soon? Of course—Javier, he has been very busy this morning.*

He groaned and pulled the bottle of migraine meds out of the bottom desk drawer.

"Armando I want you to tell me everything that has happened since she arrived, and do not leave anything out." She stressed the "do not" as she leaned back in her chair, a smirk on her face. "Start from the beginning, *por favor*," she said, in her most congenial tone.

Armando started from the beginning, with the email from the director's office asking him to pick her up at the airport. Her meeting Santiago on the plane, and her being afraid of him. Then, his inquiry into the man's business. Right up to and including what he knew about the accident. He however, did not mention anything about moving her from the hotel to his home, the pretend meeting with Javier, or what had happened last night.

He popped two migraine pills in his mouth and swallowed.

"Thank you. I will be in touch if I need anything else." She hung up, leaving Armando holding the receiver, the dial tone buzzing in his ear. After a few moments of listening to the mind numbing buzz, he punched in the extension number to call Javier.

No sense in putting if off any longer.

Javier picked up.

"Armando here. You wanted me to call?" he said impassively.

This is not going to go well. With his head pounding, Armando shut his eyes.

"Ah, yes, Armando. So good of you to return my call." Javier's voice held a veiled threat that was not lost on Armando. "The authorities will be contacting you, possibly today. You will tell them everything I told you to say last night, including your research on Carlos Santiago. That will send them looking in Santiago's direction and not here."

Armando wondered if he should mention that Lilly had called, grilling him on Darcey and the accident. Then he decided it wasn't worth mentioning, since, he was sure Javier had been the one who informed her anyway.

"Yes, I will tell them everything you told me to," he said, rubbing his eyes with his hand. The pounding increased.

"One more thing. How is what I am paying you for going?" Javier asked.

"It's going well," Armando said, smiling at his cleverness, in spite of the pounding behind his eyes. "The flow of parts and equipment through my office runs extremely slow. I have been able to delay, mis-order, or lose requisition forms for most requests. I feel that I have managed to slow work on the residential areas by at least a week now. However, I will have to process some of the requisition forms soon before Lilly starts asking questions." He frowned at that thought.

"Ah, Lilly." Javier paused. "Have as little as possible to do with her. You do know she wanted you fired after you screwed up getting the plans. It took a lot of talking on my part for you to keep your position. That put me in an extremely sensitive position, and some of the others involved were not happy with me doing that. It could have exposed their part in the plan. Your ass is on the line now, so I suggest you do not screw up again," he threatened and hung up.

Armando sat there, staring out into thin air, stunned. The dial tone buzzed in his ear for the second time in less than five minutes. "You could have at least given me a 'thank you' for the delays I have caused," Armando whined into the buzzing receiver.

Espionage was not his cup of tea, and he had to admit it was most unfortunate he had gotten caught with the stuff and then had his security clearance revoked.

"What else could I have done," he asked himself. "And just who are these 'others' Javier kept mentioning?"

Apparently, these "others" could make life very difficult for him if he did not hold up his end of the bargain.

Cold chills ran through his body as several scenarios played through his mind as just what those might entail.

He was alone in this and there seemed to be no way out. What if how he was handling the orders did not put up a substantial roadblock in the progress for completion?

Armando knew those "others" would not hesitate to do something unpleasant to him. They might even kill him, and if those "others" didn't kill him and he got caught, he would most assuredly go to prison. Neither choice appealed to him. Mulling over his self-made predicament and looking for another way out, a thought hit him—maybe if he went to Lilly and confessed, she could do something to help him out.

He picked up the phone and called Lilly.

"Hello Lilly here. How may I help you," she answered, looking at the caller ID and wondering why Armando was calling her back.

"Lilly, can we meet? I think we need to talk," he asked, popping two more migraine pills in his mouth.

"Yes. I will not be up top until tomorrow. Can we sched-ule for around two? My office?"

This should be interesting she thought marking the ap-pointment on her calendar.

"Sounds fine. I'll meet you there," he responded.

"I will see you at two tomorrow, then," she said, smiling as she hung up.

"Yes, tomorrow."

Armando hung up and leaned back in his chair, staring at

the phone. After a few minutes, he got up, walked over to the credenza, and poured himself a glass of Vodka. He gulped half of it down and then refilled the glass before he walked back to his chair and sat down.

It was not my fault things went wrong, he groused to himself. *It was not my fault I did not understand how to enter the stupid code to open the damn safe, either. It was Javier's fault. He should have told me how it worked. If I had known, it would have taken half the time to open the damn safe, and I would have been safely on the sub with no one the wiser.*

Armando eyed the orders stacked on his desk. He supposed he should do something about them.

Then, he did. He opened his desk drawer, pushed them in, and slammed the drawer shut.

I can't do anything about them if I can't see them, he reasoned, poured another glass of Vodka, and waited for the authorities.

As the day wore on, the trips to refill his glass grew tiring. On the last trip, he picked up the second, now almost empty bottle and brought back to the desk.

Should have done this sooner, he thought, sitting the bottle on his desk.

"No, they are not going to hang this on me," he said as he sat down. "I will find out just who 'they' are and give them a piece of my mind. I cannot be expected to do something right if I do not have all the information. No, sir, this is not my fault," he said, slamming his glass down on the desk for emphasis.

It was much later when he noticed the room had grown dark. The light from the outer office cast a soft glow through his half-open door. Most of the office staff had gone home. He had sent his secretary home shortly after the authorities had left and cancelled all of his afternoon appointments.

I should go home, too. He just didn't have the energy to get up and go, besides, he was just a little drunk.

໐๑໐๑

Javier hung up the phone after talking to Armando. He, too, was feeling the pressure, but from the Eastern Alliance to get the job done.

He had brought them a foolproof plan to shut down the dome and, in the process, obtain the Bio Dome and the filtration system plans. They were paying him a quarter of a billion dollars and giving him a place on the Eastern Alliance board for all his trouble.

He had derived the perfect plan that would give them everything they wanted. He would have a virus inserted into the filtration system's digital files, which would result in the files going corrupt, requiring ORCA costly time to try to repair them before the completion deadline.

Then, when they could not, ORCA would miss the deadline, resulting in substantial fines being levied against them for missing it. ORCA would then be forced to step away from the project or go bankrupt, leaving the EA to step in and rescue the project. It was the perfect plan.

Too late, Javier realized he had no one to blame but himself for the failure of the plan.

If he had had the balls at the time, he would have followed his gut and bribed one of the technicians, as he had originally planned, then ignored the EA board when they insisted the person needed to be someone with classified access to both topside and the dome. If he had tried harder to make them see that a technician was the perfect one for the job, they could have uploaded the virus, gotten the plans, and gone undetected.

If he had argued stronger against Armando when the EA suggested, no insisted, he was the perfect one for the job. If he had argued longer that Armando did not have the expertise or finesse to pull the job off, before he caved in to the EA's instance that Armando was the one.

If he had, could he have made the board see they were wrong? Probably not.

But, for some reason, someone on the board believed Armando was the best suited for the job. Then, when the inevitable happened, the EA demanded Javier pull Armando's ass out of the fire.

As the head of ORCA's Human Resources, Javier had been required to go before the ORCA Board to beg them to let Armando keep his job. All of it, at the risk of exposing himself, to say nothing of the risk of exposing the EA's involvement, as well.

Javier had hoped that the ORCA Board would not look too closely at his ties to Armando. If they had, then the EA would be exposed, also. He remembered heaving a sigh of relief when the board just took his recommendation and did not research it further. That had been a close call.

Then, what he considered a stroke of luck at the time, while talking with his friend at the Dallas office, they had mentioned, in passing, that Brad's girlfriend was coming to Lima to look for him.

Perfect, he had thought. He had asked his friend to contact the Lima office and give them the date of her arrival as two days after she actually arrived. He then emailed Armando and asked him pick her up at the airport. Then to bring her to a meeting he would set up for the day following her arrival.

Javier's new plan, which he thought was perfect again, was to hold her and trade her for both sets of plans. A perfect plan. It was simple—brains not required. *What can go wrong?* he had thought at the time.

Armando—that was what went wrong.

Armando has screwed things up one too many times. He is of no use to me anymore, if he ever was in the first place, he decided. He did not know the person the EA had hired to hack into ORCA's servers. Javier was just responsible for getting them the information they requested. The hacking and uploading the virus had been the EA's job, so if it did not go right, that was on them. They were not going to hang that one on him.

☙❧

Sometime later, Armando tossed back the last of his Vodka, got up, and cautiously walked out the door, pulling it half way closed behind him as he swayed toward the elevator.

Stumbling out of the elevator in the parking garage, he paused, trying to recall where he'd parked. Eventually, he remembered.

A few cars were left, and Armando started weaving toward them, his shuffling footsteps echoing in the vast cavern of the garage. The overhead florescent lights buzzed and blinked. The low ceilings were claustrophobic. Gasoline fumes assailed his nose, making him nauseous. It gave him the creeps, especially at night, when the place was almost empty.

"I hate parking garages," he muttered to himself.

Still not seeing his car, he fumbled the keys out of his pocket. They slipped out of his fingers and jingled as they hit the concrete floor. Retrieving them, he pushed the unlock button and watched for the car's lights to flash. They flashed and he swayed toward them.

Suddenly a second set of footsteps, just slightly out of sync with his, echoed. He turned and saw nothing. The footsteps had stopped.

Must be hearing things, he surmised, shrugging his shoulders.

He turned back around too quickly and had to steady himself on the fender of the car beside him. Orientating himself again, he moved toward his car.

Finding the car, he opened the door and fell into the seat then reached out to pull the door shut. He leaned out too far and had to grab the steering wheel to keep from falling out onto the floor. Struggling upright, he finally pulled the door shut.

On the third try, the key slid into the ignition. He sighed

and rested his forehead on the steering wheel, thinking he should just crawl in the back and sleep it off.

Tap, tap on his window. Bleary eyed, Armando turned and was staring down the barrel of a gun. That was the last thing he saw.

CHAPTER 12

Chaos and Confusion

The office was filled with police when Lilly arrived topside. She'd been told Armando's body had been found in his car in the parking garage by one of the employees that morning. No one knew what had happened or who could have killed him.

Lilly headed for her office to call Brad. She had told him the previous evening about Darcey having been kidnapped and Armando's involvement in the accident where Darcey went missing. Brad had been furious and had immediately called for Asad's security team to issue an arrest warrant for Armando.

Realizing now, he would have to come to the surface to take care of the situation, Brad told Lilly he would be up as soon as he could. It wasn't going to matter now, he guessed, if topside or anyone else knew he was here now that the virus was under control. He would leave Ty in charge. There shouldn't be any more attempts on the dome since access was now with Level One Clearance only, and Matt had put in new hacker-proof firewalls.

Shortly after noon, Brad walked into Lilly's office. She was on the phone speaking to Armando's lawyer. Armando's housekeeper had told her that Armando had no living family to notify, so Lilly hoped the attorney would take over responsibility for the arrangements.

"Yes, thank you. I will look for you around three this afternoon." Lilly hung up the phone and smiled at Brad. She thought he looked tired. "Fix yourself a drink. I think you could use one."

"Would you care for one, too?" Brad asked her.

"No, I am fine. Armando's lawyer will be here later this afternoon to handle the arrangements," she said, straightening the papers on her desk. "I do not know if the authorities will want to speak with you. They have talked with everyone in the office. You were not here when this unfortunate incident occurred, but they may wish to talk with you, anyway, since you are the project manager."

"I think we need to move fast now to find out who is behind this," Brad said. "It's my guess that the people who have tried to sabotage the project now think it's failed and are tying up loose ends." Brad took a drink from his glass. "Have you heard anything more from corporate?"

"No, I have asked everyone there I trust. I have also been trying to track down the anonymous call I received yesterday telling me about Armando's accident and his involvement with Darcey," she lied. She had not contacted corporate and already knew who had made the call, but she had to keep up appearances. "According to the office call logs, the call came from an extension in the office here. I tracked down the extension, but it came from a vacant office. No one saw anyone enter or leave that office. So a dead end there."

Lilly was not about to tell Brad that it was Javier who had called her. That would lead to too many questions that she had no intention of answering. Her involvement in the plan was too big and she was not about to jeopardize it—the stakes were too high.

"Call me if the authorities need to talk with me. I'll be in my office." Brad took his drink and left.

Asad's men had cleared everyone in the dome, but security was still tight and would be until the official opening. His request for Armando's arrest was unnecessary now. After Brad had called Asad and relayed what had happened, he asked if Asad would authorize his security squad to discretely check out the Lima office personnel as well. Asad had thought it prudent, in light of what had happened, and again asked Brad to keep it strictly confidential. Asad also placed all of ORCA's resources at Brad's disposal in his search for Darcey.

❧❧

Later that afternoon, by the time the authorities had concluded their interviews, Brad swung his chair around and turned his computer on. He logged into ORCA's extensive data bank, which was linked to Interpol and numerous other law enforcement agencies around the world.

After twenty minutes, the search for Carlos Santiago had, basically, netted nothing useable. It seemed that Santiago had kept a low profile. He was suspected of human trafficking, and he was on Interpol's watch list. But, apart from that and his questionable association with a Señor Vargas from Morocco, there wasn't much else about the man. There was a brief mention of two other men believed to be associated with him—Quin Alvarez and Ricardo Perez.

There was not much information on Alvarez or Perez, either. Neither one had been in trouble with the authorities, but each was also suspected of human trafficking. To date no solid evidence had been found. They were on Interpol's watch list as well.

However, a second look through the arrest files showed that Santiago had been arrested several times but under the name of Michael Johnson.

Now why does that name sound familiar?

Brad pulled up the full file for Santiago/Johnson and looked for a mug shot. As soon as the picture flashed on the screen, Brad knew who he was.

Johnson had been a student at the University the same

time as Brad and had applied to be on Brad's bio habitat team. But he had not been accepted. There was something about an incident on campus involving Johnson and several female students. Brad couldn't remember all of the details, but seemed to recall that the charges had been dropped, and Johnson left college shortly after the incident. Brad remembered thinking at the time that there was something not quite right about Johnson. He was too slick, too quick with excuses, and always had an alibi for everything.

Brad scanned through the rap sheet on Santiago/Johnson. All the charges on every arrest for trafficking had been dropped. He had never been prosecuted. Most assuredly, he would have had an ironclad alibi, bought and paid for, for whatever he had been arrested for, or had a slick lawyer.

Most likely the former, Brad thought. *Wonder who Johnson paid off to get the charges dropped at college.*

Bribery seemed to be a way of life here, something Brad hadn't quite gotten used to. He called Lilly to tell her what he'd found out about Santiago and what he planned to do about locating Vargas. Lilly never expressed an opinion on the situation but suggested that he go ahead with his plan and try to make contact with Vargas.

"It just might be possible that he would know something about her," she told Brad, all the while thinking she hoped he never found that woman.

Hanging up, Brad Googled Vargas. Several names came up. He scrolled through the list and their brief descriptions, but there was just one listed as residing in Morocco.

That was one Luis Vargas. Vargas was described as a self-made, multi-billionaire philanthropist, who raised Arabian horses at his ranch, Mon Rêve, outside of Agadir, Morocco. There was not much information provided, other than a short list of charities he was widely known for supporting. The only picture in the file was a small one of him with one of his prize-winning horses in the winner's circle at a horse show function.

Brad noticed that Vargas's file had been flagged with a

link back to Santiago's file. Other notations indicated Vargas's name had been added to Interpol's watch list under "Trafficking" as well.

Brad decided that he had to be the one. He called the airport and arranged to use the corporate jet the next day. Afterward, he looked up the phone number for the ranch and called.

"*Buenos días,*" the soft voice on the other end of the line said. "*¿Como le puedo ayudar?*"

He laughed. "Howdy. Do you speak English? My Spanish is a little rusty."

"Certainly, sir. How may I help you?" The female voice was mild and pleasant.

"Well now, little lady, I'm lookin' to talk to Mr. Vargas 'bout some horses," he said, in his best Texan accent.

"Who shall I say is calling?" she asked.

"Just tell him Brad Daniels with ORCA is callin'."

He figured the ORCA name would get him in quicker than his own name since ORCA was known worldwide for their excellent reputation in the business world.

"One moment please. I will see if Señor Vargas is available."

She put Brad on hold; a recording of the history of the Vargas ranch played in his ear. The recording had started on its second play through when the receptionist came back online.

"I'm sorry, but Señor Vargas is unavailable at the moment. He asked me to take your information and he will call you back shortly," she said.

"Certainly, little lady." Brad relayed his number. "I will be here the rest of the evening," he told her. "I look forward to hearin' back from Mr. Vargas."

"Thank you, he will call you shortly," she assured him.

Well now, that was easy, he thought. *We'll see what happens when he calls back.* He checked the time and decided it wasn't too late to call Lilly with what he had found out.

"Yes? Lilly here," she answered, wondering why Brad would be calling her at this hour in the evening.

"I found Vargas. He has a ranch in Morocco. I called and he will be calling me back. I used the ORCA name so it looked like corporate was inquiring about his horses," he said.

"That sounds like an excellent plan," Lilly replied.

It did not make a difference to her how he handled it or if he found that woman, but it did please her knowing that he placed value on her opinion. So much so, that he had called her at home. "Let me know how the conversation goes, please. I can make arrangements for the jet if you would like," she added.

"No, I've already got it on standby for tomorrow, assuming everything goes as planned with Vargas," he said. "I'll let you know as soon as I have solid arrangements made."

With that, he told her goodbye and hung up.

CHAPTER 13

Señor Vargas

Waiting for Vargas to return his call, Brad checked in at the dome for an update.

"All is excellent," Ty reported, "running like a well-oiled machine. Matt updated the hydroponics program, and preliminary tests show that it will perform two times better than the previous program. Hot Dog and Scott made adjustments in the atmospheric program for the hydroponics, main-street, and parks areas that allow for additional moisture control."

"Sounds great," Brad told him. "Keep me posted."

"Will do."

Brad had just hung up when the front office buzzed him.

"There's a Señor Vargas on the line for you," the operator said.

"Put him through," he told her. "Señor Vargas, Brad Daniels here. Thanks for callin' me back."

"Sí. I understand you are interested in some of my horses," Vargas answered.

"Yeah, a friend of a mutual friend said you might have what I'm lookin' for, if you catch my drift." He fudged a little on who knew who, but didn't waste any time getting to the point.

He saw no advantage in dancing around the issue.

"Who would this mutual friend be?" Vargas asked, most

interested in who might be giving out information about him.

"That would be Carlos Santiago," Brad told him.

"That is most interesting, and how does your friend know this Carlos Santiago?" Vargas asked cautiously, suspicion tinting the edge of his voice.

"They were friends in college," Brad said flatly. He could hear the wall coming up in Vargas's voice. This was not a good thing, he decided. If he didn't level with Vargas, he could lose him altogether, and any hope of finding Darcey. Brad made a split second decision to drop all pretenses and lay it all out for Vargas. He poured himself a glass of Scotch and took a big swallow. "Señor Vargas, I don't have time to pussyfoot around the issue," he said, "so I'm going to level with you. I believe Santiago kidnapped my girlfriend Darcey Callahan. She was traveling from Dallas, Texas, to Lima, Peru, to meet me when Santiago took her. I understand that Santiago does business with you. I'm not interested in anything about your ventures, and I don't care what you paid Santiago for her. I will pay you double what you paid for her or whatever price you name. I only want her back safe and sound."

Brad took another big swallow of the amber liquid, waiting to hear Vargas's reaction. It did a slow burn down his throat like his anger that was building inside him.

"This throws a different light on things," Vargas said thoughtfully.

That might explain why Santiago had called for a special pick up from Salinas.

Vargas had thought it strange that Carlos would call for a pick-up—that was not his style. He always wanted to make a delivery in person.

"Señor Daniels, I will have to check into this. I will have my manager contact you and let you know what we find out. It has been very pleasant speaking with you. Adiós, Señor Daniels. We will be in touch."

Vargas hung up and leaned back in his chair, thinking.

Daniels sounded desperate and angry. Even after all these years, Vargas could still remember the same feeling all too well. The pain was still sharp, even after twenty-five years. Nothing had been able to heal his heart after Saleem the love of his life, had been kidnapped on the eve of their wedding.

ღჯღჯ

The next morning, Brad walked down to Lilly's office to tell her about Vargas's call. He didn't know what to think now. Would Vargas help him or would he just blow him off?

Brad had not eaten breakfast and asked if Lilly would like to join him for a late one. They walked through the line in the cafeteria on the lower level of ORCA's Lima's office building. Choosing items from the vast array of choices prepared daily by the ORCA chefs was usually a delight, only this morning nothing appealed to him. One thing about ORCA, they didn't skimp on keeping their employees happy.

He had eaten only half of his bagel when his cell rang. The front desk said a Juan Cruz from rancho Mon Rêve in Morocco, was on the line.

"Put him on hold. I'll take it in my office," he told the receptionist. "I'll let you know what I find out," he said, to Lilly as he grabbed his cup of coffee and headed back to his office.

"Hello, Brad Daniels here. Thanks for gettin' back to me," he said.

"Juan Cruz, Señor Daniels. I am calling to let you know Señor Vargas would like you to come, as a guest, to his ranch in Morocco," Cruz paused, waiting for Brad to confirm.

"Thank you, I would like that," Brad replied.

"Señor Vargas believes he can help you with what you

are looking for. Will you be available to come right away?"
Cruz asked.

"Yeah, I'm available. When do you want me?" Brad replied.

"Will you be able to arrive tomorrow?" Cruz asked.

"Just give me all the particulars and I'll see you tomorrow," Brad said, picking up his pen, he wrote down the instructions Cruz gave him. He called Lilly and let her know he was flying out at first light in the morning.

∽∾∽∾∽

Fourteen hours after takeoff, the ORCA jet landed at Inezgane Airport, Morocco. Stepping off the plane, Brad saw Vargas's limo waiting on the tarmac. The driver opened the door for him and put Brad's luggage in the trunk.

"*Buenas noches*, Señor Daniels," the driver said. "We will be arriving at rancho Mon Rêve in approximately forty-five minutes. There is a full bar and tobacco products for your enjoyment. The remote for the DVD player is in the side pocket and the machine is pre-loaded with five movies." With that, the privacy partition slid silently up as the limo moved out into traffic.

Brad checked out the bar and saw that the driver was right. It was fully stocked. He tipped up a bottle of Chivas, watching as the amber liquid filled the glass.

Vargas certainly knows how to treat his clients, he thought. He settled back to enjoy the journey to the ranch.

Forty-five minutes later, the limo pulled up in front of the very imposing home of Señor Luis Vargas. The driver already had Brad's luggage in hand when he opened the limo door for him.

The driver motioned to Brad to precede him up the walkway to the front door. "This way, *señor*."

The doorman stood aside allowing Brad to enter, followed by the limo driver.

The foyer was large with twenty-foot ceilings and an ornately carved grand staircase in the center that reached a landing where it split left and right with the stairs continuing on to the second floor. Hallways leading off to the interior of the home flanked either side of the staircase. Fresh cut flowers filled a huge oriental looking vase on a carved white marble table below a mirror that appeared to be at least ten feet tall.

"*Buenas noches, señor*. Please follow me. Señor Vargas will join you in the library," the doorman said. "Your luggage will be taken to your room."

Brad followed the stiff back of the doorman through the foyer and a short ways down the hall to the library. Walking inside, Brad saw that it really was a library. The windows, doors, and fireplace were surrounded by floor-to-ceiling shelves filled with books.

Over the fireplace a massive guilt frame held a large oil painting of one of Vargas's prize-winning Arabians. Numerous trophies lined the mantle. A seating area in front of the fireplace was defined by two long facing leather sofas and two matching chairs, all centered around a beautifully carved, teak-wood table. Carved walnut shutters with copper trim covered the windows, and antique carpets softened the stone floor. It was a man's room.

Brad strolled around the room, reading book titles. He was admiring the wide range of topics the books covered when Señor Vargas entered.

"*Bienvenido a mi casa* Señor Daniels," Vargas said. "In English, that's welcome to my home. Please fix yourself a drink. I'm sure you had a long and tiring journey." Vargas smiled at Brad, assessing him. From their conversation and now viewing his body language, he could see this man was on a mission to find his woman.

"Thanks, I'm good. I had one on the way here." Brad turned and smiled at Vargas. He was pleasantly surprised to see that Vargas was not what he had expected.

Vargas had a warm, comfortable look about him, and

appeared to be in his early-to-mid-fifties. He was just shy of six foot, with the body of a man who had spent many hours with his horses. His slightly receding hairline, graying temples, and neatly trimmed beard gave him the distinguished look of a worldly gentleman. Friendly, but knowing, quick brown eyes made Brad sure they never missed a thing.

"I was just admiring your collection of books. Have you read any of them?" Brad asked, walking back toward Vargas.

"Yes, I have read every one of these," Vargas said, swinging his arm around to encompass the whole room. "I have three passions, horses, reading, and women, not necessarily in that order."

Vargas gave Brad a wicked grin. He liked this man. He was not afraid to look him in the eye—a man who had nothing to hide.

"What have you found out about Darcey?" Brad asked, eager to know anything that could help him to find her.

"Ah, yes, the reason for your visit." Vargas smiled, walking up to Brad. "I am waiting for one more piece of information, before I am comfortable telling you what I have found out. However, it is getting late and we rise early around here, so we will finish this discussion in the morning. Jose will show you to your room," he said, walking Brad toward the door, where he stopped and pulled on a long brocade sash. Within a few seconds the doorman appeared. "This is Jose," Vargas said. "He will escort you to your room. *Buenas noches*, Señor Daniels."

Vargas inclined his head slightly, turned, and returned to the interior of the room, leaving Brad feeling slightly let down and disappointed. His anticipation of the information Vargas had for him had been building ever since he had left Lima. Now it was like being sent to bed without any dinner.

"This way, *señor*."

Jose started back toward the foyer. Brad followed him up the grand staircase to the second level.

Several large oil portraits, that Brad assumed were family ancestors, interspersed with antique tapestries, lined the walls on either side of the wide hallway,

Jose opened the double doors and stood aside for Brad to enter. "This is your room, *señor.*"

"Thank you, Jose. Guess I'll see you in the morning," Brad said, before walking into the room.

"Sí. Breakfast will be served at seven. You will have a wake-up call. *Buenas noches, señor.*"

Jose gave a slight nod of the head, turned, and walked, straight-backed, down the hall.

Brad watched him go before shutting the doors. He looked around the room. It was quite large. Earth tones complemented the heavy antique furniture. It was definitely designed for a man, no frills, or lacy stuff here. He saw his luggage had been unpacked, his clothes were hung or folded away, and the bed had been turned down.

A hot shower and I'm ready to hit the sack, he said to himself.

The hot water relaxed his tired muscles. He knew he would sleep well tonight.

☙❧☙

As was his usual ritual, Vargas stopped by his office to check emails and faxes before turning in for the evening. Turning on the computer, he checked his inbox.

There was a message from his manager Nicho's assistant Jada, with an attachment. It was about the special pick-up he had sent Nicho to get. It seems the girl was not up to specifications. However, she was exquisite and Jada thought it would be worth Vargas's time to look at her.

His first inclination was to tell Jada to cancel the deal but before he replied, curiosity got the better of him and he opened the attachment.

When the image of the girl popped up, his heart almost stopped. There on the screen was a nearly identical picture of his Saleem. *My eyes must be playing tricks.* He blinked and looked again. *No, the girl could have been Saleem.*

He hesitated. What should he do? What did he want to do? If this was Brad's woman, why did she look like his Saleem?

The impossible popped in his mind—could this be a daughter? She appeared to be around the right age or had he been thinking so much about Saleem that he was seeing her in this girl?

He hit reply and sent a message saying he would take her, in spite of her being imperfect. However, he would only pay half of the previously agreed price.

Business is business, he thought.

He instructed Jada to take another photo of the girl for the binder and inform Carlos the money would be deposited in his account upon receipt of the girl. Vargas did not wait for a reply. It wasn't necessary. He had given instructions and expected them to be carried out.

Turning off the office light, he headed to his bedroom, trying to decide what to tell Brad.

Maybe things will be clearer in the morning, he thought.

ღღღ

At exactly five-thirty the next morning, one of the housemaids knocked on Brad's door. She opened the door just enough to see if he was decent before entering.

"*Buenas días, señor.* Breakfast will be at seven. Is there anything you need?" she asked looking at the floor.

"Mornin'. No, I'm good. Thanks, anyway," Brad said, sitting up and stretching his arms over his head.

The sheet fell to his waist, revealing his sculpted chest. The maid giggled, blushed, and left. Brad swung his legs over the side of the bed and got up. He did a quick shave, dressed, and left his room.

He had no idea where the dining room might be, so he

took the opportunity to explore, on the pretext of looking for it. The second floor seemed to be all bedrooms. He wondered casually which one was Vargas's.

On the lower level, he discovered there were several rooms—one was a sitting room, small and intimate, probably used for family; then a larger formal room, he guessed would be used to entertain guests; the library; and then what must be Vargas's office. On the opposite side of the hallway, was the dining room. It was light and airy. A large expanse of windows with French doors in the middle covered most of one wall and opened out onto a large patio and down a few stone steps, to a lovely garden.

The long dining table, that could have easily seated twenty people, had been set for two at the end closest to the doors Brad guessed would connect to the kitchen or pantry.

On the sideboard, were two large urns. He took a sample from the first one. It was a tea of some sort. *Ugh, way too sweet.* Taking a clean cup, he sampled the other. *Ah, yes, coffee—thankfully,* he thought, and filled the cup. It was hot and strong.

Large pitchers of juice had also been placed next to the urns along with several serving trays piled high with sweet breads and pastries.

Brad hoped the more substantial items, like the eggs and bacon he was used to, would come later. He sat down at the table and waited for Vargas to make an appearance. He didn't have long to wait. Vargas walked in a few seconds after seven.

A man who runs on schedule, Brad mused.

Vargas was surprised to see Brad already there. He had heard the Americans were excessively lazy and late to appointments.

This man must be an exception, he thought. He gave Brad a broad open smile.

"*Buenas días,* Señor Daniels, Beautiful morning. Hope you found your room to your liking?" Vargas asked, filling his own cup from the tea urn.

Brad returned the smile. "Just Brad, please, and yes I slept very well. Thank you."

"Help yourself," Vargas said as he placed pastries on his plate. "The kitchen staff will serve the main course shortly. In the meantime, enjoy some of these delicious treats, all prepared fresh this morning."

Brad refilled his cup with coffee and selected a couple of the pastries. He and Vargas sat down simultaneously. Vargas dove wholeheartedly into the pastries on his plate.

When he was finished, Vargas put down his fork, picked up his cup, and leaned back in his chair. "Now tell me, all about why you have contacted me."

Brad looked Vargas in the eye and told him about everything that he knew of what had transpired up to his coming here.

When he'd finished, he picked up his cup of coffee. It had grown cold, like the lump in his chest. Brad had studied Vargas's face while he was telling him his story. The man gave nothing away.

Vargas sat there thinking.

If what Brad has told me is true, and knowing Carlos as I do, I see no reason to doubt him. Yes, I will see what I can do to help him out, as long as it does not interfere with my business, he decided.

"All right, Señor, er—Brad, I appreciate your frankness. I do not tolerate anyone who is not honest with me." He paused and took a drink from his cup.

Just then, the kitchen staff walked in with the main course and placed steaming platters of eggs, ham, bacon, along with silver breadbaskets filled with hot bread, on the sideboard. Fresh churned butter, heavy cream, assorted jams, jellies, and fresh fruit finished the assortment.

"*Por favor*, let us eat while it is hot," Vargas said, scooting his chair back.

Brad followed suit.

Vargas watched Brad out of the corner of his eye. He felt like Brad had integrity, and he was seldom wrong about a man's makeup. It was something Vargas prided himself on. Friend or foe, he had made it a habit to know who he was dealing with.

"I will show you the ladies I have, and you can see if any of them is the one you are looking for," Vargas told Brad, as he downed a glass of juice.

"Thanks. I appreciate your help." Brad grinned slightly, putting a fork full of eggs in his mouth.

Breakfast over, Brad walked with Vargas to his office. Vargas motioned to him to take a seat in one of the chairs in front of his desk. The desk was a sharp contrast to the rest of the furnishings. It was all glass and steel. Vargas noticed Brad staring at it and laughed.

"A gift from one of my daughters. She thinks I am stuck in the eighteenth century and she is trying to move me forward." He smiled affectionately, looking at the desk. "Yes, well, let us get to business, shall we?"

He pulled a large binder from the credenza behind the desk and handed it to Brad.

"This is my entire collection. Look through them and see if any is the one you are looking for," he told Brad, even though he knew the one Brad was looking for would not be there.

Brad started turning pages. Nothing in the first pages he turned through was Darcey. He stopped at the page titled "New Arrivals." He inhaled before turning the page and exhaled slowly, continuing to turn the pages, looking at each one. All of them were beautiful women but none that could compare to Darcey. She wasn't on any of those pages either. The small glimmer of hope he had had evaporated as he slowly closed the binder.

Vargas rocked back and forth in his chair watching Brad as he looked through the pages of the binder. He noticed the disappointment and pain reflecting in his face as he turned page after page only to find that the one he searched for was not there.

Vargas knew it was cruel not to have told Brad that he

would not find her in those pages. However, he could not afford to tell him she would be arriving some time that night.

Business is business.

He had money invested in this woman and he had to see her before he decided if he wanted to show her to Brad. If he could prove she was Saleem's daughter, then that would change everything. He had to know first.

"No," Brad said, sadly, "she's not here." Despair was noticeable in his voice as he heaved a heavy sigh.

"I am most sorry," Vargas said, with pretended sympathy. "I still have one or two more who are coming that have not arrived yet. Wait a couple more days and let us see what will happen. If it is, as you have said about Santiago, then she will arrive. He called for a special pick-up and I have sent my manager to bring the woman back. I will let you know," Vargas said, putting the binder back and coming around to sit in the chair next to Brad. "In the meantime, I invite you to be my guest for the Bel Ami Gala. I am sure you will find it most informative and enjoyable. Also, please take advantage of the many amenities we have to entertain you—horseback riding, golf, swimming, tennis, skeet shooting, billiards, video games, movies, and of course reading. For any of these activities, you may have the pleasure of the company of one of my many beautiful hostesses."

Vargas looked at Brad to see his reaction. He felt you could judge how serious a man was about a woman by what he did when confronted with limitless temptation.

Brad sat staring at the desk, not really seeing it; his heart ached as visions of Darcey filled in his mind. "I'll take you up on the riding, but I prefer to ride alone, if you don't mind. Not that your ladies aren't beautiful, I'm just not interested."

As Vargas studied him, it brought back a painful memory he had tried to bury years ago. Even though he did not want to, he could feel Brad's pain as precisely as he had once felt it himself, and still did, when he allowed himself to remember.

Pushing himself up out of the chair, he looked at Brad. "My stable is at your disposal. You may ride any of the horses that you would like." Vargas reached for the phone on his desk and called the stables. "Señor Daniels will be coming down to select a horse for a ride this afternoon. Assist him, *por favor*."

"Thanks, Señor Vargas. I appreciate all you are trying to do." Brad reached out his hand to Vargas.

Smiling Vargas shook Brad's hand. "It is Luis, and you are welcome."

❦❦❦

The next morning, the new photo Vargas had requested was in his inbox when he turned on his computer. The image on the screen, even though it was slightly out of focus, did look a lot like Saleem.

Too much, to be just a coincidence, he reasoned.

The look of defiance on her face said she had a spirit that would not be easily crushed—much like Saleem. Vargas picked up the phone and called Nicho. "How soon will you be arriving?"

"No later than this evening."

"Good. Does this one have a name?"

"She was in a car accident and lost her memory."

Vargas's heart constricted at Nicho's words. "A car accident? Is she hurt? How badly?" he questioned in rapid succession.

Not understanding Vargas's over reaction to the news about this woman, Nicho calmly replied, "She has a small concussion according to Dr. Lopez. He thinks it may result in some memory loss and may only be temporary. There is no way of knowing at this point. She had a few minor abrasions but nothing that would mar her beauty."

Vargas felt a wave of relief. He made a mental note to arrange for a complete examination by his doctor as soon as she arrives. "Good. Where did she come from?"

"Carlos never mentioned her by name," Nicho said. "But as far as I can tell, she came from the United States."

"Well, since she does not have a name, I will give her one—Saleem. From now on, she will be known as Saleem. I will pass this information on to Alfredo in the morning."

But, now, what did he do about Brad? Did he tell him or keep him in the dark? He did not have proof yet that she was Saleem's daughter. He could not let Brad know about that until he had proof in hand. And if she was, could he let her go? He had many things to consider. Things that pulled at his heartstrings. Things that pulled at his purse strings.

Brad and several of the other Gala guests were just finishing breakfast when Vargas walked into the dining room. Looking around, he spotted Brad and motioned to him to follow. Brad gave him a slight nod and followed him out of the room.

Vargas was waiting for him in front of his office. "Come in," He moved aside so Brad could enter. "I have a photo of the girl who Carlos picked up for me. Please take a look and see if this is your Darcey." He turned the monitor around so Brad could see it.

"Yes! That's her but I've never seen her look quite like that, like she's ready to kill someone." Brad's heart leaped with joy. The photo was grainy, and the look on her face—it was another side of her he'd never seen. But it *was* Darcey.

Vargas smiled at Brad. "Well, she will be here this evening. After she is settled in, you may see her tomorrow at the first formal dinner. If you did not bring a tuxedo with you, I will have one sent up to you as my gift to you."

"What? What do you mean I have to wait until tomorrow?" Brad stepped back staring in disbelief at Vargas. "I want to take her home tonight."

"It is complicated," Vargas said, turning away from Brad to avoid eye contact. "There are many things to be considered. You must be patient. You do not even know if this is your Darcey—" he said, turning to face Brad.

"Yes, she is!" Brad interrupted frustrated at this turn of events.

"As I was saying, we will sort all of this out once she is here and settled," Vargas continued. "I understand from Nicho that she has been in an accident and has lost her memory. She may or may not be your Darcey. I only have your word for it." He shrugged his shoulders. "I cannot just turn her over to you because you say so. Like I said, it is complicated. We will see what happens after she arrives."

"This ridiculous," Brad fumed, pacing back and forth. "She is Darcey Callahan. She's an American citizen and you have no right to keep me from taking her home," he challenged.

"Yes, *mi hijo*, I can." Vargas looked Brad square in the eye. "She is my property, and your word carries no weight here. I have made a business deal. She is mine to do with as I please and, if she is truly your Darcey, then we will see what arrangements can be made."

"Arrangements? What arrangements?" Brad was furious. "I've already told you I will pay whatever price you want. What's a better business deal than that?"

"Like I said it is complicated. There other things to consider in this transaction," Vargas said, his voice turning hard. "We have talked enough on this. You will see her tomorrow evening or you may leave. The choice is yours."

Brad stood, running his hand through his hair. *This can't be happening,* he thought, and by the look on Vargas' face, he knew he had no choice if there was going to be any hope of getting Darcey out of here. "All right, I'll play your little game—for now," he conceded.

"That is a wise decision," Vargas said, from behind his desk. "Now, I will have that tuxedo sent to your room, and we will hear no more of this."

With a wave of his hand Vargas dismissed Brad as though he were a schoolboy in the principal's office. Brad slammed the door on his way out. After Brad had stormed out of his office, Vargas felt bad about his behavior. He truly liked Brad, but his selfish side's need to know about Saleem's daughter outweighed everything else.

CHAPTER 14

Where the Hell is She?

The phone rang and rang and rang. That was the fourth time today that Marti had tried calling Darcey. *She should have been home yesterday,* she worried. Marti hit disconnect and punched in Darcey's office number.

"I'd like to speak to Darcey Callahan, please," she told the receptionist.

"I'll put you through to her voice mail. She is out of town," the receptionist replied.

"No, wait. Is there someone I can speak to about her?" Marti asked her, wishing she could remember Darcey's boss's name.

"I'll see if Mr. Duncan is available to speak with you. One moment, please."

The on-hold music came on. Marti kept time to the music tapping her pen on her desk.

"Duncan, here," came a deep gruff voice.

"Hi, Mr. Duncan. My name is Marti Campbell, and I'm trying to locate my friend, Darcey Callahan." She paused, before going on. "I understand she is out at a job site and was expected back yesterday, but I've not been able to reach her."

"Just a moment, let me look." He paused. "No, she's on vacation. She took a week's vacation. She won't be back in the office until Monday," Duncan replied, wondering what all the fuss was about.

"I'm sorry, but that's not what she told me," Marti fumed. "She said she was going out to a job site to do some preliminary drafts and would only be gone for three or four days. It's now been five days, and I'm really getting worried that something has happened to her. She wouldn't lie to me about this. So I'm trying to find out what's going on." Marti had to pause to catch her breath.

"Well, now, we have her down as taking vacation days. She's not due back to work until Monday. I have no idea if she is on the job or not. Perhaps you misunderstood her," Duncan said, sounding perplexed.

Why do I have to be the one to get these kinds of calls? he thought. *I'm not Callahan's boss. I am just the HR assistant. How would I know if she was on a job or not? I'm going to have to have a talk with Mary Ann, at the front desk— don't put anyone through to me unless it specifically is HR related.*

"No! I didn't misunderstand her," Marti bristled, agitated and just short of shouting. "She told me she had a new job and would be gone three or four days doing preliminary drafts. Did she leave any contact information with you in case she was needed?" Marti was frustrated, tapping her pen hard on the desk leaving little tick marks on the surface.

"No, we only have her cell number. Have you tried that?" he asked, not knowing what else to tell the woman, pinching the bridge of his nose with his fingers.

"Yes, and I've tried her home phone, too. No answer at either. Oh, you're absolutely no help. Sorry I bothered you. Good bye!" she shouted and hung up.

Marti left Duncan wondering what the hell that was all about, and why he had been so privileged to be the one to handle the call, as he reached for his bottle of Pepto—it wasn't even noon. Marti laid her phone on the desk. She just knew something was not right. Darcey should have been back yesterday. She rummaged around in her desk drawer for the key Darcey had given her months ago, as a safety precaution, in case she lost hers. She found it where it had been shuffled to the back.

"I'm running over to Darcey's," she hollered at her dad on her way out the door.

He looked up from his computer and waved.

It took twenty minutes to drive over to Darcey's. Marti pulled her car up in front of her apartment house and walked up the short flight of stairs to Darcey's apartment. She inserted the key in the lock and opened the door.

"Oh geez!" she exclaimed.

The acrid aroma of burnt coffee slammed Marti in the face, when she opened the door.

Crap! She left the coffee pot on, again!

Marti yanked the plug out of the socket and gave the de-hydrated coffee pot a quick once over, wrinkling her nose at the cracked, crusty layer of charred coffee in the bottom of the pot. As soon as it cooled off, it was going in the trash.

It's a wonder the thing didn't catch fire, she thought.

Marti went around the apartment opening windows and turning on the ceiling fans. She smiled to herself. *Sometimes Darcey can be such an airhead. But I love her anyway.*

Marti sat down and turned on Darcey's computer. She looked through Darcey's browsing history to see what she had been looking at last. Just the usual stuff, but she almost missed the one for American Airlines. She clicked on it to see what was of interest to Darcey at American Airlines. The site opened on reservations, and from what she could tell, Darcey had been looking at direct flights from Dallas to Lima, Peru.

"Oh my God! She didn't, did she?" Marti threw up her hands. "I'm going to strangle that woman when I get my hands on her."

Shuffling through the papers on the desk, she uncovered Darcey's planner. The planner's day-marker was on last Sunday's date. She opened it. Written in red ink was *AA 2012 10 am Sunday* on the date.

Marti got the American Airlines number from the computer screen and called.

"Hello, can you tell me if you had a flight to Lima, Peru, on Sunday with flight number 2012?" she asked the airline representative.

"Yes, we did," he replied. "Is there something I can help you with?"

"Yes. Can you tell me if you had a passenger on that flight by the name of Darcey Callahan, please?" She waited, holding her breath.

"No, I'm sorry but we cannot give that information out," he said. "Is there anything else I can help you with?"

"No that's all and thank you," she said and hung up.

Now what do I do?

She leaned back in her chair, tapping the pen against her fingers, wondering if she should call the Dallas ORCA office. If they didn't have information on Darcey, maybe there would be something new about Brad. She found the number and called.

"Yes, we believe that Miss Callahan had arranged to fly to Lima," the receptionist at Brad's office said.

"Do you know if she actually got there?" Marti asked.

"No, we don't. Sorry we couldn't be more help. But we have no further information."

Marti hung up. *Well that answers that,* she thought. *Darcey flew off to Lima without telling me one word.*

Hurt and anger welled up.

"How could she?" Marti said, tears stinging her eyes. "I know exactly why she did it—she knew I would try to talk her out of it, and she was right—I would have." She sniffed wiping her eyes. *Well nothing left to do but wait till I hear from her,* she thought as she stood up.

Marti tried her cell one more time. A faint ring came from the bedroom—Darcey's cell was here.

CHAPTER 15

The Clean Up

Quin stood looking at the wreckage. *This wasn't exactly how I had imagined it playing out.*

Carlos had directed Quin to put together a plan to get the girl, but, somehow, he had a feeling this was not what Carlos had had in mind. However, Ricardo had missed hitting the limo directly in the back seat area, and that was a blessing. Ricardo was young, and he would learn.

Once Quin knew who she had been staying with, it was easy to find someone to bribe in order to get the information he needed. A call telling him when the girl and Armando were leaving and what road they were taking was all he needed. Quin waited for them to enter the intersection he had chosen and instructed Ricardo to "floor it" straight at their limo.

Prying the door open, Quin saw that the girl was pretty banged up. He made a quick assessment of her injuries—a large lump and a cut to the side of her head had left her face bloody, but nothing looked broken. He gently ran his finger of the lump. *This was going to need to be looked at.* The head wound would not show after healing. Her hair would cover it. The bruises and scratches would heal and leave no marks, either, a vital requirement.

Darcey drifted in and out of consciousness. She had no sense of time. Vague images and weird sounds came and went. At one point she was dimly aware something was be-ing lifted off her legs. She heard a voice echo far away.

"Be careful with her. We can't afford damaged goods."

"She looks to be in pretty good shape except for the lump. I will call Dr. Lopez to come look at it. That will take a little longer to heal," Quin said, pointing at the bloody side of her head, "but everything else should heal in a few days. It should not put us behind schedule."

"What about the others?" Ricardo questioned.

Another voice emerged from the haze.

"They are not our concern. Only the girl."

She was being lifted. She screamed—darkness envel-oped her again.

Quin lifted her as easy as he could and carried her to the SUV. Laying her down, he covered her with a blanket. They had to hurry. The authorities would be arriving soon. Even though this was a rural area, someone would have heard the crash and called for help.

Ricardo drove them to the warehouse close to the heli-port. Quin jumped out to move the girl to a gurney, then rolled her into the building and onto the elevator.

The elevator doors rattled shut and he pushed the button to the fourth floor. After exiting the elevator, Quin rolled the gurney into a small, dimly lit room where Dr. Lopez was waiting.

Pulling back the blanket that had covered her in the SUV, Dr. Lopez began his examination. He took her vitals and checked her other injuries. "Hmmm, yes, this might be a problem," he murmured as he examined some swelling on the woman's head. "I am sure she has a serious concussion. To what extent, I would not know without taking her to the hospital, and I presume that is out of the question."

"Yes."

Dr. Lopez pulled the stethoscope from around his neck and placed it back in his little black bag. "Well, it would be my opinion that you keep a close eye on her and I would keep her awake if at all possible. There is a probability that there could be some brain damage or perhaps even memory loss. Tests should be run. However, in your case, I can see where that is not going to be feasible."

"No. At this point, no," Quin replied, his mind spinning frantically, trying to figure a way out of this. *Damn. This is not going to go well. Carlos will be furious. Still, I have no choice but to proceed as planned, in spite of the risk.* Reaching for his money clip, he pulled out several bills. "I am sure there is no need to inform Carlos of this visit, is there?" he said as he slipped the bills into the doctor's hand.

Dr. Lopez grinned broadly as he closed his bag. "I was never here."

Quin heaved a sigh of relief as he turned his attention to the woman on the table in front of him. He took in her bloody and torn clothing. Gently, he removed the bloody blouse and ripped slacks and pitched them into the trash barrel. Assessing her bra and panties, he decided they would have to go, also.

Quin called for Ricardo to search through the boxes of clothes that had been selected for her, to find her some under clothes.

Ricardo wrinkled his nose and glared at Quin at being relegated to handling women's underwear as he sorted through the boxes.

Quin filled an old porcelain basin with warm water, added disinfectant, and then, washed her body, marveling at its perfection. The sensation, he felt as his hands moved over her body was like stroking velvet.

He washed the blood from her hair and bandaged the cut. It was small and would heal quickly. Silently, he apologized for the course towel he used to dry her off.

Only the finest of fabrics should ever touch this skin, he thought.

He slipped the clean undergarments onto her unconscious form and covered her with a clean sheet. Then he pushed her down the hall to the waiting area.

A bright light behind her eyelids brought her to the surface, but she couldn't find the right command to make them open. The light got brighter and then faded, then brighter and faded again, and repeated for she didn't know how long. It felt like she was moving, but she couldn't be sure. She wasn't sure of anything. Nothing made sense.

I must be dreaming. A crazy dream. I will wake up and everything will be okay. Her mind spun, drifting in and out of awareness.

"Put her in here for now," Quin directed.

The faraway voice echoed again.

"She will be okay here until the chopper arrives."

Chopper? What chopper? No, no, no! That can't be right. Oh, yeah, this is just a dream... She drifted again.

"What did you do with Armando?" Carlos questioned.

That voice cutting through the haze had a familiar ring to it. *Who is that? Why does he sound familiar and what is he doing in my dream?* she wondered.

"We left him for the authorities to take care of. He will not be a problem," Ricardo replied.

Another voice drifted in.

Who won't be a problem, she wondered. Pain, unbearable pain, entered her dream. She groaned and tried to shift her body.

"She is coming around. Take care of it," Carlos demanded.

Who is that? Why does he sound familiar?

Quin hesitated only slightly as a twinge of guilt hit him before he gave her a shot of propofol.

She felt a sharp stab in her arm—oblivion.

෨෨෨

A whirring, whoop, whoop, whoop sound broke through the darkness. She tried to open her eyes, but could only manage narrow slits.

Everything was fuzzy. She attempted to focus, forcing

her eyes open farther. Blinking didn't help. She tried to move her hand up to rub her eyes, but her hand wouldn't move. She tried the other arm, but it wouldn't move, either.

Were her arms tied down or was she still dreaming? Her head was pounding.

Did you feel pain in dreams, she asked herself? *You must, because I am.*

She closed her eyes, the pounding increased, and crimson lightning bolts flashed behind her lids. She groaned in agony.

"She is coming out of it again. I told you to give her enough so we would not have to deal with this until we reached San Lorenzo," Carlos growled.

That sounded like that man again, she thought. *Why is he in my dream?*

"I did not want to give her too much. You know what will happen if anything happens to her," Quin reminded Carlos.

The other voice.

"Let us get going. The chopper's waiting."

She was dreaming, drifting again. This time she was floating on a cloud with angels in white pushing the cloud. They were driving the cloud toward a big black dragonfly, its mouth gaping open and its wings spinning wildly. She had to get off the cloud before the dragonfly swallowed her. The angels held her down. She fought them. She had to get off the cloud.

"Hold her down!" Carlos shouted.

Another stab in her arm. She drifted again. The dragonfly turned into a butterfly. She felt euphoric.

CHAPTER 16

Awakening

Her eyes opened to a dim light. She blinked, trying to focus on her surroundings. The room was small and narrow, a couple of chairs sat against the far wall on either side of a door.

The lone window was covered with old, yellowed newspapers; bright streaks of sunlight shot through the holes in the paper, placing white spots on the rough wooden floor; dust particles danced in the light.

Stale tobacco smoke blended with the musty air of the room, making it hard to breathe. A small wooden table, with several bottles sitting on a metal tray, was beside the bed.

The bed, she was lying on, was narrow, but comfortable. A single flat pillow was under her head, and a thin white sheet covered her. Nothing about the room was familiar. She was alone.

Where is this place? What is this place? Why am I here? How did I get here?

All those questions swirled in her mind, but she had no answers.

Am I still dreaming?

Bits and pieces of crazy images drifted and floated through her memory. She didn't know what was real, what had been her brain's concoctions, or what were dreams.

She was sure she was awake now. She tried to sit up. A

shooting pain ripped through her body. She fell back on the pillow groaning through clenched teeth.

Yeah, I am awake. Dreams don't hurt that much. What happened to me?

She raised her arms and looked at them. They hurt and were covered with bluish-purple bruises.

How the hell had that happened?

She touched her face and winced then touched the side of her head feeling a large lump there. It was tender, too, and there was a bandage. She moved her legs and they hurt, too.

What's going on? How did I get hurt?

She had no answers. Whatever had happened to her, it had to have been violent. That much was evident.

She heard muffled voices coming from behind the door and tried to listen to what they were saying, but it was in Spanish and she didn't understand Spanish. She heard footsteps coming toward the door and then the doorknob turned. She closed her eyes and pretended to be asleep.

The door opened and fresh cigarette smoke drifted in, but whoever it was only opened it far enough to look in at her.

"Naw, she's still out. I gave her a little extra so she's all set till morning." The voice receded and the door shut.

Gave her a little extra—what did that mean?

She was still groggy, but she had thought it was from being not fully awake.

The 'little extra' must be what is making me fuzzy. Have they been giving me drugs? Yes, that would explain some of the crazy things I have been dreaming.

She looked over at the bedside table with all of the bottles. She reached, wincing, gritting her teeth, to pick-up a couple of the bottles. She tried to read the labels, but most were in Spanish—she couldn't read it. She put those back and picked up a couple more. One she couldn't read, but the other one she could. *Ibuprofen 500mg!*

She set the other bottle back, opened the Ibuprofen bottle, and shook out two tablets in her hand—*No, better make it four.*

She placed the bottle back on the tray and looked for something to take the pills with. She didn't see anything. She would have to dry swallow them.

Ugh.

She put the first one in her mouth as far back as she could, so she didn't have to taste it and it would be easier to swallow. She swallowed and it went down. Then she repeated the process with the other three. Now, she had to wait for them to take effect.

All was quiet. No sounds from the room beyond, or from the outside either. She wished she knew what was going on.

Why can't I remember what's happened to me? Anything, as bad as this—surely I would remember it.

There was just a big empty void in her memory.

The room gradually sank into darkness and the soft, fused light from the moon filtered through the holes in the newspapers covering the window. The pills kicked in at last, the pain eased, and she slept.

෬෬෬

"Okay, missy, time to rise and shine."

A bright light shone in her eyes. She couldn't see. She raised her hand up to shield her eyes from the light.

Rough hands pulled her up and pushed her legs over the side of the bed and into a sitting position then grabbed hold of her shoulder. Waves of pain radiated through her body. She gritted her teeth and groaned.

"Get her some clothes and shoes and see that she gets dressed. We're almost ready to shove off," a different voice barked.

There must be two of them. She couldn't see who was speaking but she could feel the one who was holding her.

"Who are you? Why am I here?" she asked as forcefully

she could through the pain. "Get your hands off me!" she snapped, at the person who had manhandled her and was now holding onto her shoulder.

She tried to move away and almost passed out from the pain.

From somewhere across the room, she heard someone move and then something soft hit her. She cringed, startled by the sudden movement, and reached instinctively to bat away whatever it was that hit her, but missed.

It landed softly in her lap. As she examined the stuff, it appeared to be some type of clothing. She held it up trying to get a look at it, but the bright light was still in her eyes, and it was impossible to get a look at the things.

"Those are your clothes. Put them on and hurry," the voice barked, again.

"Who are you people?" she asked through clenched teeth and threw the clothes on the floor. "And I'm not putting on anything!"

"Look lady, it makes no difference to me whether you are dressed or not. You are going just the same. The choice is yours. I just assumed you would like it better if you had clothes on," Quin said, amused. *Yes*, he thought, *you can go with nothing on and I would not mind at all*. He remembered the texture of her skin under his hands as he had washed and cleaned her up. She was blushing now. It looked good on her. He reached down, picked up the clothes, and tossed them back to her.

The clothes hit her again. She looked down to see what she was wearing—bra and panties.

Oh, my, gosh!

She immediately wrapped her arms around her chest. Blushing from embarrassment and cringing from the pain, at the same time, she grabbed the clothes and held them tightly to her chest. She glared at him. "Go away! Get out! I'm not putting this stuff on while you're in here!"

She hoped she was looking in the right direction because she couldn't see where he was.

"Okay, give her a few minutes to herself," Quin said, still amused.

"Hmpff," she snorted.

She heard the door shut, and the light went out. It took a few seconds for her eyes to adjust so she could see what she was doing.

She held up the pieces of clothing to see what they were. It was a pair of black slacks and a lime green sweater top. She wrinkled her nose at the lime green, but both looked to be the right size. She pulled on the slacks and sweater—they fit. She saw there was also a pair of white sneakers. She put them on and they fit, too.

How did they know my size? Better yet, who had put the bra and underpants on me? Where had they come from? They're certainly not mine. Are they? I'd never owned anything remotely like them, too expensive for my tastes. At least I don't think I did.

She was having trouble remembering.

She'd barely got the sneakers tied when the door opened again, and the bright light came back on. She heard someone walking toward her and the next thing—darkness.

A black cloth bag had been placed over her head. Instinctively, she reached up to pull it off, and her arms were instantly held down. She cringed in pain.

"No, you don't," Quin said. "Leave that on if you want to stay alive."

He smiled to himself. He could feel her body tense under his hands.

"You're going to kill me?" she screeched. Her voice went up and she was beginning to hyperventilate.

"Only if it's necessary. Leave the hood on and it won't be necessary," he said, with a smirk.

Somehow, she got the feeling he was finding the situation amusing. *Well, just let me get my hands on him and I'll show him there's nothing funny about this!*

Quin took her arm. He could feel the frustration in her muscles. He walked her out the door, chuckling, as he watched her trying hard not to stumble, clutching his arm, and hoping he would not let her trip and fall.

"Take her down to the loading dock. I'll meet you there," Carlos said.

That voice again. There is something familiar about that voice.

She knew she should know who that was, but she couldn't remember.

Quin guided her down what felt like a hallway. It had a wooden floor; their footsteps echoing as they walked. The smell of aged wood mixed with dust, stale cigarette smoke, hydraulic oil, and salt water, filtered through the cloth bag.

They stopped and she heard a whirring sound. She knew that sound—it was an elevator. Then she heard the doors rattle open—*an old elevator.*

He guided her in and turned her around so that she was facing the doors. She heard the click as he pushed the button. The elevator gave a short jerk and started down, her stomach came up in her throat. A few minutes later, the elevator jerked to a halt, and the doors rattled opened again.

The man took her elbow and guided her out of the elevator and through what she guessed was an enormous room with a concrete floor. Sounds echoed and the smells of gasoline fumes, motor oil, and fish filtered through the cloth bag over her head.

Lots of noises echoed around her. Some she could identify—busy noises, like people working, moving things…maybe, she wasn't sure.

A forklift, she knew that sound and smell, but how did she know that? She couldn't remember.

Also voices, people talking, laughing, shouting as they worked, all speaking Spanish, at least she thought it was Spanish. She tried to get a sense of where she might be.

A warehouse—maybe?

She caught the scent of salt water again, stronger, as they moved out into what she guessed was the outside.

We must be close to the ocean.

They stopped. It was outside and the sun felt hot.

"Stay put. Don't move," the man barked.

She could hear the rhythmic thumping of what sounded like boats hitting the pier as they were rocked by the waves slapping the pier.

She stood, waiting, afraid to move. Her hands weren't tied and she supposed she could have reached up and pulled off the bag, but right now, she wanted to live. She had no way of knowing if there was someone else watching her. So, she listened to the sounds around her—workers shouting back and forth to each other, speaking Spanish, forklifts, maybe overhead cranes moving cargo around, and the seagulls crying overhead.

"Ah, I see you listened to me. That was smart," he said, and she could tell he was smiling. "Let us go. This way." He took her arm and pulled her along with him.

They walked several feet and stopped. The thumping, like a boat bumping into the dock, was louder here.

"There is a step here." He placed her foot on the step. "Up you go. Walk slowly. I have you. Careful." They walked for a few more feet, the floor under her feet undulated, and she grabbed tighter on his arm. "Now, a step down. Careful. I have you."

She could tell he was trying hard to keep from laughing. She hoped she had left nail marks on his arm.

She could feel she had just stepped onto the deck of a boat. The gentle rise and fall of the vessel, made her lose my balance, again. She reached her hand out to catch herself, but strong arms grabbed her first.

"We cannot have you getting any more damaged than you already are. Here, take her below deck," he barked, to someone.

Another pair of hands took hold of her and guided her across the deck.

"Watch your step here, we are going to go down six steps. I will go in front and hold your hands. You will be perfectly safe. I will not let you fall."

A soft male voice went with the hands now holding hers. She started down the stairs, counting each step as her foot landed on it.

"There, you see—perfectly safe," the soft voice said.

"Yes, thank you," she whispered. She didn't feel intimidated by this voice. "Can you please tell me what is going on? Why am I here? Where am I?" she pleaded, with the soft-voiced man.

"No, I am not a liberty to say."

He took her elbow and guided her down a passageway; the smell of wood, furniture polish, and varnish filtered through the bag. They stopped, and she heard him slide open, what she guessed to be a door. He moved her over and entered the room first.

Taking her hand again, he guided her into the room.

"Come in. This will be your room for the duration of the voyage. As soon as we are underway, you may remove the bag, but not before. Is that understood?" he asked pointedly.

She nodded.

"Fine, I will leave you now. Remember, only after we are under way. You will know when that is."

"Will you show me where to sit before you go, please?" she asked.

He took her hand and led her over to what felt like a sofa when she sat down.

"Thank you," she said politely but glared at him, even though she knew he couldn't see her.

If he thinks I'm going to sit here with this damn bag over my head, he has another think coming.

CHAPTER 17

Why Me?

As soon as she heard the door slide shut, she pulled the bag off, flung it across the room, and let her eyes adjust to the sudden brightness. It was a state-room, an extremely luxurious one. There was original art-work on the walls, rich carvings, and antique carpets on the floor. The bed was larger than king size. It sat on a small riser with gauzy netting hanging from the ceiling at all cor-ners. A baby grand piano stood beside the sofa where she sat. From her vantage point, she could also see the marble and gold interior of the bathroom.

Why am I here? She got up and walked to the big win-dow. The only thing she could see was the ocean, lots, and lots of blue water. *Where are we going? Where have we come from? Why is this happening? I have to have some answers.*

She went to the door and tried to slide it open. It was locked. She pounded on the door with her fists.

Bam! Bam! Bam!

"Let me out of here," she shouted. "Open this goddamn door!"

Bam! Bam! Bam!

She waited, listening, but heard no one. She pounded on the door and shouted several more times again. Her fists were hurting, and still no one came.

She turned around with her back against the door and slid down to the floor, drew her knees up and rested her head on them.

What is going on?

She wanted to cry, but couldn't. Tears eluded her. She sat there for a while rolling over in her mind everything that had happened to get her to this point.

She searched her memory for that one thing that would make sense of why she was here. But, the only things she remembered up to this point were waking up in that dirty little room with a bright light in her eyes. Then discovering she had no clothes on except for some underwear that didn't seem to belong to her. Then being told to put on clothes that was not hers. A black bag stuck on her head and voices telling her what to do and where to go. And, finally, getting on this damn boat. Before that, her mind was a total blank, not just about, how she got here, but about her whole life.

Getting up, she looked around searching for a clock or something to tell her what time it was. She looked at her wrist, where a watch should have been but wasn't.

Did I even own a watch?

She couldn't remember.

She looked out the window, it looked like the sun would be setting soon. It must be late afternoon. Her stomach began protesting about not being fed, for how long she didn't know, but it must have been quite a while. She did know she hadn't had anything to eat since this morning. Before that, she didn't have a clue.

She went to the door again and pounded—Bam! Bam! Bam! "Hey! How about some food! Are you going to starve me to death? Hey! I'm hungry!"

Bam! Bam! Bam!

No one answered.

Has everyone abandoned the boat? Am I here alone?

A few minutes after her last outburst, she heard a noise in the hallway outside. A loud bang on the door caused her to jump.

"Pipe down in there! You will get something to eat soon enough," barked the familiar voice that had been telling her what to do all day.

She examined the room. She sat down on the bed and lay back, resting her head on the mountain of pillows. The sea blue coverlet felt like silk and the pillow coverings looked to be the same.

Sliding off the bed, she looked over the desk, pulling out the draws, one after the other. They were all empty.

Wooden double doors, on the wall next to the bed, opened into a closet full of clothes. Shelves and drawers were full of clothes and shoes as well. She picked a pair of slacks from one of the shelves and held it up. Reading the label—it was Dior! They were her size! She flipped through the rest of the hangers and shelves—they all were her size—all designer labels!

What the hell is this? I've been kidnapped, put through hell, and then, dumped in this damn room with a freaking closet full of designer clothes, all in my size? I would consider myself in heaven if it weren't for the fact that I didn't know what was going to happen to me, or how soon—

Her thoughts were interrupted by a light knock on the door,

"Dinner will be served in one hour. Please select something appropriate from the closet to wear. I will call for you then." It was the man with the soft voice.

It would be nice to have a bath. She knew she needed one. It had been a long day and she had to take care of the necessities, too. She walked over the antique carpets to the bathroom—or was it called "the head" on a boat—she couldn't remember that either.

Necessities first. Then shower. She glanced in the mirror to see how bad she looked. She came to a dead stop. The face looking back at her—she didn't know it. She didn't recognize the person in the mirror. She carefully studied the reflection.

Who is this person?

The reflection had short, spiky, copper-colored hair, tanned skin, hazel eyes, straight nose, and full wide lips. She appeared to be approximately five foot eight or nine and had a graceful figure with curves in all the right places. Except for the bruises, this person looking back at her was rather beautiful, but she still didn't know her.

Pulling off the sweater and slacks and dropping them on the floor, she surveyed the rest of the body, seeing lots of bruising, some already turning yellowish. The body looked like it had been beaten, and rather severely.

Realistically, she knew the person reflected in the mirror had to be her, but she didn't have a clue as to who she was. She had no recollection of a life before today.

She turned away from the mirror. Regardless, the person in the mirror still needed a shower.

Her body felt like one big bruise and the hot water felt wonderful. She towel dried her hair careful of the bandage and patted her body dry. It was still very tender.

She checked out the drawers under the counter and found makeup, hairbrushes, toothpaste and brush, and other toiletries.

She ran a brush through her hair, applied a little blush, and some lipstick.

On the counter sat a crystal tray, with several bottles of perfume—not cologne, but the real stuff. She chose a bottle of Joy and dabbed some in the hollow of her throat and on her wrists.

Walking into the closet, she was amazed at the selection of clothes. Flipping through the hangers with the evening gowns, she chose an embroidered black silk dress by Dior. It fit perfectly.

She found black strappy heels and a drawer full of jewelry. Everything appeared to be genuine. The dress had a plunging V neckline, so she chose a diamond pendant on a slender gold chain that rested just above her cleavage. There were earrings to match.

She surveyed herself in the full-length mirror. She didn't

know that woman in the mirror but thought she certainly cleaned up nicely in spite of all of the bruises. Smiling, she twirled around sending the skirt flaring out—

She came up short. *What the hell are you doing? You can't let all of this go to your head. For crying out loud, girl, you've been kidnapped, and to top it off, you don't even know who you are! You don't know what they are going to do with you. These people could be human traffickers.*

A chill went up her spine and she had goose bumps. She had never thought of that!

What if they are?

Were they going to sell her to someone who would dispose of her as soon as they grew bored with her? Or to someone who would lock her up and make her commit horrendous sex acts? Or to someone who would make her a slave and beat her? She had read articles about this sort of thing. At least she thought she had, maybe in her past life?

She sat down in the middle of the closet floor, the skirt of the dress billowing out around her. She drew her knees up to her chest and hugged them, rocking back and forth.

This can't be happening to me—whoever 'me' is. Well it is, so you're going to have to deal with it. You can't go off the deep end. Pull yourself together. They'll be here soon to get you for dinner. You're strong. You can handle this.

CHAPTER 18

The Beginning of the Nightmare

She heard a small tap, tap, and someone began unlocking the door.

"Are you ready?" the soft-voiced man asked.

She got up off of the floor, straightened out the dress, and walked out of the closet. She smiled, but she was sure it didn't reach her eyes. "Yes, I'm ready."

"You are enchanting, *señorita.*"

The soft-voiced man couldn't have been much more than nineteen or twenty. He was just a little taller than she was and his olive skin covered an athletic body. His black hair was long and tied in a ponytail at the nape of his neck. His dark brown eyes were assessing her admiringly.

"Thank you." She blushed, in spite of the talk she had just had earlier with herself. "Do you have a name?" she asked.

"Ricardo." He smiled and held out his arm for her to take.

Manners. Who would have thought?

He allowed her to step into the hallway first. He turned and closed the door then offered her his arm again. Escorting her to a stairway, he then preceded her up the stairs. Upon reaching the top, he turned and offered her his hand to hold while she climbed the six stairs.

Ricardo left her on the deck and returned below deck.

She saw they were on the deck of the boat, only it wasn't just a boat. It was an enormous yacht!

The soft light, from the deck's indirect lighting, revealed a table set for three. A snow-white linen tablecloth, with a sea blue stripe around the edge, covered the table; matching sea blue napkins, silver charger plates, ornate silverware, and crystal wine glasses completed the setting.

The owner of this yacht must be rich, she thought as she took in the table setting.

She wondered who the other two were. She assumed she would find out in due time. Soft music was playing while she wandered across the deck to the railing and peered over.

The wind carried the spray from the wake up and over her; it felt incredible. She took a deep breath, inhaling the fresh scent of the sea. They were moving at a fast clip, if the wake was any indication.

A touch of vertigo hit her, as she noticed just what a long way it was down to the water. She gripped the rail to steady herself, as footsteps sounded on the deck behind her.

"There you are. You look very stunning this evening." It was the Barking Voice man.

She turned around to face him. He was not at all what she had expected from the sound of his voice, and how he had been treating her. He was handsome, in a rugged sort of way. He stood maybe six foot four of five. His olive skin covered a finely sculpted body that was evident beneath the tailored white shirt and black slacks he was wearing. Soft brown eyes looked back at her admiringly. His black hair just touched his shirt collar. And, the scar on his left cheek was not at all distracting. It made him dangerous and fascinating, all at the same time.

❧❦❧

Quin stood admiring the vision before him.
Too bad, she is just a job, he thought.

He would love to spend some time with this one. Usually, he did not get so up close and personal with his "jobs" as he had been forced to do with this one. She fascinated him more than what was healthy for his sanity. He couldn't get her out of his mind. But she would be delivered, as promised, in perfect condition. They were going to have to stay at sea a little longer than usual to let the wound on her head heal.

"Thank you." She hesitated, eyeing him suspiciously. "Why am I here?" she demanded. "Who are you?"

"All in due time." He smiled calmly. "Please, come, sit." He held a chair for her and inclined his head in the direction of the chair. "Let us eat."

She walked over and sat down in the chair he was holding. He handed her the sea blue napkin and she placed it on her lap.

"Wine?" He held a glass and bottle ready to pour.

She nodded. He poured a half a glass and sat it in front of her. She stared at it, wondering. *Has it been drugged?*

"Come, drink. It is safe. You will enjoy it." He smiled, showing beautiful white teeth and taking a drink from his glass as if he knew what she'd been thinking. "I see you found the clothes to your liking. You chose well. That dress complements your figure," he said, admiringly.

She had the figure to be a model. He wondered if she was. Carlos never gave him any background on the "jobs."

She tried not to blush. She couldn't let herself be taken in by stupid, empty compliments, designer clothes, and diamonds. These people had ulterior motives in regards to her future, and she had to find out just what they were up to. More important—she had to know who she was.

Footsteps behind her indicated the third person to this dinner party had arrived. She looked up as he pulled out his chair and sat down.

He had a swarthy complexion with piercing brown eyes, high cheekbones, and short-cropped black hair. He looked like someone she should know, but how and from where?

She couldn't remember if she'd ever seen this man in her entire life.

"Good evening, *señorita*." Carlos leered at her, mentally licking his chops. "You make a lovely addition to our dinner this evening."

She smiled back, sort of. He gave her the creeps. Even though he hadn't touched her, she felt dirty.

"Ricardo!" Quin shouted. "I hope you like calamari and scallops. Ricardo prepares them to perfection," he said, smiling at Ricardo.

Ricardo carried in a large tray and placed it on a small serving cart next to the dining table. The delicious aroma caused her stomach to remind her just how hungry she had become. She was ravenous. She hadn't eaten in she guessed what had been at least over twenty-four hours, maybe longer. She tried to maintain some decorum, but she couldn't keep herself from devouring the food as quickly as possible. Both men stared at her, an amused look in their eyes.

"What are you staring at?" she demanded. "Haven't you ever seen a starving woman eat?"

Much to her chagrin, they laughed.

"Here, have more wine to wash it down." Grinning, Quin poured more wine into her glass. "It is good to see you enjoy Ricardo's masterpieces. He will be pleased."

"Yes, he is an excellent chef," she agreed, taking a swallow of wine. She was stuffed. Her stomach was full, and her head, a little fuzzy. Feeling a lot braver, thanks to the wine, she glared at both men. "Who are you people?" she demanded, staring at the man she thought of as Barking Voice. "What do you want with me?"

"All will be revealed in due time," the other man replied, leering at her, "but you do not need to worry your pretty little head about it now. It is not in your best interest."

"Why not? Why isn't it my best interest? I'm the one it concerns. I'm the one you've kidnapped. How the hell, can it not be in my best interest? And I suppose you're going to tell me it's in my best interest not to know what you're going to do with me, too?" she snapped sarcastically.

She turned and glared at the swarthy man she thought of as Creepy Man because he gave her the creeps.

"I am afraid that is on a need-to-know basis, and you are right, you do not need to know," said Barking Voice, the smile fading from his face.

This is going to turn into a scene if I do not put a stop to it right now, Quin thought.

"Why the hell don't I need to know? This is all about me, isn't it?" she demanded, stronger this time. "You didn't kidnap me just for fun, did you?"

"We do have a purpose, but that purpose does not concern you at the moment," Creepy Man said, with an edge to his voice.

"What do you mean it doesn't concern me? It most certainly does concern me! I'm the one who's been kidnapped!" she shouted, jumping up, her chair tipping over and landing with a bang on the deck. She placed her hands on the table and glared at both of men. "I want to know what the freak is going on! Why do you have me here?" she said, in a measured voice; gripping the edge of the table, her knuckles turning white. She wanted to hit something, preferably one of them!

"Ricardo!" Quin yelled, standing up, anger reflecting in his eyes. "Ricardo! Please take our guest back to her room," he said, through clenched teeth. *Why does she have to be so damn persistent? Why can she not be like the other jobs I have had: afraid, compliant, and easy to control—no trouble.*

Ricardo took her arm and tried to pull her away from the table. He looked apologetically at her. "Please, *señorita,* come with me."

"Hmppfft," she snorted and jerked her arm away from Ricardo.

She followed him to the stairway and heard Creepy Man laughing as she left.

"She is a little spitfire, is she not?" he said with an evil laugh.

Ricardo walked her back to her room in silence. She was still fuming when he opened the door to let her enter.

"*Buenas Noches, señorita.* Sleep well." With that, Ricardo closed and locked the door.

Well, that certainly didn't go well.

She was no closer to knowing who, or why, than she had been this morning. All she had managed to do was anger them. It was obvious they had plans for her, but they weren't about to divulge them.

Why not? What difference did it make now? They have me locked up. Where am I going to go? We are in the middle of the ocean, for crying out loud. She paced the floor, fuming.

They probably thought she would try to harm or kill herself if she knew. She vaguely remembered, dreaming, in one of those crazy dreams she had, something about someone not wanting damaged goods. Maybe she was the "goods" they didn't want to be damaged.

Possible.

The events of the past hours, she didn't know how many, were descending on her. Suppressing a yawn, she unzipped the dress on the way to the closet. She was too tired to look for something to sleep in. Bra and underpants would have to do.

She shoved the mountain of pillows off to the floor, keeping one, pulled back the coverlet, and fell in.

CHAPTER 19

Who Am I?

She woke up screaming, her heart pounding in her ears. What seemed like only seconds after she screamed, she heard the door slide open with a loud thunk as it hit the stops. The overhead lights came on, and footsteps rushed into the room. Shielding her eyes, she tried to focus on who was standing by the bed.

"Are you all right?" Barking Voice asked, out of breath. "Are you hurt?"

"No." She shook her head, still groggy. "It was a nightmare. It was awful."

She looked into his eyes with tears streaming down her face. She pulled the cover over her head, trying to shut out the visions that kept recurring.

Quin sat down on the edge of the bed, reached over, and pulled the cover away from her face. Tear stained, red eyes, and nose—she was still beautiful. He shook his head. *Get those thoughts out of your head*, he scolded himself.

"Tell me about it," he said softly. "It might help." She shook her head and sniffed, wiping the tears away with the back of her hand. He reached over and took her hand in his. "It will be all right, *niña*. All will be over soon, I promise," he said, cradling her hand in his and pulling it to his lips. An impulse he could not stop. "You will be well-taken care of. Nothing will happen to you, I promise." He smiled and put her hand down. "I will leave you now. Go back to sleep."

He rose and walked to the door, forcing himself to put one foot in front of the other. If he stayed any longer, he knew he would never leave.

The light went out, the door closed, and the lock clicked.

What the hell just happened? Her mind was in a whirl. *This makes no sense. Why did he kiss my hand? And, why all the reassurance over how I'm going to be treated when I get to wherever I'm going, like he really cared? Why should he care what happens to me?*

After what just transpired with the man she called Barking Voice, the conflicting feelings it had stirred in her, and the terrible dream, she was clinging to sanity by a single thread.

Turning the table lamp on, she got up, paced the floor, and noticed that sometime between dinnertime and now, someone had left a crystal glass and carafe of water on the bedside table. She poured herself a glass and gulped it down. Then she had half a mind to throw the glass across the room, but didn't. Instead, she fell on the bed, buried her face in the pillow, and screamed, pounding the mattress with her fists.

After her tantrum had run its course, she rolled over and stared at the ceiling. Nothing made sense. She had been kidnapped, but from where and by who—she didn't know.

They had been treating her like royalty, except they kept her locked up—why?

Some time and some place she had been injured—where and when she didn't know.

She knew it was important to them that she was in perfect condition—she remembered that from the dreams, she thought.

Then there's the nightmare she just had. It was disjointed and jumbled up—a man, whose face she couldn't see; a black car trying to run her over; her, flying through the air; dark things falling and hitting her; horses, strange people she didn't recognize; and a big dragonfly. Then she was

falling and falling and falling, reaching for something that was just out of her grasp—

That's when she jerked awake, screaming.

She turned off the light and lay in the dark, still trying to sort things out. Maybe things would look better in the morning. Maybe she would be able to find something out then.

Maybe.

☙❧

A light tap, tap sounded on her door, the lock clicked, and the door slid open.

"*Buenos días, señorita,*" Ricardo said, walking in with a tray of the most delicious aromas wafting from it. It smelled like breakfast.

She grinned at him. "Good morning, Ricardo. That smells amazing."

Pulling her knees up in front of her, she sat up in bed, conscious she only had on her underwear.

"I will leave it here for you," he said, setting the tray on the table next to the window. "I will be back to collect it in an hour or so."

He looked away, trying to hide a smile, as he walked out the door and locked it.

She jumped out of bed, hurried to the table, and sat down. Everything looked delicious. There was fresh fruit, freshly baked rolls, butter and jams, slices of ham, eggs, and—coffee—a whole big pot of coffee. She poured a cup and took a sip, closing her eyes and enjoying the flavor.

I may not know my name, but I know I love coffee.

Frowning, she tipped the coffee pot up and watched the last little bit of coffee trickle into her cup. The food was delicious and she had devoured as much as she could hold.

When Ricardo comes back to get the tray, I will ask if I can have another pot.

What do I do now? Read a book?

She looked around to see if she had missed anything. She had already checked the desk and it was empty. The drawer in the bedside table was also empty. There weren't even any magazines. She would also ask Ricardo if there's something to read on this stupid boat.

She had showered and dressed by the time Ricardo came to retrieve the breakfast tray. She asked for another pot of coffee and if there were any books or something, she might be able to read. He said he would check about the books and would bring the coffee shortly.

She stood at the window watching the ocean speed by. A wave of loneliness swept over her.

Do I have parents? Do I have friends? Do I have a boyfriend? Am I married? Do I have any children? Do I have a job? Do I have anyone who would miss me? Is there anyone looking for me?

She was deep in thought and didn't hear the door open or the footsteps that were muffled by the carpet until she felt a hand on her shoulder. She jumped and spun around, her eyes wide with fear.

"I didn't mean to startle you. I thought you would have heard the door open," Barking Voice said, standing just a foot away from her, searching her face. He reached up and touched her cheek, running his thumb gently across it. The feel was incredible, like velvet. "Why so sad, *niña*?" he asked softly.

She shrugged and pulled her head away from his hand. "I'm just fine," she sniffed and stepped to the side so she could go around him.

He placed a hand on her arm. "You are in no danger here. I told you that. You have nothing to worry about. I will make sure nothing harms you," he said, still searching her face.

"Well, isn't that just peachy?" she countered, narrowing her eyes. "I have nothing to worry about? Well, how about the fact, that you kidnapped me? How about the fact that I don't even know who I am and I don't know who you are and I don't know—oh, just go away, and leave me alone!"

She put her hands on his chest and shoved as hard as she could, her voice rising as she shouted at him. She closed her eyes. Tears seeped from under her lashes and rolled down her cheeks.

He reached out, wrapped his arms around her, and pulled her close. She buried her face in his chest and sobbed. He picked her up, carried her to the sofa, and sat down, still holding her. Cradling her in his arms, he kissed the top of her head as she sobbed.

¡Dios! She feels wonderful in my arms. Fool, what are you doing, he thought.

What am I doing? She thought. *I should be fighting to get away from this man who kidnapped me.*

Strangely, though, she didn't feel threatened; instead, she felt only comfort.

She turned her head and looked up at him. He was smiling as he brushed her tears away.

She halfway smiled, her heart doing crazy things. "I'm sorry, looks like I've gotten your shirt all wet."

He lifted her off his lap and sat her on the sofa. "It will dry." *This has to stop. She is a "job" and that is all she is.* He knew that, yet he still had a hard time releasing her. He turned his head so she would not see the desire smoldering in his eyes. "Now, I believe you asked Ricardo for something to read? Well, if you will accompany me, I will take you to the salon where you may select something."

He stood and offered her his hand.

She placed her hand in his and he gently pulled her off the sofa. Holding her hand, they walked to the door. She felt safe.

They went in the opposite direction of the way she had been escorted to dinner last night. A short distance down the passageway and up a few stairs, they walked into a large salon flooded with light from a row of windows on both the starboard and port side walls.

He tapped on a carved panel at the side of the back bar.

It sprang open to reveal several shelves filled with books. "Come, take your pick." He waved his hand at the books. "Feel free to read any of these. When you're finished, Ricardo will bring you back to select more."

"Thank you." She smiled with genuine warmth. *Maybe, with a little too much heat,* she thought as he looked at her with a mischievous grin. She looked away quickly and started reading the titles.

"Would you like to sit in here for a while?" he asked admiring her curves as she studied the titles of the books. "You can stay here while I check on a few things. You can go from here back to your room or up to the area where we dined last evening. But, nowhere else. Can I trust you to do this?" He placed his hands on her shoulders and turned her around. He looked her straight in the eye. "Can I trust you to do this?" he repeated.

She nodded, hoping her face didn't give her away. This was the opportunity she had been waiting for. Left to her own devices, maybe she could find out something.

"I will leave you then."

He turned and disappeared up the small stairway beside the bar.

She did a quick three-sixty, surveying the salon again. She would wait, giving him time to get to wherever he was going before she started snooping. It didn't look like there was anything in here that would be helpful.

No, they would have that stuff hidden away, out of sight.

She decided to go back to her room and leave the books before checking out the two doors she had noticed on the way to the salon.

Cautiously, she moved to the first door. She tried it. It slid open smoothly. It was another stateroom.

She slipped inside and quickly slid the door closed behind her. Several papers were strewn on the desk. Some looked like maps. She sorted through them, trying to keep them in order. The maps appeared to be nautical charts.

One showed the Pacific side of South America with an

island off the coast of Peru circled—San Lorenzo. Another place had been circled on the map; it was Salinas, Ecuador. There were notations on the map in Spanish that she couldn't read, but guessed it had something to do with traveling from San Lorenzo to Salinas. This must be where they are going—Salinas.

Most of the papers were in Spanish and she couldn't read them. One of the papers had what appeared to be dates and times. That didn't help either, as she had no idea what today's date was. She placed everything back in what she hoped was the correct order. As she turned to leave, she heard voices in the passageway, getting louder as they got closer to the door.

Her heart stopped. She froze. She couldn't breathe. *Hide, hide, hide! Where? Try the closet. Oh, super! That'll be the first place they look! They won't look if they don't know you're here!* She opened the closet doors. *Ugh, it's full of men's clothes. Whose room is this?*

The voices were getting closer. *Hurry up pull the doors shut! Get way in the back. Get behind that pile of clothes. Pew! It's dirty laundry! Just hold your breath! It's no big deal, just some dirty clothes.* Tunneling through the stack of dirty laundry a pair of men's briefs fell across her face. *Oh yuck! Underwear!* She shuddered and carefully removed them with two fingers.

She rooted under the pile of dirty clothes and pushed herself as far back as possible into the corner, keeping as many of the pieces as she could covering her. She ducked her head, drew her knees up, and hugged them as tight as she could, making herself into a ball, but how small of a ball could a five foot nine inch body make? *Small enough*—she hoped.

The voices stopped outside the door and were loud enough for her to hear.

"We should be there by tomorrow night. Can we load everything on the plane before dawn? We do not want anyone becoming nosey." It was Creepy Man talking.

Oh, crap! This is probably his room.

"What time are we scheduled for takeoff?" That was Barking Voice.

"Five. Can you have everything together by then?" Creepy Man asked.

"Everything will be loaded well before takeoff time. The special cargo will be loaded last, just to make sure nothing goes wrong before takeoff," Barking Voice again.

Special cargo? What do they mean special cargo?

"Good. I have calls to make to let them know we are on schedule," said Creepy Man, as his voice faded. "I know they are going to be pleased."

"Right, I will see you on deck as soon as I get that chart. Have Ricardo bring up some drinks. Make mine bourbon." Barking Voice slid the door open.

Geez! I'm in Barking Voice's room. This is bad.

She heard his muffled footsteps as he crossed the carpet and stopped at the desk. Papers rustled as he shuffled through them. She heard him cross the room and stop in front of the closet doors.

Oh, shit, shit, shit! Don't breathe. Keep still. Don't move. Her heart was pounding so hard that she was sure he must be able to hear it.

Barking Voice opened the doors, sorted through several hangers, and pulled something off one. She could hear him moving around, and guessed he was changing clothes.

She squeezed her eyes shut like a little kid. *If I can't see him, he can't see me. Not likely,* but she hoped.

Well, it must have worked, because she felt a piece of clothing hit the pile of dirty clothes she was under. He shut the door and muffled footsteps headed away. She heard the room door slide open and then close.

Whew! That was close. She let her breath out, not realizing she had been holding it. She waited a few more minutes before she pushed the dirty clothes aside. *Ugh! I need a shower.*

She pushed the closet doors open and crawled out on her

hands and knees right into two deck shoes with jean clad legs extending up to a blue chambray shirt with muscled arms folded across the chest and up to the glaring, angry face of Barking Voice.

She stopped and closed her eyes. *I'm doomed.* Rising up on her knees, she opened her eyes and looked into the face of Barking Voice. Anger, disappointment, confusion, and worry flashed across his face.

"*Maldita sea mujer!*" he said through clenched teeth. "You gave me your promise! If he finds you in here, you will be bound and gagged till we reach our destination. He will not kill you, but he will not treat you kindly. I will not be able to protect you. He will not trust you with me anymore. You have put us both in a dangerous position."

Quin could not believe that this one woman could be such trouble. Of all of the women he had handled for Carlos, this one had caused more trouble for him than all of the others put together.

"I just wanted to know what is happening to me. I have every right to know what you intend to do with me," she said, glaring back at him. "Besides, everything is in Spanish and I don't know Spanish, so your damn secrets are safe. I still don't know anything! Does that take you off the freakin' hook?" she snapped at him.

He reached down, grabbed her arms, and pulled her up. He gave her a small shake and wished he could shake her harder. "How many times do I have to tell you, you are safe with me? Your situation would not be changed, even if you had found out something." Holding her a little too tightly, he saw her wince and released her, exasperated. "I have to go. Wait till I have gone, then go directly to your room. Do you understand? If no one saw you come in here, we may have avoided complications. Can I trust you this time?"

She nodded. "How did you know I was here?" she asked, hesitantly, searching his face.

"Your scent gave you away, and the only place, you could have hidden was the closet." The corner of his mouth turned up into a wicked little grin. "Whatever you are wearing, it suits you. I like it."

She ducked her head and blushed.

With that, he turned on his heel and walked out of the room. She stood just long enough for the sound of his footsteps to fade before she slid the door open. With care, she looked out into the corridor before she slipped out and slid the door shut behind her.

Bolting the few yards to her room, she opened the door and ducked in. She threw herself on the bed, conflicted over her treatment by Barking Voice.

Why is he so worried about my safety? What am I to him?

It made no sense to her why he would feel responsible for her safety. He and Creepy Man were planning to hand her over to some other people. She was sure of it. The "special cargo" they were talking about was her.

Maybe when we reach Salinas there will be an opportunity for me to escape.

CHAPTER 20

Rocking the Boat

She didn't know how long they had been at sea, maybe four or five days. The days faded one into another. Last night, she overheard Creepy Man say they should be reaching port tomorrow. She found herself looking forward to feeling solid ground under her feet again.

It had started to rain and she stood at the window looking out at the foamy whitecaps forming on the waves. On the horizon, dark and threatening storm clouds were forming.

How can anything so beautiful be so dangerous? she wondered.

A wave of fear and excitement swept over her as the rolling motion of the boat increased slightly.

A gentle tap on the door sounded and then the lock clicked. Ricardo stepped through the opening.

"Lunch will be served in the salon," he said, waiting for her by the door.

"Lead the way," she quipped, smiling at Ricardo.

She didn't know why, but she was looking forward to seeing Barking Voice. Frowning, she noticed the table was only set for one.

Ricardo placed a plate of stuffed crab and a shrimp salad in front of her. The crab smelled and looked delicious, but she had no appetite. The last few hours had tied her stomach in knots.

Ricardo left the salon as soon as he had served her lunch, giving no explanation as to why the other two were absent. She was alone. It was not like them to leave her by herself. One of them was always watching.

No use sitting here, she decided, tossing her napkin on the table.

Heaving a sigh, she picked up her wine glass and headed back to her room.

It was raining harder now and the swells were getting larger. The boat lurched as she started down the stairs and it threw her hard against the wall, causing her to lose her balance. The wine glass flew out of her hand and splintered on the floor as she tumbled down the stairs, bumping her head on the floor.

Ow!

Her head and arm hurt where she had hit the wall and then the floor. Pulling herself up, she sat on the bottom step for a moment, before trying to get up.

Keeping her hand on the wall for balance, she moved slowly down the passageway. Once inside her room, she looked at herself in the mirror. There was a bump forming above her right eye. She touched it gingerly.

Ooooh, that's going to turn purple. I'll be lucky if my eye doesn't also turn colors.

She ran some cold water in the basin and wet a washcloth to hold over the bump. The cool water eased the throbbing. Maybe it wouldn't be too bad. She pulled the cloth away and checked it again. So far it showed only a slightly reddish tint.

The rain and swells increased.

Looks like the storm has finally caught up with us, she thought. Looking out the window now, she could barely make out the dark roiling waves. Her stomach was beginning to feel a little queasy. She lay down on the bed—not a good idea as the queasiness increased. She went over to the sofa, sitting upright was a much better idea—at least, her stomach settled down some.

The door slid open and Barking Voice came in with something orange gripped in his hand—a life vest.

"Here, put this on. The storm is getting worse. This is just a precaution. We will be fine, but I do not want to take any chances," Quin said, tossing the vest in her direction. Concern showed in his eyes as he walked over to examine her. "What, has happened to your head?"

"The boat went up and I went down," she said, shrugging. "It's nothing, just a little bump."

"That is more than a little bump. I will get you an ice pack for it," he said gruffly, walking out of the room. "Stay put!" he growled over his shoulder.

She went to the mirror.

What's he so upset about? Looks just fine to me.

Coming back, Quin handed her the ice pack. The cold felt much better than the washcloth had on her eye. The cold eased the throbbing.

"Thank you."

She looked up at Barking Voice. His brown eyes were looking her over carefully, like he was trying to memorize everything about her. "What's wrong? Have I damaged something else?" she snapped at him. "I'm fine. Wherever you're taking me and to whoever you're handing me over to will just have to live with this little bump. Shouldn't inconvenience them for more than a day or two." Sarcasm dripped from her voice.

"No, they will not be happy about this if it turns into a black eye. We stayed at sea long enough for your head and other bruises to heal. I do not want to have to explain to them how you got a black eye just before we reached port. You are to arrive in perfect condition," he said, quietly taking her chin and turning her head from side to side, examining the damage. Thankful that the bump showed no signs of turning purple.

The boat listed to the port side and back, throwing Barking Voice off balance. He fell headlong into her. She reached out to keep him from crushing her. He put his hands out to stop his forward motion by placing them on either side of her against the sofa back.

His face was only inches from hers. Desire flooded his body as he looked at her. Quin knew he was going to kiss her and he could not do anything to stop it—he did not want to. Still looking into her eyes, he softly placed his lips on hers. She gave a little gasp and closed her eyes. He deepened the kiss, parting his lips and touching hers with his tongue. Her lips opened without hesitation. His tongue invaded her mouth, their tongues met, and the heat rose.

Her total surrender took Quin by surprise. His heart skipped a couple of beats and his desire skyrocketed. Backing away from the sofa, he took her with him. Her arms reached up and wound around his neck. They were now standing. He bent down and scooped her up, carrying her to the bed. His lips never left hers.

Her fingers played through his hair as he kissed her under her jaw. Quin could feel her heart doing wild and crazy things as he kissed her neck. A soft moan escaped her lips as she wrapped a leg around him. He was kissing her neck when the boat listed again, tumbling them both to the floor.

Quin sat up with a startled look. "That should not have happened." Still breathing hard, he covered his eyes with his hand. "You will say nothing of this!" Pulling his hand down, he glared at her. "You understand? Nothing, you will say nothing! You are my charge and this never happened!"

She stared at him wide-eyed and mouth opened. "Wow, what was that?" she asked, breathless. Her heart had not come back to normal. She was still feeling the adrenaline rush from the kiss.

"It was something that should never have happened." His teeth clenched. "You will forget all about this. Understand? Forget it!"

She nodded, but how was she going to forget it? "You just can't kiss someone like that and then tell them to forget it," she said, emphatically. "It's not humanly possible."

"You will make it possible," he ground out. "I have to

check on the rest of the boat." He jumped up and left her still lying on the floor. He slid the door closed so hard it bounced in its track when he left.

¡Mío Dios! What was I thinking? Quin thought as he stormed up the stairs to the upper deck. *That could get both of us killed. If Carlos knew what had just happened, he would toss me overboard without a second thought, let alone what he might do to her. Although, it might not be that bad for her since Carlos really wants this deal.*

The client was only paying if the girl was in perfect condition—flawless body and a virgin. That was one of the reasons for taking the long way. They needed the time for her head wound and bruises to disappear. Quin headed topside to make sure things had been battened down.

৵৩৵৩

He must be out of his mind if he thinks I can forget that. What's more, I don't want to forget it, she fumed.

She crawled to her feet and put the life vest on. It was dark and she couldn't see anything out the window. She had no idea what time it was.

The books, she had earlier placed on the table by the sofa, had tumbled to the floor. She picked them up and sat down, hoping she could read a little and get her mind off of him.

Several pages into the book, she realized she didn't remember anything she had just read. Her mind kept drifting back to him.

I wish I knew his name.

She tried to force her mind away, but it kept coming back to how his arms had felt around her, how his lips had tasted, how she couldn't believe her uncontrolled response to him.

Was it just physical attraction or an answer to my situation?

She didn't know. She reached over and turned the lamp off plunging the room into total darkness.

Sometime later, she felt herself being lifted and carried. Her eyes flashed open. A dark figure was holding her but she couldn't see who. She started wiggling and lashing out, trying to make whoever had a hold on her to put her down.

"Put me down!" she shouted. She squirmed, kicking her feet and flaying her arms at the dark figure. She hit something solid.

"Umph. Cut that out," Barking Voice hissed and tightened his hold. "I am just putting you to bed. It is late and we have an early call in the morning. I did not think you would want to wake up with a stiff neck in the morning. The sofa is a little short for you." Smiling, he sat her on the bed.

"I'm sorry, you startled me. I couldn't see you," she apologized. "I am sorry if I hurt you."

"Nothing to worry about. I will call for you in a few hours, so sleep while you can," he instructed. "I will lay out some clothes for you to put on in the morning. Everything else will be packed and moved out. Now go to sleep." Quin bent over and placed a kiss on her forehead.

"If you want me to forget about what happened earlier, you'd better stop doing things like that," she teased.

"I couldn't resist. There will not be another time," he said, pushing away.

"You're right there won't be, so what's wrong with now?"

Reaching out, she grabbed the front of his shirt and jerked him down, planting a kiss of her own on his lips. He resisted briefly, inhaled deeply, and put his arms around her, then pulled her tight against him.

"You do not know what you are doing," he groaned. The taste of her lips and the scent of her pushed him over the edge.

"Oh, yes I do," she breathed into his mouth.

Her arms found their way around his neck and her fingers wound themselves in his hair.

He trailed hot, burning kisses down her neck and inside the opening of her shirt. Slowly he moved his arm from around her and began unbuttoning her shirt. Pushing the material aside, he kissed the rounded tops of her breast that pushed up above her bra.

"You are perfect," he breathed, trailing his tongue over them.

She caught her breath. Never had she felt anything like this. Liquid fire burned in her veins. She wanted this man. She didn't know his name. She didn't know if she would ever see him again. It didn't make any difference. She wanted him—now.

White hot flashes of passion enveloped them both as they sped headlong into sweet oblivion. They lay in the tangled sheets, arms and legs wrapped around each other.

"That should not have happened," he whispered, in her ear. "You do not know what you have done to me."

She moved her head to look in his eyes. "I don't regret one minute of it," she said, kissing his lips again. "I'm sorry that you do."

"I do not regret any of it. What I do regret is, that I cannot have you for my own. In the morning, you will be gone and I will see you no more." His eyes were sad, as he caressed her cheek. "Where you are going, you will be well-taken care of. But if he ever finds out about this, you will be beaten and I will be tracked down and killed."

Quin buried his face in the curve of her neck and inhaled, storing her scent in his memory. He held her tight as if he would never let her go, then, suddenly released her, shoving her away as he swung his legs over the side of the bed and sat up.

"What kind of people are you taking me to? How can you stand by and let this happen? What kind of man are you?" she demanded, her voice louder with each question.

"I am a man who was hired to do a job," he said, looking back over his should at her. "That's what you were to me— a job to complete. I picked you up to transport you to my employers, nothing more," he said, running his hand through his hair. "Then, you got under my skin. I saw your beautiful, bruised naked body. I undressed you and cleaned you up and dressed you again. I loved the feel of your flesh under my hands. Never have I had a woman who took my breath away just from feeling her body." His eyes were searching her face as he reached for her again, sadness in his voice. She moved into his arms without hesitation. "You became an obsession to me," he breathed into her hair. "I felt responsible for you. Then it reached the point where I had to hold you. I had to know your body. I told myself it was insane to even try. The consequences were too high, for you, for me. But, then, in a weak moment, I let my guard down. You responded to me and I was lost." He pulled away, looking deep into her eyes, knowing what he was going to say next would hurt her. "Now you are a job again. This never happened. You mean nothing to me now. Tomorrow you will be gone and I will take another job." His eyes turned hard as he let her go and thrust her away. He put his clothes on and walked out the door, never looking back.

She felt cold, abandoned, and sad. She hugged her knees, the tears flowing freely.

Shortly after he left, there was a tap, tap on the door. Ricardo walked in with two other men who she had never seen before, carrying boxes she guessed were to be used to pack her belongings.

She kept her head down, hiding her tear-stained face. "Ricardo can you wait till I dress, please. It will take me just a few minutes."

"Yes, that will be okay. We will come back in fifteen minutes. Please be ready by then." He gave a slight bow and motioned to the others to follow.

Jumping off the bed, she rummaged through the closet for some slacks and a top. She found a pair of slacks and a silk blouse. Closing the bathroom door, she quickly showered.

CHAPTER 21

The Trouble Maker

Ricardo and his two friends came back, packed everything, and carried the boxes out. Minutes after they left, Barking Voice came to get her.

"I need to know your name. Please, tell me your name." She looked in his eyes, pleading. At that moment, nothing else mattered except her need to know his name.

"Quin, my name is Quin. You cannot let anyone know that you know," he whispered.

She smiled up at him. "It's an agreeable name for you, I like it. Thank you,"

"Do not look at me like that," Quin barked, at her. "Be angry, hate me, but *do not like me*! For your sake and mine, you have to hate me!" He pinched her arm hard.

"Ow! Now that's going to leave another damn bruise," she snapped, lashing out at him. "What the hell's the matter with you?"

"That's better." He grabbed her arm and pulled her along.

Sometime during the night, the boat had docked. Several boxes had been unloaded and were now sitting on the dock.

It was just beginning to get light and a slight chill lingered in the air. She shivered, goose bumps forming on her arms as she wished she had thought to throw on a light jacket. The gulls were starting to squawk and fly overhead searching for their morning meal. A large transport truck rumbled to a stop on the dock and she watched as the men loaded the boxes into the back of the truck.

Quin stood beside her on the deck, still holding her arm a little tighter than she would have liked. She tried to pull it away and he only held it tighter.

"Ow! Do-you-mind?" she hissed at him. "You're hurting me."

"Not as much as they will if you make a scene," he said, inclining his head toward a group of four men standing on the dock in conversation. "They are here for you."

"Are they your employers?" she asked as a chill ran up her spine. She noticed that one of the men was the Creepy Man. She had a terrible sinking feeling this wasn't going to end well.

"No, they are here to make sure you are in perfect condition and to travel with you to your final destination. I will not be taking you any farther. You will go with them. This will be the last time you will see me."

"What does the man who dined with us have to do with this?" she asked.

"He is a broker," he stated.

"Broker?" she asked. More cold chills.

"He finds the merchandise for a buyer. You are the merchandise," Quin's voice was full of contempt.

"I—I'm the merchandise? I've been bought and sold?" Total disbelief filled her voice.

"No, kidnapped and sold," he said with a sharp edge.

"Who bought me?"

She couldn't breathe. It hurt to breathe. She started shaking; her head was spinning. She knew she was going to faint.

They are *human traffickers*, she thought, her knees beginning to buckle.

Quin held onto her arm to keep her upright.

"Pull yourself together!" he hissed, at her. "I do not know who bought you and nor do I want to know or care. I have been assured you are going to be well taken care of. That is all I care about. That's the end of it for me."

Quin couldn't believe he just said that to her.

Hell yes, I care what happens to her, he swore to himself. *But she will never know.*

More than he cared to admit, if he could find out who bought her, he would try to get her back, but there wasn't any chance of that. Carlos kept his deals secret. Quin should have taken his chance when he had it. Too late now. He would have to live with it.

The group of men on the dock broke up when a big black SUV pulled up behind the transport truck.

"There is your ride." Quin started forward pulling her with him. She held back trying to pull her arm from his grasp. He jerked her forward down the gangway.

"Do not make a scene," he whispered furiously in her ear. "Your trip will be much more pleasant if you cooperate. There is nothing you can do now. Your fate is sealed. It was sealed the first time he saw you."

And Dios, my fate was sealed the first time I touched you, he thought.

"Where did he see me? I've never laid eyes on that man," she asked, in a panic, racking her brain, looking for somewhere she could have seen him before that first night on the boat. But, she couldn't remember life before waking up in that dirty little room.

"I'm sure I've never seen him. Where did he find me?"

"I do not know where or when he first saw you. I only know I was told to pick you up."

She tried to pull away. "Where? Where did you pick me up?"

He jerked her back. "Shush! They will hear you."

They were moving faster now, getting closer to the SUV. Quin couldn't wait to hand her over and be rid of her. He had to get her out of his system. "You are no longer my responsibility." His fingers dug into her arm. She winced. "Just a little something to remember me by." He glared at her then shifted his eyes to the men as they approached.

Quin had hesitated just a second before he released her arm to Carlos. He hated the thought of the man touching her, even if it was only for a few moments. This was the first time in two years he regretted what he was doing.

"Well, well, how beautiful. Nicho, here is your merchandise in perfect condition." Creepy Man leered at her as he took her arm from Quin. She felt dirty and cringed from his touch.

"Your payment will be transferred to your account after inspection of the merchandise," Nicho said, eyeing her with a raised eyebrow.

She is much more beautiful that we were led to believe. Señor Vargas will be pleased. He may keep her even if she is not perfect, he mused.

"She's all yours." Creepy Man released her arm and gave her a shove in the direction of the three men.

Nicho reached out and took her arm. "This way, *señorita.*"

Her head was spinning. Too many things were bombarding her all at once for her to clearly grasp what was going on. She looked back to see where Quin was, but he had already disappeared below deck. Loneliness and a sinking feeling set in, as the new man pulled her along.

Had Creepy Man called him by name? She tried to remember. She thought so but couldn't be sure. She'd had trouble concentrating on things. Anxiety over the situation was beginning to overwhelm her.

Nicho? Was it Nicho?

She stumbled as they headed for the SUV and was caught up by a strong arm.

"Watch where you're stepping," Nicho growled at her.

As they walked, she studied him out of the corner of her eye. He was tall, maybe six-four, tanned and appeared to have an athletic build under his brown leather sports jacket. His unkempt, dark brown hair was collar length and it gave him that roguish look. His eyes were a lighter brown, almost amber, and his nose appeared to have been broken at some time, but healed back a little crooked. He had strong looking hands—a workingman's hands. She wondered what he did besides transport someone's merchandise.

The other two men had reached the vehicle ahead of them and the back door was already open.

"*Por favor*," he said, motioning that she should climb into the SUV.

She reached for the handhold to pull herself up, but he put his hands on her waist and lifted her up, as if she weighed nothing, then waited for her to settle herself before he closed the door. He walked around to the other side and climbed in.

The other two were in the front seat, with the youngest looking one in the driver's seat.

Passenger seat guy turned and looked at her then said something in Spanish to the tall man who smiled. She looked from one to the other in confusion.

Nicho smiled, his eyes admiring her. "He just said you are more beautiful than we had been told."

In spite of everything, she blushed. She didn't have a clue as to how tolerant these men would be if she started asking questions. Quin said she should cooperate. *Maybe just asking where we were going would be all right. Probably just tell me like on the boat—it's on a need-to-know basis and I didn't need to know. But, I'll never find out if I don't try.*

She looked over at the tall man and smiled. "Can you tell me where we are going?"

"No." Nicho looked straight ahead, thinking *this one is going to be trouble.*

"Well, can you tell me who you are least?" she asked, still looking at him.

"No," Nicho said, his jaw clenching. "It is no use to ask questions. I will not give you answers. It is best that you just sit there and enjoy the ride." *Yes, definitely, this one is going to be trouble,* he thought.

Nicho could see she was not intimidated, by him or her situation. That combination definitely spelled trouble any way you played it and that he did not need.

Enjoy the ride! Yeah, like that's going to happen! She fumed.

They followed the transport truck to the airport and drove out to a waiting private jet, sitting on the tarmac just outside a small hangar. The SUV pulled into the hangar and stopped.

"Wait here, *por favor*." Nicho exited the vehicle.

She tried to see where he was going, but he walked behind the SUV and disappeared through a doorway.

A few minutes later, he reappeared with a woman by his side. He opened the door and held out his hand to help her down.

"You will go with Jada now," he said, pointing to the woman beside him.

She eyed the woman warily. Jada extended her hand toward the door and indicated for her to precede her. She headed for the door and Jada fell into step beside her.

"This will only take a moment, *señorita*." Jada smiled, what she probably thought was a reassuring smile, but at that point, nothing was sure.

She stopped a few steps inside the room. The smell of antiseptic was overpowering—this was a sterile room with an examination table in the middle surrounded by privacy screens and a metal table on wheels with several examination items on it. *Whoa, this is sooo not going to happen!*

She stopped dead in her tracks. The hairs on the back of her neck were standing up. "*No!* I'm not getting on that table!" she screamed at Jada, pointing at the table, and started backing out the door. She bumped into a solid object, which turned out to be Nicho.

"Yes, you are." Nicho's voice gave no room for argument, his arms on her shoulders. "My employer requires proof of perfection before the transaction is complete. You will submit to this."

¡Maldito! I knew it. Trouble. He felt her stiffen.

"I'm a person not an animal! I have rights," she shot back, twisting out of his grasp and whirling around to glare at him. "You don't treat a person like this. I'm not something to be bought and sold. I-am-a-person!" she shouted. "You don't sell a person. This is the twenty-first century not the seventeenth century!"

"Makes no difference, you will submit or I will make you. The choice is yours." Nicho glared at her and spoke to her like she was an unruly child. *"¡Mío Dios!* Why me? Vargas will hear about this," he grumbled under his breath.

"No. I won't! I'm not afraid of you!" she screamed again backing away from him. "You leave me alone!"

She continued backing farther into the room, frantically looking for a way out, but there was none. Only one door and no windows. Jada moved quickly to try to get behind her. She sidestepped Jada, just in time. She saw there was enough space between the tall guy and the door that if she could get around him, she could run. She faked right and the big man went with her, but she zipped back left and made a mad dash for the door before he realized she was gone. It didn't take him long to recover and he was out the door after her.

"¡Maldito! Stop her!" Nicho shouted, to the other two men. "Stop her! Don't let her get out of the hangar!"

She was running as fast as she could with them right behind her. Just a few more feet and she'd be out the hangar door. She looked back over her shoulder to see how close they were, and she ran into the arms of a big burly man.

"Lookie here what I've caught. Well, aren't you a sight for sore eyes." He gave a wicked chuckle.

She squirmed and kicked, flaying her arms and legs, trying to get loose, and hoping she'd land one in his face.

"Just settle down, girlie. You ain't gonna go nowhere." He held her tighter.

She was so frustrated and mad; she let out a scream that would have shattered glass, if there'd been any around. A hand clamped over her mouth. She was still struggling, when she saw Jada coming with a needle.

She kicked even harder and her foot caught the younger guy somewhere below his belt. He doubled over in pain. The passenger seat guy grabbed her legs and held them. Jada had moved around behind her and stabbed the needle in her arm. She was still struggling, when everything went dark.

"Get her inside," Nicho ordered. "Jada get this over with, now. We are close to being behind schedule."

Nicho ran his operation on a strict time schedule. The one thing he hated most was running behind time, and this piece of trouble was close to causing just that.

He was just doing this as an extra job for Señor Vargas. He had intended to spend some time in the south of France, relaxing and enjoying some well-earned time off, but Vargas had called and asked him to handle this particular pickup. They would be at Vargas's this evening. He would deliver her and take off for France, as soon as he could get a flight out the next morning.

They carried her in and put her on the table. Jada quickly did her examination and took photos for reference.

"I will call them with the results and email the photos," Jada said. "I will let you know what they say."

❦❦❦

Her head was pounding. The antiseptic smell burned her nose. She squeezed her eyes tight then tried to open them. The light was bright. One eye opened, the other wouldn't cooperate; she rubbed it with her hand and that seemed to help some.

Looking down, she saw she was on the exam table that she'd fought so hard to avoid. *Lotta good that did me.*

The privacy screens surrounded the table. She could see someone pacing back and forth, their shadow, reflected on the cloth of the screen.

"Well what did they say?" That sounded like Nicho.

"He is not happy but after viewing the photos, he is willing to go through with the transaction," Jada replied. "However, he will only pay half the price for her now. That will be deposited in Carlos's account. He also wants another photo for the binder."

"Good! Let us get things ready. This little escapade has now put us behind schedule," Nicho said, exasperated.

"She should be coming around any moment now," Jada said. "She's already dressed. You hold her up and I'll take the picture. Then you can carry her out or wait for her to wake up."

"I'll carry her, we've lost enough time." He strode across to the privacy screens and shoved them back.

She heard the metal legs of the screens screech across the concrete floor as someone shoved them aside. She closed her eyes as the tall man approached the table. He put one arm under her shoulders, one under her knees and scooped her up. With the sudden jolt of being lifted, her eyes flew open.

"So, you are awake. Good." He put her down abruptly. "You can walk. Jada needs to take a photo of you before we go. Jada! Take the picture, now!" he shouted at her.

She saw Jada pick up the camera and walk toward her.

"Stand still," Jada commanded.

The camera flashed in her eyes, leaving bright spots floating in her vision. She glared at Jada, and, if looks could kill, Jada would've been long dead.

She can take that photo and shove it.

Nicho grabbed her arm pushed her toward the door.

"What did you do to me?" she turned and glared up at the man. She felt violated.

"We only determined if you were in perfect condition," he said, shoving her toward the door.

"Well, did I pass inspection?" she asked, sarcastically.

He shoved her again. "You are not perfect, but they will take you anyway," he said. "Move along."

"What do you mean, I'm not perfect?" she demanded.

"Your skin has scars and you are not a virgin," he stated, as a matter of fact.

"I could have told you that! All you had to do was ask," she said, through clenched teeth. "You didn't have to subject me to this humiliation. I would have just told you, I haven't been a virgin since I was eighteen."

Now how did I know that? she thought. *I can't remember anything else, so how do I know that?*

"That would not have been good enough," he said. "They needed proof from medical personnel."

"So what does this mean now? Are you going to let me go?" she asked as they walked out of the hangar heading for the plane idling on the tarmac.

She already knew what he would say because she had overheard his conversation with Jada.

"No. You have been purchased and will be sold immediately because you are not perfect. You will not bring as much as you would have, had you been perfect," he said, studying her. "But with your looks, you should garner a handsome price anyway. Had you been perfect though, you would have brought fifty times the purchase price."

"You're going to sell me?" she yelled wide-eyed. "What kind of people are you? Selling people—that's—that's against the law!" she yelled at him.

He stopped and looked at her, smiling a crooked smile. "Only if you are caught, and we have never been caught. There is always someone willing to be bribed."

They reached the plane. He took her elbow and helped her up the stairs. Once inside the aircraft, he directed her to a seat.

"Sit here. Put your seat belt on. I will be back." Nicho walked toward the cockpit.

He gave the pilot the destination and the pilot radioed the tower for takeoff instructions. Heading back toward to the lounge, he watched her.

How could anyone this beautiful be so much trouble?

Trouble he hadn't bargained for and could do without now. He noticed she had put her head back on the seat and closed her eyes. It looked like she was crying. He watched as she pulled up the tail of her blouse and wiped her eyes. Nicho grabbed a box of tissues from the overhead and tossed it in her lap as he passed.

Despair set in as she closed her eyes. She had to reconcile herself to what fate had chosen for her. She could see no way out. It was hopeless.

Why was this happening? What did I do wrong? Am I going to finish out the rest of my life as someone's property? Will I ever know who I really am?

The plane engines roared to life and began to taxi to the runway. It paused and then accelerated, pushing her back into her seat. The plane was in the air carrying her to her final destination where fate awaited.

∽∾∽∾

It was dark when the plane taxied into the hangar at a small private airport. Nicho had left her alone most of the flight, only bringing her something to eat and drink. She drank the water but didn't touch the food.

There was not much communication between Nicho and the pilot and co-pilot, but when they spoke, it was in a language she was not familiar with. She had tried to catch a name or something that would let her know where they were going.

Stepping out of the plane's doorway and descending the stairs, she saw a limo waiting for them. Nicho assisted her into the limo and climbed in beside her. The limo pulled smoothly away down the tarmac and turned onto an outer road.

She knew it would be useless to ask questions. There would be no answers now.

The day had finally caught up with her, but she couldn't

relax. She knew if she did, she would fall apart. She didn't have a clue as to what was going to happen to her, where she was headed, or who she was. She was in limbo with nothing to hold on to, nothing to ground her—nothing.

Nicho heaved a sigh. It was almost over. Another couple of hours and he could wash his hands of this woman. He must have been out of his mind to let Vargas talk him into doing this.

His phone vibrated and he pulled it out of his pocket. The hotel was calling to confirm his reservation. He made a mental note of the confirmation number.

Nicho watched the woman. She sat up straight, her body tense, and her hands folded on her lap. She was so tense, he felt if he touched her she would fly into a thousand pieces.

They traveled for close to an hour and she was getting thirsty. "Would it be possible to have some water?" she asked.

Nicho pressed a button and a panel opened, revealing a small refrigerator stocked with bottled water. He handed one to her.

"Thank you," she whispered, then, opened the bottle and drank deeply.

He said nothing.

The limo slowed and turned onto another road.

"We are here," he said as he opened the door and got out.

Someone opened her door and Nicho came around to her side.

"We will go this way," he said, pointing toward a long narrow stone walkway.

He started and she followed. Night sounds filled the air, off in the distance a horse whinnied and a dog barked.

Several yards down the walkway, they stopped at an iron gate. Nicho unlocked the gate, the metal hinges groaning as he pushed it open, and motioned for her to enter. Following her in, he locked the gate, and they continued down the walkway as it meandered through a garden. The fragrance from the flowers floated on the gentle night breeze, crickets stopped their songs as they walked by.

He pointed, toward a massive wooden door. "This way."

She stared up at the door. It had to be at least fifteen feet tall. She felt dwarfed by its size and intimidated by the darkness surrounding them. The moon's silver light did not penetrate the dense foliage of the trees lining the walkway in front of the door. She shivered, even though the night air was warm.

Nicho knocked on the door, using the huge, iron ring doorknocker. The lonely sound of the knocker echoed behind the door. Shortly it opened, and they entered a cavernous foyer. A slight man stood holding the door as they entered.

"*Buenas tardes, señor.*" He inclined his head. "Everything is ready,"

"Gracias, Jose. Lead the way, *por favor.*"

Jose shut the door. The sound echoed through the foyer and reverberated down the hallway. The sound sealed her fate.

"This way." Jose started down a long, dimly lit hallway, their footsteps echoing on the stone floor. Dampness and the smell of wet stone gave her chills. Several yards down the hall Jose stopped in front of two heavy-looking wooden doors, and pushed them open.

"This will be your quarters," Nicho said, looking at her. "You will find everything you need in here. You'll be given instructions in the morning as to what will be expected of you."

With that, Nicho turned on his heel and left. *Good riddance!* he thought as he strode down the hall.

He could not wait to get out of here. Too bad, there wasn't a flight out tonight. He would be on it.

"*Buenas noches, señorita,*" Jose said as he pulled the doors shut and locked them.

After Jose closed the doors and the echo of the lock had faded, she stood dazed, staring into space. Her mind had slipped into neutral. She saw nothing. She made no connections to the surroundings. Nothing made sense. Her body was numb. She felt nothing. She didn't even feel the pain as she collapsed and her knees hit the stone floor.

CHAPTER 22

Nicho's Drop Off

Nicho went to Vargas's office to tell him the woman had been delivered and found him sitting behind his desk, looking out the window behind it at the moon, high in the sky over the mountains.

"She is in," Nicho said, falling into one of the chairs in front of the desk. "She is a handful. I am glad to be rid of her. Mind if I pour myself a drink?"

"*Por favor*, and one for me, as well," Vargas told him, as he turned around. He noticed Nicho looked a little stressed. *She must have really been a handful to upset Nicho so.* Vargas chuckled as he took the glass from Nicho's hand. "Tell me about this woman who has you in such a state."

"She was trouble from the time we picked her up. Always asking questions, demanding to know who we were, and where we were taking her. How I would have loved to tape her mouth shut. We had to sedate her for the examination. She fought like a wild animal. I am glad to put her in your care," Nicho said, swirling the amber liquid around in his glass before taking a big swallow.

"Where did Carlos get this woman?" Vargas asked, setting his glass on the desk.

"I do not know. Carlos did not talk much about her except to say she was a real beauty. That part he got right." Nicho got up to refill his glass.

Vargas sat back in his chair, his fingertips together in a teepee fashion tapping his lower lip with them. "What is your assessment of her?"

"She is worth what you have paid for her and probably much more. She is not like the other women. She is not afraid. She fought me and would have scratched my eyes out if she could have reached them. She has spirit and I do not think you will want to break her. She would die first, that I am most sure of." Nicho looked Vargas in the eye and noticed he was paying strict attention to what he had just said.

"Do you actually think she would kill herself?" Vargas asked.

"Yes, I believe she would. This is one you will want to take special care of." Nicho got up and walked toward the door. "It is time I was on the road. I have an early flight out in the morning, for my much-needed holiday."

"Have a nice time. I will have a job for you as soon as you get back." Vargas raised his glass to Nicho. "See you when you get back."

Vargas sat for a while after Nicho left, thinking about the woman...

☙❧

Earlier, he had opened the message from Jada concerning the special pick-up from Carlos. Unfortunately, Jada had written, she was not up to specifications, but she was exquisite and Jada had attached images. Vargas's first inclination had been to tell Jada to cancel the deal, but thankfully, curiosity caused him to look at them anyway.

His heart almost stopped. There on the screen was an almost identical image of his Saleem. Beautiful, Saleem, his soul mate, abducted on the eve of their wedding, twenty-five years ago. His eyes must be playing tricks he had thought. No, she could have been Saleem. He hesitated.

Why did she look like his Saleem? Then the impossible had popped into his mind—could this be her daughter…

⁓∽⁓

It was too late for him to go meet the woman tonight. He would to do it tomorrow, probably, after Alfredo had met with her. He was disappointed that Nicho did not have any more information about her. He would push Carlos for more information.

Vargas picked up his phone and punched in Carlos's number. The phone had rung twice before Carlos picked up.

"Tell me about the woman you sent me today, the American."

Vargas dispensed with the greeting, getting directly to the point of his call. He could hear the intake of air from Carlos.

"Ahem…what would you like to know?" *This is unexpected*, Carlos worried. Vargas never wanted to know anything about the women he brought to him.

"First, I want to know why you picked this particular woman," Vargas said.

"I am not sure what you mean. I saw a beautiful woman and thought she would be perfect to add to your collection." Carlos was beginning to wonder where this was leading.

"Did you find out any information about the woman, say, her name perhaps?" Vargas inquired.

"Well, yes, I guess I did. I met her on a flight down to Lima from Dallas. I think she said her name was Diane or something like that. I do not remember."

Carlos had never been interrogated like this before. He was beginning to get very uncomfortable.

"Tell me, Carlos, how did you apprehend her?" Vargas asked.

"Well that was a bit sticky. We were supposed to only divert the car she was in, but there was an accident. Unfortunately, when she came to, she had lost her memory. That's all I know to tell you." Carlos hoped that was the last of the interrogation.

"Are you sure you do not have any more information on the woman? Specifically her name?" He pushed Carlos again for a name.

"I will see if I can find out some information about her. A friend of mine knew the other passenger in the vehicle with her, when the accident happened," Carlos hedged. He would call his stepmother and get her name. "I'll call you in the morning."

"I will be looking forward to it," Vargas replied and hung up.

If she has lost her memory, what are the odds she would remember her parents? Again, he was not any closer to finding out about Saleem than he had been twenty-five years ago.

Still it might be possible to have a DNA test performed that might tell if she were Saleem's daughter. He would make inquiries in the morning of the possibility of obtaining samples from Saleem's mother, who was still alive.

It was late and he needed to go to bed. He rang for Alfredo to tell him he would like to meet with the new woman, Saleem, tomorrow after he had met with her. Vargas got up, refilled his glass, and took it with him to his bedroom.

CHAPTER 23

Instructions

She had no idea how long she had lain on the cold floor before her senses came back. She vaguely remembered arriving here and entering the room, but nothing else.

What is wrong with me?

Her mind refused to let her remember, precisely, what had happened. It was a nightmare, one she was never going to wake up from.

She sat up and looked around her. From the soft glow of several lamps, she could see the room was large with a twelve or fourteen foot ceiling and was furnished in what must be expensive antiques.

The bed was huge. It was a canopy bed and had to be at least ten feet tall, with ivory lace gracefully falling to the floor from the top of the canopy at each corner of the bed. The walls were hung with beautiful tapestries and antique carpets partially covered the stone floor. What looked like floor-to-ceiling windows, were covered with heavy, ivory brocade draperies.

She finally stood up, rubbing her knees where they had hit the floor, and turned off all of the lamps, except the one by the bed. She lay down on the bed, reached over, and turned that light off, too.

It was dark. No light filtered through the drapes. She

wrapped her arms around one of the pillows, hugged it to her chest, and fell asleep.

She woke up screaming. It was the same nightmare she'd had had on the boat. Only this time no one came to hold her hand. She was alone. Sobbing, she drifted back asleep.

༼ঌ༽

A key rattled in the lock waking her up. The doors opened and two dark skinned women entered the room. One went directly to the windows and flung back the drapes. She shielded her eyes as the brilliant sunlight flooded the room.

The other walked across the room and opened a door that led to a bathroom, where the woman turned on the tap and started filling the tub with water. She laid two fluffy, ivory-colored towels on the wide lip of the marble tub and then walked over to the bed.

"Your bath is ready, *señorita.*"

Turning, she motioned to the other woman, and they left, closing and locking the doors.

She sat up, stretched, and yawned. Her knees throbbed and her body hurt from lying on the cold floor last night.

She walked into the bathroom, tested the water. It was just right. Leaving her clothes in a pile, she climbed into the tub and slowly sank down into the water. It was wonderful. The hot water seeped into her sore, tired muscles, and she relaxed.

She was borderline pruney when she finally pulled herself out of the tub and wrapped one of the big fluffy towels around her. Looking for something to wear, she walked into the dressing room/closet combination and began flipping through hangers. *These look familiar. Yes, they are! They are the ones I had on the boat. They really did ship them here. Everything is here! At least I won't go naked.*

Somehow, that seemed to comfort her. Her clothes were the only familiar things she could connect with.

After selecting a pair of slacks, a silk blouse, and a pair of flats, she toweled dried her hair, put on a little blush, lipstick, and a dab of Joy. Dressed, she was ready for whatever they had in store for her.

The windows overlooked a walled-in courtyard with a fountain, made of mosaic tiles, in the middle. Palm trees lined the outer wall. At the far end of the courtyard, were a couple of orange trees heavy with fruit.

She heard the door unlock and the two dark skinned women, who had been there earlier, came in carrying a tray of food and a coffee service. The one with a tray placed it on the table by the windows and set the plates and bowls of food on it. The aroma made her realize just how hungry she was. The other woman carried the coffee service and sat it on the table next to the food. They both left without saying a word or looking in her direction. The lock clicked.

The food was delicious but more than she could eat. However, what she thought was coffee, was a horribly sweet, green, mint tea. She'd have to see what could be done about that.

The lock clicked and the doors opened. She was expecting the women back to get the dishes. Instead, in came a very distinguished looking, portly gentleman, maybe in his sixties, with olive skin, gray, almost white hair, a matching mustache under an aquiline nose and a square jaw.

"Buenas días, señorita." He inclined his head. "I am Alfredo. I have come to acquaint you with what will be expected of you during your stay here."

He walked across the room and took the chair opposite her at the table. Moving the plates and bowls over, he opened his leather portfolio.

"While you are here, it is Señor Vargas's request that you be known as Saleem. Now, you will be here approximately three more weeks. This is when the next Bel Ami Gala will be. Until that time, you will be expected to be available whenever you are summoned. You will be expected to dress appropriately for dinner each evening that your presence is requested, and you will never refuse an invitation to dine."

He paused and looked at her with raised eyebrows. She must have been staring at him with her mouth open.

"Do you have a question or may I continue?" he asked stiffly.

She shook her head too dumbfounded to think of even one question. She was still trying to process that she was to be called Saleem. *What kind of name is that?*

"Well then, let us continue, shall we? Should your presence be requested at other times, you will be expected to dress appropriately for each occasion. You will not refuse any of those requests either. Should you not know what is appropriate, please let someone know, and they will assist you. Your closet should have everything you should need to comply with a request. At all instances, you will act with grace and decorum. You will not embarrass Señor Vargas or any of his guests. You will speak only when spoken to. If no one is speaking to you, you will sit quietly. You will not initiate a conversation, nor will you ask any questions. It is forbidden. Are we clear on this?" he asked, looking directly at her.

She nodded.

"Your time here is short so your presence may not be required for all functions. You will be notified approximately three hours before your presence will be necessary. You will be given the time to be ready and you must be prepared at the time designated."

He was flipping pages in his portfolio as he spoke.

"I believe I have covered everything except to show you where to find the intercom, and to tell you it has been activated. You will use that to communicate with the kitchen and the housemaids. Oh, yes, you are forbidden to leave your quarters unless accompanied by Señor Vargas or one of his guests. This is most important. Any violation of this will result in immediate discipline." He leaned back in the chair, folded his hands over his round belly, and looked smugly at her. "Do you have any questions?"

"Is there anything else expected of me other than to act as a dinner companion or a companion for an outing?"

She looked him directly in the eye, her face expressionless. She had a feeling that the "requests" entailed more than this guy was telling her.

"Had you been perfect, I would say no. However, since that is not the case with you, I will say that whatever the request might be, you must comply without hesitation," he said, as a matter of fact not to be disputed.

"You've got to be kidding!" She jumped out of her chair. "I. Am. Not. A. Whore. And. I. Will. Not. Be. Treated. As. One! You can do whatever you want with me, but I will not—I will not be forced to do that!" she screeched. She felt her face turning red and her fists were in tight balls at her side. "So if that's what you expect me to do, you better bring out the whips and chains to beat me and chain me up, because I will die first!"

She shook her fist at him. He sat as far back in the chair as his chubby body would allow, his eyes and mouth wide open.

She turned on her heel, ran into the bathroom, slammed the door, and turned the lock. Her back against the door, she slid down to the floor, wrapped her arms around her knees, and sobbed.

CHAPTER 24

Locked In

Vargas swung his chair around, looking out toward the paddock area, while he decided what to do about the news Carlos had just given him. True to his word, Carlos had called this morning with the name of the woman.

Darcey Callahan.

Yes, that was the name Brad had given him, too, but was it really her? He decided not to tell Brad about this, at least not until he had had a chance to do the DNA test.

Vargas swung back around and picked up the reports he had been working on when Carlos had called. Minutes later, Jose rushed in out of breath.

"You have to come quick, *señor*. The new *señorita* has locked herself in her bathroom and will not come out," he related, panting and trying to catch his breath.

"What has happened to cause this uproar?" Vargas asked, getting up and helping Jose to a chair, then he poured him a glass of water. "Here, rest, catch your breath."

"Gracias. Alfredo had just given the new *señorita* her instructions. Then she asked a question, and she did not like the answer. She locked herself in the bathroom and she will not come out." Jose finished his glass of water.

"Come, we will go and check this out." Vargas chuckled, helping Jose up and heading for the women's quarters.

They walked through the hallways over to the women's quarters in the south wing. Walking into Saleem's room, Vargas was surprised to see Alfredo. He was quite pale and standing against the wall clutching his leather portfolio like a life preserver. He stared at the bathroom door as if a monster lurked behind it.

"Now tell me what is going on here?" Vargas asked, looking at Alfredo.

"Sh—she attacked me," Alfredo stammered. "She raised her fist and shook it at me."

"I am sure she did not attack you, Alfredo. Now tell me what happened," Vargas said with a chuckle. He was used to Alfredo's theatrics and overreactions to situations.

"I gave her all of the instructions, and she asked if she had to do anything other than be a companion, and I told her since she was not perfect, she had to do anything that was asked of her, then she went crazy and locked herself in the bathroom," Alfredo said, all in one breath.

"Well, let us see what we can do about getting her out." Vargas laughed. He motioned to Jose, "Go get one of the other women to see if they can coax her out."

Jose left and returned quickly with another woman.

"This is Marla," Jose said.

Vargas smiled at Marla and motioned toward the bathroom door. "Well, Marla, it seems we have a situation where our newest arrival has locked herself in the bathroom. Let us see if you can coax her out."

"I'll do my best, Señor Vargas," she said. Marla walked over to the door and tapped lightly on it.

"Go-away!" Her teeth gritted together as she replied. "Just leave me alone."

"*Señorita, por favor.*" It was a female voice. "You must come out. I have to speak with you. It is *muy importante, por favor.*"

"Go away. I don't want to talk to you or anyone else; not now or ever," she said, flatly.

She was worn out, and no longer cared what happened to

her, but she was not going to be a whore for anyone. She would die first.

"*Por favor*," Marla said, pleading now.

"No. Go. Away."

"If you do not come out I will have Manuel come and take the door down and then you will not have a choice," she said.

"Go ahead and have him take the damn door down because that's the only way I'm coming out," she shouted back.

She heard the woman speaking to someone else in the room, but could not understand what they were saying, it was in Spanish. Then there was silence.

"This is getting us nowhere," Vargas said. "I will handle this."

He turned and walked out of the room, pulling his phone out of his pocket. He scrolled through the names in his address book, found Nicho's number, and hit the call button.

Nicho felt his phone vibrate. He pulled it out and looked at the caller ID. VARGAS.

Now what the hell is he wanting? I'm going to regret this, he thought.

"Yes," he answered.

"Nicho, we have an emergency. I need you to come back and take care of it right now." Vargas's tone did not leave much room for saying no.

"What is wrong?" Nicho asked.

He really did not want to know, and he knew now, he was definitely going to regret taking this call.

"The new woman, she has locked herself in her bathroom. We cannot get her out. I need you to come back and take care of this. She trusts you, so I am sure she will open the door for you," Luis said, in his most cajoling voice.

"Have you tried taking off the door?" Nicho asked, thinking that would be the obvious solution to the problem.

"We cannot take the door off. The hinges are on the bathroom side of the door and short of chopping down the door, you are my only hope of getting her out. Besides I have not paid the purchase price yet, so technically, she is still your responsibility."

Vargas delivered the punch line and it hit Nicho like a punch in the gut.

"I am going to regret this, am I not?" Nicho smiled to himself. Somehow, Vargas always got his way. "I will see you in a couple of hours."

Nicho pulled over, turned around, and headed back.

Yes, I am going to regret taking that call.

ↅↄↄ

"Right this way, *señor*." Jose motioned Nicho to follow after he shut the door. "We have had quite a bit of excitement. The new lady, you brought has locked herself in her bathroom. We cannot get her out. Have you come to help?" Jose asked hopefully, following Nicho.

"I am going to do my best," Nicho answered, turning the corner to the women's quarters.

Nicho opened the door and walked in. Vargas and the woman Marla were still trying to get her out. Alfredo was standing, looking like he had seen a ghost.

Vargas gave him a brief overview of the situation and explained the reason for her outburst.

"I will leave her in your capable hands," Vargas told him as he left. "Oh, yes, she will be your dinner companion until the Bel Ami Gala."

Nicho glared at Vargas's back, squared his shoulders, and walked over to the door, shaking his head. He was right, he already regretted answering the call.

ↅↄↄ

She pushed her legs out in front of her and leaned her head against the door.

Let them come and take the damn door down.

They would have to drag her kicking and screaming to get her to go to bed with anyone she hadn't given permission to. She may not be a virgin, but she was no whore either. In truth, she'd only had sex with one person that she could remember and that was Quin. She guessed that there were others, but she couldn't remember. She did remember that she hadn't been a virgin since she was eighteen, so there had been at least one before Quin.

She had no idea how long it had been since she locked herself in the bathroom; she had no watch. Then she heard voices back in her room.

Bam! Bam! Bam!

The thumps on the door vibrated through her body, jarring her back to reality.

"Open this door—*Now!*" the voice shouted.

I know that voice. It's Nicho, who brought me here. Oh great!

"You will come out now!" Nicho commanded.

He couldn't believe he was back here. He had only gotten halfway to the airport this morning when Vargas called him back.

"No! I won't!" she shouted back.

"Yes, you will. I will be here. You will be in my care, again. No one will force you to do anything you do not want to do. You have my word on it."

He sounded sincere, but could she trust him? At least he was someone she felt she kind of knew. On the other hand, how long did she think she could stay locked in here?

How long have I been here anyway?

She reached up and turned the lock then scooted over, out of the way of the door. She would not go out, they would have to come in.

The door opened slowly and stopped when it hit her leg. Nicho stepped around the door and shut it, looking down at her. "What have you done now?" he asked, with a scowl.

Trouble, he said to himself.

He didn't need this. He knew she would be trouble the

minute he had taken custody of her at the docks. She was too much of a spitfire, and she wasn't afraid to stand up to him, or anyone else, for that matter.

"I've done nothing. It's what they want me to do." She drew up her knees and hugged them again, putting her forehead on them. "They want me to—to have sex with men I don't know. I'm not that kind of person, and I will not turn into one. I will die first." She raised her face to look at him. "Please don't let them make me."

Nicho squatted down in front of her, took her hands, and pulled her up. She was a pain in the ass, but until the purchase price was paid, he still was responsible for her. It was not like Vargas to delay a payment. There must have been a particular reason, other than just to annoy him.

"You will be okay. I will see that you will not have to do anything you do not wish to do," Nicho said, looking her in the eye. "I will have to postpone my holiday to stay here and take care of you, but I will stay only until the Gala. You are still my responsibility." He dropped her hands and sighed. "Come, let us go into the other room. I am afraid you gave Alfredo quite a scare. I believe you are the first not to be afraid, let alone throw a tantrum. He did not know quite how to handle it." Nicho chuckled close to her ear as they left the bathroom.

Alfredo was standing by the door now, clutching his leather portfolio and looking quite pale. Nicho turned and assured him everything was going to be fine and that he could leave.

Poor Alfredo, he must have been standing there the whole time I was in the bathroom.

Alfredo looked ready to collapse. He gave a quick bow and left the room as fast as his short legs could carry him. She smirked as she watched him leave. Nicho turned and looked at her, running his hand through his hair. She couldn't read his face. It could have been exasperation, it could have been anger, she couldn't tell.

"What am I going to do with you?" Nicho said, more to

himself than to her. "I thought I was through with you. You are most certainly more trouble that you are worth."

"I'm sorry I'm such a problem and I'm sorry you regret having to take care of me. But, I'm not the one who wanted to be kidnapped. I didn't want any of this. I just what my life back! I don't know what it was, but I want it back!" she screamed, on the verge of tears again.

"Well, there is nothing that can fix that now. For that, I am truly sorry for you," he said putting his hand on her shoulder and looking her in the eyes. "Were it in my power to grant you that, I would, only because you are such a pain in my ass. I will be glad to be rid of you. I will leave you now. You will be fine. No one will call for you except me, and you will not be expected to do anything other than to be my dinner companion. Please, be ready by eight. It is a formal dinner this evening."

He started for the door.

"If I'm such a pain in your ass, why don't you just let me go? Then you could take your goddamn holiday and I'd be out of your hair," she said, gritting her teeth.

"Oh, you do not know how happy that would make me, but unfortunately, it is not up to me. Señor Vargas owns you now. You might plead your case to him, but it is doubtful he will listen. He is not one to let good merchandise go," he said, his hand on the doorknob.

"Fine!" she huffed. The door closed and she heard the lock click.

CHAPTER 25

Brad and Luis

It had been two days since Brad had arrived at Mon Rêve. Despite the blowup over Vargas not releasing Darcey to him, they had enjoyed each other's company over meals and drinks after dinner. Several other guests had arrived in anticipation of the Bel Ami Gala, Vargas explained over drinks one evening.

"Many years ago, when I was much younger, my betrothed, Saleem, was kidnapped, on the eve of our wedding, by white slavers, much like your woman. The only exception was that I was never able to locate her..." Vargas's voice trailed off as he remembered. Taking a deep breath, he continued. "My family and hers searched for months and could find no trace of her. Until one day my mother was at the market, she noticed a woman wearing the necklace I had made special for Saleem for her birthday. Mother admired it and asked where she had gotten it; the woman said it was a gift from her fiancé. My mother told her it was lovely and would like to know where he had purchased it. She would like to buy something similar. The woman said she would ask her fiancé. Mother suggested that they should meet for tea the next day and she could tell her about the necklace. They settled on a time and place. Mother was so excited when she got home, telling me all about the woman. I began to have hope we would find Saleem."

Vargas paused, swirled the liquid in his glass, and took a drink. "We arrived the next day at the appointed time and place, but the woman never came. That was the last information we ever had about her. In hindsight, I can see we were both naïve in handling the situation." His eyes glistened and a tear slipped slowly down his face, his face turned hard, as he spoke. "That is when I formed my elite squad of enforcers. I sent them out with two purposes—one to rescue women who had been forced into prostitution or slavery and to find out what they could about Saleem. Over the years, we have saved several thousand women from the clutches of that sort of vermin." Vargas paused and looked at Brad with hatred in his eyes.

"Did they ever find anything out about Saleem?" Brad asked, leaning forward in his chair.

"No. It was as if she had never existed. We could only guess that she had been shipped overseas and hoped she was alive, somewhere. We continued to wipe out as many of the slavers as we could. The women we rescued were given the choice of returning to their previous lives or staying here. Several of the women chose to go back to their families, but the majority decided to stay. They were ashamed of what had happened to them and afraid they would not be accepted back. Understandable, but they were welcomed here—we ask no questions, make no judgments. Alas, I soon ran out of room for all these lovely women—my 'lost jewels.' That is why I started the Bel Ami Gala, offering these beautiful creatures to a very select clientele. My invited guests are put through an extensive background check and vetted to the smallest detail. They are allowed to socialize with my ladies before the Gala so the best matches can be secured. The women offered at my Gala are to be taken care of like beautiful jewels—no exceptions. My elite squad of enforcers is frequently checking on all the women who leave here. They make sure all of my requirements are kept." Vargas emptied his glass, got up, walked to the bar, and filled it again.

He turned and, looking at Brad, saw that he was still trying to digest what he had just heard.

So, it was just as well I did not tell him about my private collection, just yet, he decided. "Refill?"

Brad nodded. He had to admire him in his dedication in helping those women who had been sold and degraded, beaten and forced into prostitution. From what Brad gathered, Vargas's elite forces were well-trained mercenaries—swift, silent, and deadly. Vargas saw the Gala as his way of giving these women back their lives. Maybe not the one they had before, but a better life than the one they were rescued from, and a guarantee they would never have to worry about that again. Brad was also sure Vargas wasn't above making a little profit out of this venture, either.

Brad watched as Vargas stood staring at the portrait of his horse over the fireplace. "How does this Gala of yours work?"

"Well, for starters my guests are invited here for three weeks before the event," Vargas said, turning around. "They spend time with my ladies. There is a formal dinner each evening that all are required to attend. The guest may select a lady from the evening list for his dinner companion. There is also an afternoon list for those who wish to enjoy some of our outdoor activities," he said, taking a drink from his glass. "On the night of the Gala and before dinner, all guests may exchange ladies to visit with any lady they may not have had a chance to meet prior." He turned and walked back to his chair. "Then after dinner, the bidding will take place. The bidding will continue until one bid has remained unchallenged for five minutes on the board. That bid will be the winning bid for that particular lady." He stood up and drained the last of his drink. "It grows late, and time I bid you good night. Till the morning." He raised his empty glass in Brad's direction.

"Yes, I think it's time I called it a night also. In the morning, then." Brad sat his glass on the table and stood up. "Thanks for the telling me about Saleem; I'm sorry for your loss." He turned and walked toward the door. "Oh, yeah, thanks for the tux. You really shouldn't have, you know," he said, over his shoulder.

Brad sprinted down the hall and took the stairs two at a time. He needed to check in with Lilly to see how things were at the dome, before it got any later.

CHAPTER 26

Penguin Suit

Brad eyed the tux lying across the foot of the bed with disdain. "If there is one thing, I hate worse that sitting through the weekly staff meetings, it is going to some kind of formal affair where I have to wear a penguin suit, he grumbled as he walked past the bed to the desk to call Lilly.

He hit the speed dial number for Lilly's personal phone and waited. She picked up on the third ring just as he was beginning to wonder if he had missed her.

"Hello, Lilly here. How may I help you?" she answered in her usual no-nonsense voice.

"Brad, here. Just checking in to see how things are going," he said, sitting down in the chair next to the desk.

"Everything is going well. We are still on schedule for completion," she assured him. "The hydroponic area is functioning better than expected. They will be able to start planting there next week. That is two weeks ahead of schedule," she said with a hint of pride in her voice.

Lilly very seldom became emotionally involved with any of the projects, but this hydroponic section of the Bio Dome held a particular fascination for her. Brad wasn't sure why, but she seemed to have taken great care to make sure it worked better than expected, or so he thought.

"That is good news," he said. "Well, looks like I'm going to be here at least three more weeks. Vargas's man has brought Darcey here, but Vargas won't let me talk to her. He said she has lost her memory in an accident and it would be better not to rush her. I think he's hiding something."

"Do you have any idea of what it might be?" Lilly asked, not really interested. However, to keep up appearances, she would act *very* interested.

"Don't know, just a feelin' I've got," he said thoughtfully. "Anyway, I'm going to a dinner tonight where I will have a chance to talk with Darcey. I will keep you posted," he told Lilly and hung up.

Brad sat there, staring at the tux, wishing he could just go in a regular suit and tie, but that wasn't how things were done for this event.

Oh well, when in Rome. He headed to the bathroom to clean up.

Vargas had told Brad he would seat him close to Darcey so he might be able to visit with her during the dinner. There were no guarantees, however. He also told him that he still hadn't heard anything from Santiago about what the woman's name might be. It was a deliberate lie, but, it was not the first bit of information he had kept from Brad.

Brad checked his watch. It was ten till eight. He walked out and headed for the banquet hall. He hadn't had butterflies like this since he first saw Darcey walk through the door at the Sweetwater Bar and Grille back in Dallas.

∽∾∽

Nicho had said eight—be ready by eight. How am I to know the time when I don't have a watch or a clock? What had Alfredo said—something about an intercom being active? Now if I were an intercom, where would I hide?

She looked around the room.

Where would be a good place for an intercom? On the wall? At the desk? By the door?

She looked in all of those places and didn't see anything she thought resembled an intercom.

Maybe by the bed?

She hadn't looked there.

Ah ha!

On the bedside table was a small black box with a speaker and an on/off button.

She turned the button to on. "Hello?" She waited.

"Yes, how can I help you?" a voice crackled through the black box's speaker.

"I would like to know what time it is and if I can have a clock in my room, please," she asked, as nicely as she could.

"The time is six-thirty. I will see that a clock is sent to your room. Will that be all?" the voice asked.

"Yes, thank you for the clock," she said and turned the button to off. *Where has the day gone? Had I locked myself in the bathroom for that long? I must have. Well, I have an hour and a half to get ready. That should be plenty of time.*

She finished a leisurely bath and went to the closet to select something to wear. Looking through the evening gowns, she chose a floor length one and the diamond pendant and matching earrings, she had worn on the boat.

She finished dressing and came out to wait for Nicho. The clock she had asked for was setting on the table by the window and it read seven forty-five. Fifteen minutes. Panic began to rise as the minutes ticked away. She had no idea what to expect.

Finally, the lock clicked and Nicho opened the doors. She stood up when he entered, not knowing exactly what she should do. Her stomach was tied in knots.

"Good evening, Saleem. You look enchanting," Nicho said running his eyes over her from head to toe. *Why does one so beautiful have to be such a pain in my ass?* he thought, exasperated. "I will be the envy of every man at the dinner," he said, giving her a crooked smile.

"Thank you," she said hesitantly.

It was the first time she had been called by the new name. It sounded strange.

"I am still your companion for this dinner thing, right?" she asked skeptically. "You're not going to hand me off to someone else, are you?"

"No, I gave you my word. You will be my companion until the Gala. No one else will touch you," Nicho promised. *That's a promise I should not have any problem keeping,* he said to himself. Trouble or not, he realized, he would enjoy every moment. He motioned for her to precede him out the door. "Come, it is time to go."

She was nervous, her palms were sweating, her heart was running wild, and she was on the verge of hyperventilating.

"Take some deep breaths," Nicho said quietly. "You will be fine. You do not have to do anything but sit, eat, and smile. You will not be required to do anything more than that."

She swallowed and nodded. She wanted to believe him, but the way things had been happening, she couldn't be sure.

They continued down the hall they had first entered last night, but in the opposite direction. The hallway ended and intersected with another. They took the left corridor and climbed the gently winding staircase. As they climbed, they could hear music and people talking.

She looked at Nicho. "What language are they speaking? I can't understand a word."

"Some Spanish, some Arabic," he said. "You do not need to understand what they are saying as you will not be conversing with any of them. You are to smile and look beautiful."

That irked her quite a lot.

"Humft!" she snorted. "I'm not some dumb bimbo to be paraded around for everyone to admire! I have a brain. I can carry on an intelligent conversation, I just don't know Spanish or Arabic."

"I know." Nicho looked at her. "But tonight you are to

play the part of a 'dumb bimbo.' It is no reflection on your intelligence. This is the first time the invited guests have a chance to view you. Intelligence is not what they will be interested in."

She glared at him. "In other words, I'm a piece of meat on display for the wolves!"

He smiled. "Your words, not mine."

"How else would you describe it?" she hissed at him

"They are looking for an investment."

They had reached the top of the stairs and the chance to continue their conversation evaporated.

The banquet hall was full of several well-dressed men and an equal amount of women all dressed as she was, in designer gowns, and adorned with jewels. She guessed the other women were in the same position she was.

How many are there?

She quickly counted in her head—maybe twenty.

She looked up at Nicho, her eyes questioning. He held out his arm for her to take and escorted her into the hall. All eyes turned as they entered.

"Did I not tell you, I would be the envy of every male here?" Nicho whispered to her, all the while smiling greetings to several of the men who he seemed to know quite well.

"How do you know all of these men?" she whispered back.

"They are all business associates. At one time or another, I have procured an investment for them."

Oh great! He's just like Creepy Man.

She immediately felt dirty and tried to pull away, but he held her arm tightly. Then, she remembered the directives that Alfredo had given her. If she pulled any harder, she would cause a scene. A scene would cause an embarrassment to Señor Vargas, and that was forbidden.

She returned smiles half-heartedly and tried to ignore the leers. Nicho had been right—the majority of the males here did not attempt to hide their envy.

Several waiters in black slacks, white waistcoats with gold buttons and white gloves, were circulating throughout the hall with massive silver trays laden with drinks and hors'd oeuvres. She noticed the drinks were offered only to the gentlemen, and if he chose, he could offer one to the woman he was with.

The hors'd oeuvres were offered to everyone. However, she declined. Her stomach was too upset. She was afraid she would not be able to eat the meal. The mixture of smells—food and fragrances—men's cologne, women's perfume—weren't helping either.

"Would you like some wine?" Nicho asked.

"I don't know if I could keep it down."

He patted her hand. "Well, take one anyway and just hold the glass."

They continued circulating around the hall, visiting with several of the men. She could not understand any of the conversations but gathered most were about her, because of the looks and laughs. One group of four men even raised their glasses to Nicho and smiled, knowingly at her.

They had gone full circle of the hall when a gong sounded. She presumed that was to indicate that dinner would be served shortly. Everyone leisurely navigated toward an enormous archway, she and Nicho included.

They walked up and down the long banquet table looking for their place cards. Finding them, Nicho seated her, and then himself. She could tell this was going to be a long ordeal by the number of pieces of silverware that made up the elegant table setting.

The meal progressed through to the dessert without incident. She only picked at her food.

Nicho had been watching her intently. He leaned over and whispered in her ear. "You must eat. It is an insult not to."

"Well which is the lesser insult, me throwing up or not eating," she hissed through clenched teeth.

He gave a big laugh. "I see your point."

The people closest to them looked on with interest. All through the meal, she had noticed the man seated across from her kept frequently glancing in her direction. It wasn't a stare, but a look with interest, as if he was trying to figure out if he knew her.

She attempted to keep her eyes diverted, but it was not always possible. He was heart-throbbingly handsome, tanned, with broad shoulders, and he appeared to be very tall, maybe six foot seven, or eight. His hair was a collar-length dark auburn, and a wayward lock lay sexily across his forehead. His eyes were the most beautiful, intense emerald-green she'd ever seen. The few times she had allowed herself to stare at him, there was no air for her to breathe when she looked into those eyes.

Several times, out of the corner of her eye, she had caught Nicho glaring at the man. She didn't know if the man saw him. If he had, he didn't let it bother him.

CHAPTER 27

Dancing

Brad noticed that Darcey's escort had been watching him closely, making no attempt to hide his interest in him. Brad thought the guy was just a little over protective. He never left Darcey's side and seemed to be catering to her, which Brad had noticed that none of the other male escorts did.

Brad tried to keep from staring outright at Darcey during dinner. He had to resist the temptation to reach across the table and take her hand, because he could see she had no idea who he was and that hurt more that he had imagined. He had steeled himself for the disappointment he was going to feel when she didn't recognize him, but this was an actual physical pain in his chest and totally unexpected.

Vargas had said she had lost her memory in an accident. That had to have been the accident with Armando. Anger boiled up inside of him every time he thought about it.

Brad needed to talk with her. He needed to make her remember him. His only hope was that their connection had survived and would trigger her memory of him.

She nudged Nicho's leg under the table to get his attention since she was not allowed to initiate a conversation. Nicho turned and looked at her with questioning eyes. He smiled raising one eyebrow. "Yes, what do you want?"

"Do you know that man sitting across from me? He

keeps looking at me. He hasn't looked at any of the other women since we sat down," she whispered, keeping her eyes glued to her plate.

"No, he is new to the Gala. Is he bothering you?" Nicho asked, ready to teach the man a lesson if he was bothering Saleem.

Nicho had also noticed the man across from her and it worried him. Nicho thought maybe he had seen him before, but wasn't sure. He didn't know why, but he felt this man had an agenda different from the other guests present, and he was sure it involved Saleem.

She looked up, smiling at Nicho. "No, I was just curious because he seems fascinated with only me."

Just then, the waiters began serving the dessert course, and their conversation ended. She decided she needed to talk more with Nicho about the man after dinner.

Sometime later, a gentleman, she presumed to be Señor Vargas, stood up, gently tapped his glass with his dinner knife, garnering the attention of the diners.

"Gentlemen, please join me in the salon." He inclined his head in the direction of the large set of double doors at the opposite end of the room away from the archway through which they had entered through.

Nicho leaned over and whispered in her ear. "You will stay here." He inhaled her scent. "I will be back shortly."

All of the men followed Señor Vargas out of the room. The women stayed seated at the table. But, as soon as the doors closed, the women started chattering amongst themselves, moving around creating little conversation groups.

She stared in bewilderment—she couldn't understand anything.

Am I the only American here?

A beautiful blonde who was seated two chairs down from her looked at her with wide eyes. "You're her!" the blonde exclaimed, quite loudly.

Several of the women closest to them turned and stared.

"I beg your pardon?" she said, not smiling.

The blonde laughed, pointing at her. "You're the one who threw Alfredo into a tizzy!"

"I'm sorry, I don't know what you're talking about," she lied, looking away embarrassed. She didn't need to be reminded of the humiliating incident.

"Oh, come on. Really? We've all heard what you did. Locking yourself in your bathroom and refusing to come out." The blonde laughed again. "That's priceless! I was the one who tried to get you to come out."

"What did they do to you?" another of the women asked anxiously.

"Nothing." Saleem said quietly. She was embarrassed and turned to look at the blonde. "You were the woman at the door?"

"Yep, that was me. I'm Marla. They did nothing? Really?" she asked skeptically.

Saleem looked away again. "No. But they did call the man who brought me here to come take care of the situation."

"I've seen him here before, but never at a dinner with one of us. That must be why you're with him, instead of one of the other men." Marla studied her thoughtfully. "Boy, I wish I'd had the nerve to do that when I first got here," she said regretfully. "But I was too afraid."

"How long have you been here?" Saleem asked, eyeing Marla. *She must be American also.*

"I have been here a year," the blonde said. She looked down sadly. "I will be here as long as Señor Vargas wants me. Then I will go to a Gala."

"Are you an American?" she asked.

"No, Canadian," Marla said, extending her hand in greeting.

Saleem shook it, "American." Two other women came over to join Marla and Saleem's little group; Laurie, a brunette from England; and Monique, also a brunette, from France. "How did you find out what I did?" Saleem asked Monique.

"We overhear things from the house staff, *mon ami*. They were all a twitter about Alfredo. He had to lie down for the rest of the afternoon and he took his evening meal in his room. Poor Alfredo." She made a pouty face and all the women laughed.

"Where are your rooms?" Saleem asked, looking at them.

"Our rooms are all on the same hallway as yours," Marla said with a giggle. "We get to gather in the courtyard once a day in the evening, when it cools down. That's where we share the gossip we pick up from the house staff. Most of us speak Spanish, but they don't know we do, so they speak freely in front of us."

"Well, I won't be able to contribute much. I can't speak or understand Spanish," Saleem said, frowning.

"Not to worry, *mon ami*," Monique said. "We will share with you."

An hour or so later they heard the doors to the salon open and the women scattered back to their seats. The smell of tobacco wafted in through the open doors. The men collected their women and strolled back to the hall. Saleem could hear music playing now.

Nicho stopped at her chair and extended his hand. She took it. The lingering tobacco smoke on his jacket softly invaded her nose as they walked out of the dining room.

"Would you care to dance?" Nicho asked, turning her around to face him.

She smiled up at him a heart-melting smile. He couldn't take his eyes off of her.

Does she not know how beautiful she is? She seems genuinely unaware of the effect she has on the opposite sex. Nicho mentally shook his head. *This is going nowhere,* he thought.

"Yes, that would be nice," she said before she thought, *Do I even know how to dance?*

The small orchestra was playing a waltz and they joined other couples already on the dance floor. Nicho was an excellent dancer; she didn't even have to think whether she knew how to dance. The music ended and they walked over to one of the sofas.

Nicho smiled, looking at her. "Would you care for something to drink, now?"

She nodded and he signaled a waiter who brought over an ornate silver tray with an assortment of drinks.

"Wine or something harder?" Nicho asked assessing the drinks on the tray for himself, as well.

"I would prefer sparkling water if they have it."

Her stomach still had not settled, even though she had only eaten enough to be polite. Now, the little she had eaten hadn't decided if it was going to stay put.

What I wouldn't give for a bottle Tums, right now!

"Sparkling water it is." Nicho nodded to the waiter and he left, only to return shortly, with a glass with sparkling water.

The orchestra was playing again.

"Shall we?" Nicho took her hand, and they headed for the floor.

For her, this was turning out to be the best part of the evening. She forgot all about the bad stuff and felt almost normal, or at least, what she imagined was normal for her. While Nicho held her in is arms, there was nothing but the music and the feeling that she was safe.

Brad watched as Darcey and her escort glided around the floor. He decided it was time to ask for a dance. He walked up to them, tapped her escort on the shoulder, and smiled at Darcey. "Mind if I cut in?"

She looked at Nicho. She had that "you promised me" look in her eyes. As much as she didn't feel threatened by this guy, she still didn't want to be left alone with him—not even for a dance.

"I'm afraid not. The lady is all mine for the evening," Nicho said curtly. He gathered her closer and whisked her away, leaving Brad standing in the middle of the floor.

She watched over Nicho's shoulder at the man glaring after them and suddenly felt a rush of guilt.

She doesn't recognize me. I am a stranger to her, Brad thought, dejected. His heart sank as he turned and walked off the floor.

Frustrated, he knew he would have to wait until tomorrow evening to see Darcey again. He had already checked Vargas's afternoon list for the available women, and she wasn't on it.

"Do you know that guy?" she asked Nicho. She had a feeling that maybe Nicho and that guy knew each other. It had been in the way they looked at each other—not like strangers, but not friends either.

"You have asked enough questions for one night," Nicho said. "You were not supposed to ask any, remember?"

"I'm sorry. Must be a force of habit I guess," she said, looking him in the eye and smiling. "Am I forgiven?"

He laughed. "Of course. How silly of me. I forgot you are an American. Americans do not follow the rules."

"Humft," she snorted, wishing she could punch him.

"You cannot do that either," he said, still laughing.

He must have guessed what she was thinking.

They danced one more dance and every time they circled the floor, that man was watching them. He made her nervous—not threatened—just nervous—and she had no idea why.

They left the hall and slowly descended the stairs. Nicho walked her back to her room, said good night, and locked her safely behind the doors.

Nicho stood staring at the doors after they were locked.

There is no way I am going to endure three weeks of this, he decided, shaking his head.

Something about this one had touched his protective side, and that was dangerous. It meant he had feelings for her, and he couldn't afford to have any feelings that interfered with the job.

He turned and walked down the hall, still trying to figure

out why he felt so protective of her. It made no sense. She had been a pain in his ass ever since he had picked her up.

Another thing that bothered him was why he had taken such an immediate dislike to that man at dinner. Normally he would not have given him a second thought, but this man irritated him beyond reason. Something in the man's eyes rankled him more than he wanted to admit to himself.

Nicho thought maybe he had seen him before, but was not sure, he would ask Vargas about him. Nicho was well aware that Vargas did not invite anyone who did not meet his high standards.

ᘓᘔᘓᘔ

Saleem leaned against the door for a while, sorting out things in her mind. It had been a very pleasant evening, all things considered, except for that man who kept looking at her all through dinner. She was hoping he wouldn't be at the Gala.

From the unfortunate first meeting with Alfredo, she had already figured out that the Bel Ami Gala was where the women were bought and sold. And, since that man was here tonight, then he probably would be at the Gala.

She frowned. Maybe Señor Vargas would change his mind about selling her. He had changed his mind about buying her. Maybe he would do it again. *Why do I have to be in this situation? Why couldn't Quin or Nicho be my knight in shining armor and buy me?*

CHAPTER 28

DNA

Vargas woke up earlier than usual, feeling in a fantastic mood. He had dreamt last night that he had found Saleem. Maybe it was a sign. He wanted to contact Saleem's mother first thing this morning to see if she would be willing to give a sample of her DNA for testing against the woman here.

He had not talked to Aicha Kaddur, Saleem's mother, in several months. She had been traveling, but she should have returned by now. He called her number.

"Hello," Aicha answered. She was surprised to see it was Vargas calling. She had not heard from him since the first of the year.

"Aicha, Luis here. How have you been?" he asked. He liked her gentle ways. He knew in his heart that Saleem would have been just like her.

"I am fine, Luis. What do I owe this call to?" she asked.

"I know you do not exactly approve of my business," he conceded, "but a woman has come into my possession who looks so much like Saleem, that I feel she could be her daughter. She was in an accident before coming to me and has lost her memory, so there is no use in asking her about her parents," he explained. "I am not calling to get your hopes up, but I would like to do a DNA test to satisfy my soul. I am calling to ask if you would give me a sample of yours for comparison," he finished hopefully. There was silence on the other end. "Aicha, are you still there?" he asked.

"Yes, I am still here." She paused. "Are you sure, Luis? It has been twenty-five years. Your memory is not what it once was." Her voice was hesitant, and sad.

"My memory is just fine," he replied stiffly. "I will get you a photo of her for you to look at, and let you make up your own mind. Regardless, whether you feel as I do, I still want to do the test. Will you give me a sample?" he asked again, just short of demanding.

"Luis, I understand your reasoning, however, I feel you are grasping at the wind with this, but I will look at your photo. And yes, I will give you a sample for comparison," she told him.

Aicha felt sorry for him. Although his business life had been a great success, his personal life had never been the same since he had lost Saleem.

There had been many women in his life and he had several children. He loved them all but was never able to commit to any of their mothers—they were not Saleem. Then there was the dirty business he had let himself slip into while looking for Saleem. It became an obsession with him to find her.

"Gracias, Aicha," he said, relieved. "You have made my day. I will have my personal physician bring the photo with him when he comes to take your sample. You cannot possibly know how much this means to me." He thanked her again and hung up.

Immediately, he called his physician and arranged with him to collect the sample. Then he called the photographer to come and take a photo of Saleem within the hour.

ೞೞ

The lock clicked. The two maids came in with the breakfast tray and, this time—coffee—she could smell it. She poured a cup and inhaled with her eyes closed.

Ummmm. Heaven.

Her stomach felt much better this morning; breakfast had been delicious. She showered and dressed.

What do I do now? I have nothing to keep me occupied. In my other life what would I be doing?

She didn't have a clue. She knew she liked reading, so maybe there might be some books she could read here.

She went to the intercom and asked about the books. Several minutes later one of the maids brought in a box full of books and sat them on the table.

She sorted through them and found several that looked promising. Choosing one, she curled up on the sofa and started reading.

One of the covers that had caught her eye looked familiar. It was a James Patterson book—*12th of Never*. She couldn't remember if she liked the author, but, as she started reading, the story was exciting and parts seemed strangely familiar, like she had already read them.

How could that be? Deja vu? In my past life?

She looked up when she heard the click of the lock. Señor Vargas walked through the door with a man carrying a camera. She must have had a startled look on her face as Señor Vargas smiled at her. She immediately placed her feet on the floor and stood up.

"Everything is just fine, Saleem. We are here to take a photograph of you. Please stay seated, it will be fine for the photograph," Vargas said, stepping aside so the photographer could move forward in front of her.

Bewildered, she sank back down on the sofa. The photographer stood in front of her and took several shots. Turning to Vargas, he said he got what he needed.

"Sorry to have interrupted your reading. We have a full library, so you may select more from there if you wish. Just ask Nicho to take you. *Buenas días*, Saleem," Vargas said, closing and locking the doors.

She stared at the doors, more bewildered than ever.

೧೨೧

The photographer dropped off several photos he had taken that morning. Vargas was pleased with the shots and thanked him. He sat looking at the photos for several minutes, staring into the face of his beloved Saleem. Heaving a sigh, he picked up his phone and called his physician.

"The photographs are ready."

The physician had picked up the photos, and left for Aicha's over an hour ago. Vargas paced the floor, anxiety growing with each passing minute.

The phone rang.

"Vargas here," he quickly answered.

"I have delivered your photos and collected the sample. When would you like me to get the sample from the woman?" the physician asked.

"As soon as you get here. You can do it now. I want this done as quickly as possible." Vargas said, excitement in his voice.

The physician arrived a half hour later. Vargas met him at the door and they walked over to the south wing. Unlocking the doors, Vargas motioned to the physician to enter.

Saleem stood up, as soon as they entered the room.

"Not to worry, Saleem, we are here to take a swab of your cheek for tests, to make sure you are healthy." Vargas reached out and took her hand. "It will be fine."

"But I am just fine. Why is it necessary? I'm sure I don't have any diseases either," she said, pulling her hand away and backing up.

Vargas smiled at her reassuringly. "Do not be afraid, *por favor*. This will not hurt, and it is for your own safety," Vargas said. "I do this for all of my ladies. Just think of it as your insurance policy where you do not have to pay the premium."

She had backed up against the chair leaving her nowhere else to go, so she just sat down. The physician took the swab out of the sterile wrapper, swabbed the inside of her cheek, and put it another sterile container for transport.

"I will take this directly to the lab. You will have your results in a few days." With that, the physician left. She watched as the physician hurried out the door, wondering what that was all about.

"*Buenas días*, Saleem." Vargas gave a slight bow, pulled the doors shut, and locked them. Back in his office, he called Aicha to find out what she thought about the photos.

"Hello," Aicha answered.

She knew it would be him. She had been sitting, staring at the photos that he had sent over. She could not believe her eyes, this woman really did remind her of Saleem. Her bone structure was the same, her coloring, all could have been Saleem's.

"Luis here. Have you had a chance to look at the photos? What do you think? Does she not look like Saleem? I am sure I am right about this."

He was so anxious to know what she thought but was not giving her the chance to answer.

"Yes, I believe she does look very much like Saleem. What color are her eyes?" she asked him. "I could not tell from the photo."

"I do not know. I have never looked her directly in the eye. She always keeps her head and eyes turned away or down. I will make it a priority to see her eyes," he said. "I have had the samples taken to the lab. They tell me the results will be ready in a few days. I will call you as soon as I know." He hung up the phone.

෨෨෨

The past two weeks had flown by, even though Brad had become more frustrated with each day that passed, by not being able to speak or even get close to Darcey. Night after night, sitting just a few feet away from Darcey, he had been thwarted at every turn by her escort.

Damn him! Always in the way, Brad had thought bitterly many times.

Then Vargas had called earlier in the morning and asked Brad to come to his office at ten. It was now ten-fifteen. It was not like Vargas to be late.

Brad paced the floor waiting for him. He hoped Vargas would tell him today that he could be Darcey's escort for the evening. He had tried several times to ask why she was never on the list of dinner companions. He wanted to have her as his dinner companion so he could talk to her. But Vargas had always managed to evade giving a direct answer to the questions.

Brad heard booted footsteps coming down the hall. No sooner, had he turned to face the door, than Vargas came rushing in with a large manila envelope clutched in his hand.

"Sit, sit. I have wonderful news to share." Vargas was ecstatic, grinning from ear to ear. "I have the most wonderful news! Your Darcey is my Saleem's daughter!" He paused to catch his breath.

Brad stood there his mouth open, eyes staring at Vargas in disbelief. "What? What do you mean she's Saleem's daughter? Are you crazy? How do you know this?" His mind was in a whirl. He shook his head to clear it. Had he heard right? How could this be?

"Here, sit, sit. Let me get you a drink." Vargas placed the envelope on his desk and rushed to the bar to fix Brad a drink. "I am just so excited about the news, and yes, I am most sure." Vargas handed Brad a half-full glass of Scotch and placed his hand on Brad's shoulder. "Is this not the most wonderful news?"

Brad stared at Luis "How is that possible, I mean I know how it's possible, but how is it possible that all of this has come together now? Here? Are you sure?"

"Yes, I am sure. I have the DNA tests to prove it," Vargas said, pointing at the envelope on the desk. "There is no mistake." He poured himself a drink. "I have yet to tell Saleem's mother, Aicha, but I know she will be as excited as I am about finding her granddaughter."

"Just how do you plan on breaking the news to Darcey?" Brad wanted to know. "She doesn't even know who she is and you're going to lay all of this on her, too? You can't throw this at her right now. You've got to give me a chance to bring her memory back. She's no good to anyone in the state of mind she's in now. You've got to give me the chance to bring her back," he pleaded.

"Patience, my friend. I have no intention of telling her now," Vargas said. "I agree that it would be too much for her to handle. It may even be too much when she regains her memory."

"So you are not planning on telling her now?" Brad asked, taking a big swallow of Scotch. It burned as it ran down his throat burning away the rest of the fog Vargas's news had created in his mind.

Vargas walked around and sat down behind his desk. "No, first I need you to tell me everything you know about Darcey's family. Who are her parents, especially?"

"I am afraid I can't tell you all that much. Her parents were killed several years ago in an accident. So I never got to meet them. I do know that Darcey was raised by her father's brother, Jack, but I have never met him either. I do know that her mom was an art teacher in the Dallas school system. That is about the extent of what I know of her family."

Not wanting Brad to see the deep disappointment in his eyes, Vargas swiveled his chair around to look out his window. "This is extremely disappointing. I had hoped I had found my Saleem," he said softly. Turning back around with purpose, Vargas finished off his drink and sat the glass on the desk. "Nevertheless, I have given this much thought over the last few days as how it should be handled. My plan, if you are agreeable, of course, will be to let things continue, as they are now. I will give you an opportunity to talk with Darcey to see if she remembers you, before the Gala. If she does not, the Gala will go on as planned. You will bid for her as you originally planned."

"And, if she remembers me, I can take her home, right?" Brad asked hopefully.

"Yes, but she must remember who you are, for that to happen. That would be the only reason I would take her off the list." Vargas paused. "I know this must seem harsh and cruel, but I have rules, and I follow my rules just like I expect everyone who works for me to do—just like I expect you to do. I do not take a woman's name off the list for any reason other than she has been claimed with proof by a family member. This has happened only once in all of the years I have been doing the Gala. So you can see with her not remembering you and you not being a family member, I must follow my rules."

Vargas grinned at Brad. He watched Brad trying to digest everything he had just told him. "Let me continue. Since I am sure she will not remember you and you will have to bid for her, I will put enough in your account to guarantee that you will have the winning bid. Once that is accomplished, you will take her with you. You will then have all the time you need to help her regain her memory." He picked up his empty glass and walked over to refill it.

"Why are you doing this?" Brad asked, turning in his chair to look at Vargas. He was still trying to wrap his mind around the fact that Darcey was Saleem's daughter. Let alone that Vargas wouldn't take Darcey's name off the list and was going to give him the money to bid with. It was bizarre!

"As I said earlier, I have rules, and I have not told Aicha, her grandmother and I will not tell her until the Gala is over and you have left Morocco. By doing it this way, I will avoid a nasty scene with her grandmother. The Kaddur family is very protective of their women, and they would want to keep her here, regardless, whether she remembered her past life or not. This way, she will be long gone before they know, and I will make sure they do not know where you have taken her." Vargas watched Brad, waiting for some sign that he was on board with the plan. Vargas knew this was a good plan all around for everyone and was confident that Brad would agree after he had thought it through.

"Okay, let me sleep on it tonight. I think it will work, but I need time to digest all of this." Brad drained the last of the Scotch from his glass and set it on the edge of the desk. He looked at Vargas, who had sat down in the chair by Brad. "Who all knows about this?"

"Besides you and me, my physician and my photographer. Both are trustworthy. And, of course Jose, but, he would go to his grave before he told anyone what he knew." Vargas reached over and put his hand on Brad's arm. "It will all work out, my son. Not to worry."

If I do not watch myself, Vargas thought happily, *I will be welcoming Brad into the Vargas family. I may anyway. It would be good to have a son after six daughters.* He sat there feeling very self-satisfied with his plan.

Brad pushed himself up, out of the chair, walked to the door, then turned around to face Vargas. "One more thing. Why can't I get Darcey for a dinner companion? It's the same guy every evening with her. He won't let me get close to her. What's the deal with that?" he asked with a raised eyebrow.

"You do not need to concern yourself with that. It is nothing you need to know about. Rest assured that everything is being taken care of and she is safe." Vargas again successfully avoided giving Brad a direct answer.

CHAPTER 29

Bel Ami Gala

Days passed into weeks. Now, there were only two days left before the Bel Ami Gala. The house was all a twitter with anticipation. Saleem wasn't.

She knew she had exactly two days left before she became someone's property. The highest bidder would buy her. Who knew where she would wind up? She made a promise to herself that she wouldn't go quietly—no matter what.

Alfredo had finally ventured back to her quarters after that first week since Vargas had assured him she would not cause any more trouble.

So on the morning before the Gala, Alfredo came to her room to inform her what she would be expected to do the next day and at the Gala. He walked in, placed his leather portfolio on the table, and sat down, waiting for her to sit down also.

She slowly sank down in the armchair next to the sofa. She was not about to get any closer to Alfredo than necessary. In her opinion, he was nothing but the bearer of bad news. Nothing good ever came from one of his visits. She watched as he opened his leather portfolio and sorted through the pages inside. She gripped the arms of the chair anticipating the worst—and it came.

"Tomorrow a photographer will come to take photographs of you in the nude," he stated without emotion, reading from the pages in the portfolio as if it were a grocery list. Alfredo turned slightly in her direction as a short gasp escaped her lips, her mouth forming a perfect O. "This will be the last formal dinner and it will be followed by the auction. Before the bidding starts, you will be placed in a room where you will stay until the auction is over."

He heard her gasp again and quickly looked up at her. Alfredo noticed that her body had stiffened and she was gripping the arms of the chair tightly as if she was trying to hold herself back from jumping up and scratching his eyes out. A look of pure hatred stared back at him. A tiny droplet of sweat trickled down the side of his face.

His hand trembled as he turned a page, cleared his throat, and continued. "You will be expected to be on your best behavior." His voice wavered, but he continued. "You will speak to no one before entering the room, and only to the buyer, if spoken to, after the transaction has been completed." He paused, nervously looking at her again before continuing. Her hands still gripped the arms of the chair and his blood ran cold at the look in her eyes. "You will not be coming back to this room. You will be taken to whatever transportation your buyer has provided, and leave with them."

Alfredo finished in one swift breath, quickly closing the portfolio as he raced across the room and out the doors. He escaped before she had the chance to do something terrifyingly horrible to him.

She sat staring at the doors Alfredo had just raced through and had forgotten to close and lock in his rush to escape.

A bubble of laughter welled up and burst through her lips followed by another and another until she was laughing uncontrollably. The laughter swiftly turned into tears and she sobbed bitterly. Her arms wrapped themselves around her waist and she rocked back and forth to stop the pain. A pain, that went deep into her soul.

"Will this never end?" she sobbed.

Now she knew there was no way out—no hope. She didn't even have a past life to grieve over. All she had were these past few weeks to call a life. Worse, she didn't know if anyone would miss her. Would anyone look for her—her family, or friends, boyfriend, or husband? Did she have a job? What was it? Where had she lived? She would never know any of that. All she would ever have was what waited for her from here forward and, at this moment that didn't look too promising.

⚜

That evening, after Alfredo had left and her tears had faded, she waited quietly for Nicho to come escort her to the courtyard one final time.

It would be a sad time. Some of the women would not be seeing each other ever again. Marla, who she had come to rely on, was now her best friend, and she would miss Marla the most. She was thankful that Marla would be staying.

Nicho left her at the gate to the courtyard with a nod, telling her he would be back later to get her. He watched her slowly walk toward the others who were already there. He could feel the sadness in the air and a sharp pain pricked his heart. Turning on his heel, he walked stiffly away.

This has to stop. Now, he scolded himself, running his hand through his hair.

The women talked, cried, and hugged each other. Good-byes were said for the last time. None of them knew what tomorrow would bring. But, unlike her, the other women knew who they were, where they had come from, and what their lives had been before. She knew none of this, and maybe it was better that way.

She was sad because she knew she had had a past life, but not what it had been. So, she really didn't know exactly what she was missing—her pain did not, could not compare to theirs. But, oh, how she would have welcomed that pain just to know who she honestly was.

One by one, the others left as their escorts came to collect them. She was the last one left and she sat down on the edge of the fountain watching the Koi fish swim blissfully unaware of anything beyond their small world inside the fountain's basin.

Trailing her fingers in the water, she attracted several of the fish. They came to nibble on her fingers, in the hopes it was food. She let her mind drift, and for a blissful moment, she was someone else, somewhere else. She closed her eyes and let herself escape the confines of her nightmare.

෴

Vargas had given Brad directions to find the women's courtyard, and permission to approach Darcey. Finding his way to the courtyard, he walked under the archway and stopped at the vision before him.

Darcey was sitting on the edge of the fountain trailing her fingers in the water. She seemed ethereal in the moonlight, which only complimented her beauty. Her eyes closed, her face relaxed made her appear to be a million miles away from this place.

Brad's heart was pounding and he found it hard to breath. She had always had that effect on him, ever since the first time he saw her. Now, he hoped she would also feel it—she had to.

"Hello, *señorita*."

The man's voice startled her. She jumped and his strong hands grabbed her arm, keeping her from falling into the fountain.

"Who are you and what are you doing in here? It is not allowed!" she said breathlessly, her eyes wide. Trying to keep her voice under control, even though her heart was still in overdrive, she turned and looked up to see who this man was. She gasped, an instant reflex, as she looked at the handsome face of the man who had sat across from her at every dinner. *He is even more handsome up close.*

Brad released her arm and sat down next to her, inhaling her perfume as it floated on the gentle evening breeze. "I had to see you before tomorrow night. I need to know if you know me. Have you ever seen me before?" He searched her face for any sign of recognition.

He knew she was his Darcey. She had to remember him. If she could remember him before the Gala, he could claim her before the auction. Vargas had said so. He had no idea if her memory would come back, but he had to depend on their connection to help her remember.

"No, I don't know you," she said, slightly out of breath as she stared into his green eyes. Her train of thought evaporated, as she was pulled deeper into the depths of his emerald green eyes. The overwhelming urge to reach out and touch him fled when she blinked, breaking the connection and the disturbing shock waves that were running through her whole body. "You better go before my escort comes back. It would not be good for you to be found here," she cautioned him breathlessly, staring at her hands, confused at the sudden urge she had had and without any explanation for it. She couldn't look into his eyes again. It was too disturbing, too confusing what she saw there.

Brad heaved a heavy sigh and stood up. It had been worth a try. *Now, I will have to follow through with Luis's plan,* he grumbled to himself. This was not what he wanted, Vargas had assured him, there would be enough money put in his account to purchase her. He would have his Darcey, and Vargas would not have broken his rules.

Brad watched her sitting there. His arms, his body burned to touch her, to smell her essence, to feel her skin on his, but he couldn't, not just yet. Anguish twisted in his stomach. Just one more night, and she would be his. He closed his eyes and inhaled her perfume. That would have to be enough until tomorrow night.

Nicho walked up to the courtyard entrance expecting to see Saleem waiting for him, but instead he saw her seated on the edge of the fountain with that man from the dinner standing over her. From the angle of his view, the man looked menacing. It only took Nicho a few long strides to reach them.

"What the hell are you doing here?" he growled, glaring at Brad. "You are not allowed in this area. You will leave immediately!" he said, in a very low, menacing tone.

All this man had to do was to make one misstep and Nicho would enjoy rearranging his face.

"I was just leaving." Brad gave a little bow in Darcey's direction, "*Buenas noches, señorita.*" He turned and glared at Nicho. Walking past Nicho, he purposely ran into his shoulder on his way out.

"Who is that man?" she asked, searching Nicho's eyes as he offered her his hand to help her up.

"I do not know," he said as he watched the man walk out of the courtyard. "I have been unable to find out very much beyond his name. Señor Vargas has assured me he has been thoroughly checked out, but he has not made that information available to me," Nicho said, turning to look at her. "Not to worry, he will not bother you again. Come, it is time you were returned to your quarters."

Nicho let her precede him out of the courtyard, watching the graceful sway of her body, as she walked.

The past three weeks have been torture, he reflected. He didn't know what it was about her. Everything he had prided himself on—handling each one as a job, with no name, no face, only nothing more than a paycheck. Now, his resolve to never become involved with the merchandise was on the verge of disappearing.

There was something about her that drew him in, and would not let him go. He couldn't explain it, and, at this point, did it really matter?

Nicho had played the gentleman, never touching her, always polite, careful, never letting his guard down in front of her. Always keeping an eye on the other guests, in case they became too interested, putting himself in between her and that guest, if necessary.

He had no idea how she felt about him, other than she looked to him for the protection he had promised to give her. How much better it would have been, if he had just told Vargas he couldn't come back, climbed aboard that plane, and never looked back. Instead, he had felt a responsibility to Vargas to finish the job, regardless of how he had felt about her.

When they had reached her room, he opened the doors and waited for her to enter.

"I will escort you tomorrow evening to dinner. Please be ready by eight. *Buenas noches*," he said, short and to the point, inclining his head toward her.

She smiled and placed her hand on his arm, feeling the muscles tighten under her fingers. She searched his face. It was a mask. She couldn't read anything. "Thank you for everything. I appreciate everything you have done for me, protecting and caring for me, when you didn't have to. You will never know just how much you have made this situation bearable. Without you, I know I would have gone insane or killed myself. And, maybe that would have been better in the long run. I don't know if I can survive after tomorrow." She took a ragged breath and closed her eyes. "Thank you."

Turning slowly, she walked through the doors.

It was the hardest thing Nicho had ever done. Shutting and locking the doors to her bedroom had a ring of finality. He wanted so much to rip the doors off their hinges, scoop her up, and spirit her away from here, right now, tonight. However, he knew that could never happen, no matter how much he wanted it.

Nicho had not planned to stay for the auction and was going to leave right after dinner. Now, he knew he had to see it through to the end. He had to be sure whoever purchased her would take care of her. He could not live with himself if anything happened to her. He could block the thought of someone else touching her, holding her, kissing her. Yes, he could block all of that out, if he knew she was safe. He turned and walked slowly down the hall.

ოოო

She took a long hot soak in the tub, hoping it would relieve the tension that had built up since that strange man had confronted her in the courtyard and then the goodbye she had given Nicho.

She knew there would not be time to say the things she wanted to say tomorrow, so she had tried to say them tonight, but she couldn't say everything she wanted. It would have done no good to tell him how she really felt. She was going to be sold tomorrow and would never see him again.

I will miss him. Will he miss me? Probably not. How often has he told me I was more trouble than I was worth? Too many times to count on one hand. He will be glad to see the last of me and move on to the next job.

She slipped under the surface of the water. How much better to just stay here and never come up. Just to drift peacefully into oblivion, never having to worry about who she was anymore, where she came from, who she loved, or who love her. Yes, it would be much better for everyone, especially her.

Then her body's self-preservation took over, and she came up sputtering and gasping for air.

That was stupid. What was I thinking? I'm no coward. I'll face whatever comes tomorrow, as I always have Damn the torpedoes. Full speed ahead. Now where did that come from? Was that something from my past life? Have I always been stubborn and determined when confronted with a difficult situation?

Wherever it came from, it bolstered her resolve to still try to find some way out of this nightmare.

CHAPTER 30

Photos

The photographer had to come back in the afternoon to retake the photos. Something about the others did not turn out to Señor Vargas's liking, and he wanted them retaken. He went through the routine again. Several shots standing—front and back—some provocative shots on the sofa, the bed, and sitting in a chair. By the time he left, she felt dirty and violated again. It was humiliating.

Just another day in the life as a piece of meat!

As soon as he left, she fled to the bathroom to bathe.

☙❧

The trusty little clock on the bedside stand said it was seven forty-five. Nicho would be here shortly. She was nervous all over again, just like the first dinner she had attended with him. Her stomach was tied in knots and her heart was trying to beat its way out of her chest. She took several deep breaths, hoping to calm down. Then she put her head between her knees. That seemed to help. She was in that position when the doors opened.

"Saleem, are you all right?" Nicho rushed over to her, placing his hand on her back. He had to put himself in check to keep from doing more than touching her back. It wasn't easy.

"Yes, just hyperventilating here." She tried to smile. "Nothing serious." She looked up and felt herself blush. She straightened up and smiled. "I'll be fine. Are you ready to leave?"

Concern in his eyes, he took her hand and held it in both of his. "When you feel ready, we will go, but not until you do."

She looked down at their hands and then up into his eyes. She didn't know what she saw there—confusion, sadness, desire? They were all there and then were gone in a flash. Maybe they hadn't been there at all.

She took a deep breath. "I'm ready. Let's get this over with."

Time to shift my mind into neutral, she thought, *and block out all that is going to happen tonight. This is going to be something I don't want to remember. Ever!*

They climbed the stairs to the ballroom one last time. It was indeed a festive occasion, at least for the guests. Not so much for the women who were being put on the block. All the women were immaculately and beautifully dressed and wearing their prerequisite smiles.

Nicho spoke to several of the other guests. Most were ones who had been at the dinners off and on over the past three weeks. He never strayed from her side. In fact, he placed his arm possessively around her waist several times when speaking with some of the guests. She didn't know what that was all about and Nicho just smiled when she asked.

They were standing a short distance away from the crowd of guests. Watching as the men and women circulated through the room, she felt Nicho's body stiffen.

She looked at him and then turned her gaze in the direction he was looking. Just reaching the top of the stairs was that man from the courtyard. He had a beautiful woman on his arm but seemed totally oblivious that she was there. She heard Nicho let out a hissing sound as the man walked toward them.

Before the man could reach them, another guest intercepted the man.

She elbowed Nicho in the side to get his attention. "Did you find out any more about that man?"

"Just his name. He is from Peru. I could not find out where or anything else for that matter. Don't worry, I won't let him bother you."

She looked up at him and smiled—thankful for his presence. "What's his name? You said you found that out," she asked, looking at the man and woman heading in their direction.

"Brad Daniels," Nicho said through clenched teeth and his arm tightened around her.

His eyes narrowed as the other man approached. Nicho was ready for a fight if necessary. This man clearly had plans for Saleem and Nicho wasn't going to let him get any closer. It was obvious from the look on the man's face he only had eyes for her. He didn't even acknowledge the beautiful woman on his arm.

"Good evening," Brad said, looking at her first and then at Nicho. "I would like to visit with your lady. I understand she will be one of the offerings tonight." He smiled at Nicho, but the smile never made it to his eyes. "Señor Vargas has said we may exchange ladies for the purpose of examining the merchandise prior to dinner, and I wish to visit with your lady."

His voice had a slight edge that wasn't lost on Nicho. Saleem felt Nicho stiffen, and his arm tightened around her. The rules of decorum applied to the guests as well as to the women. Then, knowing he had no choice, Nicho exchanged women with the man.

"Certainly," Nicho dropped his arm and gave Saleem a little shove in the direction of the man.

She shot a quick look back at Nicho.

He smiled. "It will be fine."

Brad handed the woman on his arm over to Nicho and extended his arm to Saleem. She turned and looked back at

Nicho as they walked across the floor to the seating area in front of the balcony doors. Brad motioned to her to sit and then sat down beside her on the sofa. She moved over to put some distance between them.

As she did, he smiled. "There is nothing to be afraid of," he said. "I will not hurt you. I merely want to get to know you. I have tried several times before this evening, but your escort has blocked every attempt. This is the only opportunity I will have to visit with you before the auction. Now, tell me about yourself."

Brad cocked his head to the side and smiled a lopsided grin that did crazy things to her insides.

"I don't have anything to tell. I don't know who I am or where I come from or how I ended up in this nightmare." Looking at her hands in her lap, she felt on the verge of tears and she couldn't let that happen. She took a ragged breath and exhaled slowly. She looked up at him, surprised to see such a look of pain in his eyes, emerald green eyes— eyes that held hers. Time stood still. She shook her head to break the connection. *This is crazy.*

"Tell me exactly how you wound up here." A look of determination crossed his face. "I want to know everything."

"As best as I remember, I woke up somewhere far away from here in nothing but my underwear. I was bruised all over, like I had been beaten. Then they put me on a boat, and we sailed for several days. Then I was flown here— wherever here is."

She looked around the room and then at him. His face was hard.

"I was told I had been kidnapped and was going to be sold to the highest bidder. That's where you come in." She took a deep breath and let lose all the frustration she had locked away since her long journey began weeks ago. "Well take a good look." Her teeth clenched and her eyes narrowed as she glared at him. "Do you like this piece of meat? Do I meet with your approval? Do I look worth the price you might have to pay? Do I?"

She was on the verge of shouting, but gripping the edge of the sofa kept her from leaping off it and screaming.

Brad jerked back, startled, by all of the anger directed at him. What had they done to her? How could his sweet optimistic, fun-loving Darcey been turned into this hard, cynical woman in such a short time?

It had only been two months since Armando had reported her missing, and then he had been vague on the particulars of how it had happened. From the looks of Armando, it had been a bad accident. Too bad he had been murdered. It robbed Brad of the pleasure of doing it himself. Never again would he let Darcey out of his sight. He never should have left without her in the first place. *Hindsight is always 20/20,* he thought.

She looked around to make sure no one had seen her throw her little tantrum. No one but Nicho had, and he wasn't overjoyed, judging by the look on his face.

She looked back at the man. Apparently, he was upset by her rant. He seemed to be working something out in his mind.

"I am truly sorry for your misfortune. If I am lucky enough to be the high bidder for you this evening, it will be my pleasure to take you away from all of this and give you your normal life." He grinned, placing his hand on hers.

His touch sent an electric shock up her arm. She gave a little gasp.

That's unreal. What was that?

She jerked her hand away.

Looking up, she saw Nicho walking toward them, the other woman following behind. Saleem instantly felt sad for the other woman. Two very handsome men were falling all over themselves over her, and totally ignoring the other beautiful woman.

What do I have that any other woman in the room doesn't? I can't see any difference between them and me. I don't like it.

Nicho reached them, and held out his hand for her to

take. She did, and they walked off leaving the man and the other woman staring after them.

Nicho put his arm around her waist when they walked off. He might not be able to bid on her, but he would hold on to her as long as he could. He had asked Vargas if he could bid at the auction, but had been told that employees could not participate in any of the auctions.

Just then, the dinner gong sounded and guests and their companions made their way to the dining hall. Again, the man was seated directly across from her and Nicho.

Saleem sighed. *How can this be? I will have to spend the whole meal again trying to look everywhere but at him.*

She felt that it was going to be a long meal, but it wouldn't delay the inevitable.

Brad took his seat across from Darcey and her escort. Vargas had again arranged for his place card to be across from them. Brad watched as she sat down. Her escort glared at him over the top of her head after she was seated.

This is going to be a fun evening, Brad thought as he watched Darcey trying to look everywhere but at him.

That pleased Brad. He made her nervous and he could see she felt something every time he had been close to her.

The meal finished, the women were escorted out of the dining hall. She turned to look for Nicho, one last look at her protector, and she saw he was watching her.

She smiled.

The women were led into the holding room, a large semi-circular room with twelve numbered doors. She guessed these doors opened to the rooms they were to stay in until the auction was over.

Alfredo was there to greet them and placed each one of them in the small room behind the numbered doors. He hesitated before cautiously escorting her to hers.

The room, if it could be called a room, was more like a small closet, maybe six feet across and about eight feet deep. There was a comfortable looking chair, in gold brocade, next to a marble topped table with a crystal lamp. On

the table was a carafe of wine and a glass, also several magazines and a couple of books. Obviously, it was going to
take a while for the auction to conclude.

⁊

Nicho watched as the women were led away. He had
wanted just one more look at Saleem before she was lost to
him forever. He saw her turn and smile back at him. It was a
sad little smile.

How foolish, for him to care so much for her. He did not
even know if she felt the same way. What did it matter
now? It would all be over in a few hours, and he would be
on his way to the south of France for his vacation. All of
this would be as if these past three weeks had never happened.

Nicho looked around for the man from Peru—Brad Daniels. Where had he gone? Nicho headed for the media room.
If he couldn't buy her, he could indeed make sure whoever
did knew the consequences if they harmed her in any way.
As he took a seat at the back of the room, he spotted the
man at a table close to the front.

The lights dimmed and the first offering of the evening
flashed on the huge screen. Numbers representing the bids
flashed in a box in the upper right-hand corner. Bidding had
started at one million and progressed from there, each bidder logged his bid electronically on the panel in front of
him, then it would appear instantly on the big screen.

However, Nicho could not see who was placing bids
from where he was sitting. He got up, went through the door
marked *Private*, and entered the hot room where all of the
bids were registered.

From here he could watch the monitors and see who was
bidding and how much.

The man from Peru had not been bidding. It was obvious
to Nicho who he was waiting for. She would be coming up

next and he was sure Peru would have some stiff competition.

Her nude images flashed on the screen. Nicho felt a stab of jealousy as a low rumble of approval went through the room. The bidding started at ten million, but it wasn't Peru, who logged the first bid. In seconds, the bid was up to fifty million, still climbing, and still Peru had not bid.

Nicho wondered what he was waiting on, not that he wanted him to win, but it was strange that he had not registered one bid so far. The bids were still climbing.

When the bid had reached one hundred fifty million, the bidding slowed. Peru logged his first bid at one hundred sixty million. The bid stayed on the screen for two or three minutes and then it went to two hundred million.

Peru logged his bid at two hundred ten million. The room had grown quite. Two hundred fifty million flashed in the box.

Nicho looked to see who the other bidder was. The bids were coming from a computer that was not in the media room. He found the monitor and he couldn't believe it. It was Vargas, bidding on his own merchandise. That didn't make sense. He could have just kept her and not put her in the auction. Peru logged his next bid—two hundred seventy-five million. Vargas recorded his next bid at three hundred million.

Brad couldn't believe it was going so high. Who was bidding against him? He still had his reserve if it came to that. He punched the keys—three hundred ten million. A soft gasp went through the room. Brad held his breath and waited.

The rules were if the current bid held for five minutes that was the winning bid. The electronic clock on the screen ticked off the minutes and seconds far too slow for Brad. Four minutes fifty seconds, fifty-one, fifty-two, fifty-three, fifty-four, fifty-five, fifty-six, fifty-seven, fifty-eight, fifty-nine—five minutes. He exhaled visibly. His bid held. He had Darcey.

Nicho could not believe she had brought so much or that Vargas had been bidding. He had to find Vargas and ask him. In the meantime, he would keep an eye on Peru. He would make sure at the first sign of anything that would hurt her, he would slit Peru's throat and bring her back.

CHAPTER 31

Going Home

Brad was still recovering from the adrenaline rush of winning the bid for Darcey when the directions for completing the transaction flashed on his computer screen. His name and bidding number had already been registered, so to complete the transaction, he typed in the information for the transfer of funds into Vargas's account. He waited anxiously as the transaction was processed, knowing soon as it was complete he would be free to collect Darcey.

Brad waited for the words *Transaction Complete. Please meet your attendant at the door.* to appear on the screen. He found the attendant waiting. Brad smiled, told him his name and the merchandise number.

The attendant smiled and gestured for Brad to follow him to the holding room. "Right this way, sir."

"You will find her in room number seven. Please have a pleasant journey home." The attendant gave a slight nod and backed out of the room.

Brad turned and looked at the door with the gold number seven on it. His heart pounded as he took a deep breath and walked toward the door. No matter how much he wanted to rush in and gather her up, he couldn't—not yet. Did he have the will to hold himself in check?

Brad had mixed feelings about opening that door, especially since she would be within arms' length at that point. Could he resist the temptation to hold her? Could he wait until she remembered who she was? Could he? He closed his eyes and ran his hand across his forehead brushing that wayward lock to the side, the indecision of the moment weighing heavy on him.

It's going to be pure torture now, much more than these past three weeks. Now she will be with me twenty-four seven. Can I resist? I have to.

His desire had to come second. No way around it. He loved her too much to risk doing anything that would push her away from him. He had lost her once through no fault of his, but now, if he rushed things and lost her, it *would* be his fault, and that was something he wasn't willing to risk.

Reaching for the gold door handle, Brad wondered what her reaction to him would be as he opened the door, and she saw who it was that had purchased her.

❧

She looked up from her book when she heard the latch on the door lift. In that split second her heart stopped.

This is it. This is the person who bought me. This is what my future holds. She closed her eyes. She couldn't look. *But, one thing for sure, I will not go quietly!*

"Hello," a soft velvet voice said to her, the voice of the man from the courtyard, from the dinners, from the talk on the sofa. Her eyes flew open. It was *him.* She couldn't breathe.

Noooo, it can't be. No, no, no! her mind screamed.

Brad gave a slight bow and extended his hand to Darcey. "Please, come with me. We have a plane to catch."

Brad waited for her to take his hand, holding himself in check, pushing down the urge to hold her, and tell her everything was going to be all right. He could see the fear as well as determination in her hazel eyes, and a fleeting glimpse of Darcey reflected there.

She placed her hand in his, hoping he couldn't feel how much she was shaking. Her hand touched his and a thousand tiny pulses of heat surged through her body. She tried to pull her hand away, but he held it tighter. Glaring at him, she took a deep breath, and reluctantly let him lead her out the door.

Her stomach churned.

ℰᎾℰᎾ

Nicho had positioned himself by the holding room door, watching as Brad went to claim her. Earlier, he had gone to see Vargas to find out why he was bidding.

Vargas had chuckled. "I noticed how much you were taken with the woman and decided to reward you for your loyalty. However, when I decided to do that, it was too late to remove her from the program. And, unfortunately, the man from Peru seemed determined to purchase her. I'm very fond of you, Nicho, but three hundred million is the limit to my fondness," he'd said with a laugh, slapping Nicho on the back. "You will find another, but, next time be sure you let me know before the auction," he said, as he walked off, leaving Nicho staring after him.

Walking away, Vargas felt guilty about not telling Nicho the truth about Saleem, but it was his and Brad's secret as to the real reason Brad was here. Vargas had only bid against Brad to make sure no one else bid. Now he was sure Saleem's daughter would be safe. He would worry about the future tomorrow.

ℰᎾℰᎾ

Leaving the holding room area, she saw Nicho standing by the door. She jerked her hand out of the man's and ran, throwing herself into Nicho's arms. She wrapped her arms tight around him and buried her face in his chest, sobbing.

Nicho put his arms around her and held her for a couple of minutes then firmly pulled her arms from around him and gently pushed her away.

He looked into her eyes. "You must go. My job is done. You are no longer my responsibility. You must go," he said softly, his voice full of pain and sadness. "I will miss you, but you will be safe where you are going, I promise."

A piece of his heart splintered off. "Noooo," she cried, pounding her fists on his chest in frustration. "You promised you would protect me, you would keep me safe." She couldn't stop the tears streaming down her face. Her heart ached as an emptiness grew inside of her. "You promised," she sobbed.

"No, I can no longer do that. You have been sold. You no longer belong here. You must go with your new owner. He will be good to you, I promise you that." Nicho pushed her arms away, took a step backward, glaring at Brad, knowing he had overheard her pleas.

Brad walked over, took her arm, and drew her close as he looked into Nicho's eyes. "She will be well-taken care of, you have my word."

Brad gathered her up, flipped her up on his shoulder, and headed for the door.

"No! Nicho, please. Don't let him take me, please." She reached back for Nicho as Brad carried her out the door. She began kicking and screaming, pounding her fists on Brad's back. "Put me down, asshole! Put me down, you sonofabitch!" *I promised myself I wouldn't go quietly and I won't.*

This is totally unexpected, Brad thought in amazement. *Who would have thought she was such a spitfire?* He chuckled to himself as he tossed her unceremoniously into the back of the waiting limo. It was a side of Darcey he hadn't seen before.

"Stay there!" he commanded. "I'll be right back. And don't think about running. The doors can only be unlocked from the outside."

Brad headed off in search of Nicho. He had to ask what her connection to him was and figure out the best way to handle the situation. He found Nicho in the foyer where he had been watching out the window as Brad had loaded Darcey into the limo.

Brad searched Nicho's face. "Nicho, I know you don't care for me. I think you know the feeling is mutual, but we do have something in common. That is we both want to make sure nothing happens to her. Am I right?"

"Yes, I suppose we do. What is it you want?" Nicho asked, running his hand through his hair.

"I know who this woman is, where she comes from, and I know who kidnapped and sold her to Vargas. I have no intention of pressing charges against Vargas, but I cannot guarantee I will be so generous with those who kidnapped her. I want this over and done with." Brad's voice held an edge of finality. He softened it. "She is very special to me, and I will do everything in my power to see that she regains her memory. What I need from you is information about your relationship with her. I can see she is very attached to you. She may even be in love with you, I hope not, but I can't tell." He watched Nicho's face as he spoke.

"Our relationship was strictly business. I was her escort and she was my charge. I would not have any idea if she fancied herself in love with me. She was just a job to me."

It was ripping Nicho apart lying to this man, but he could not allow anyone to know exactly how hard he had fallen for her.

"Thank you. I will go on the assumption that this is a one-sided affair, then." Brad was going to take him at his word, even though his gut told him different. He could see the pain in Nicho's eyes. Brad smiled as best he could, considering the situation. "I will need some form of sedatives for her in order to get her on the plane. The thought never occurred to me that she would react this way, so I did not bring any with me. If you would be so kind as to give me something, we will be on our way."

"Please, wait here. I will have Alfredo bring you some. Would you prefer tablets or intravenous?" Nicho asked, the pain in his heart constant now. He couldn't wait to leave. An unopened bottle of bourbon waited in his room.

"Intravenous, might be better."

Drugs in hand, Brad returned to the limo. He did not like the idea of giving Darcey drugs, but he could see no other way of getting her on the plane without them. She was distraught and on the verge of hysteria. He would have to have his chauffeur help give her the shot.

Bracing himself for an onslaught, he unlocked the limo door. Darcey was crouched up in the far corner of the seat, like a tiger ready to pounce. She was glaring at him, and, if looks could kill, he would have died a thousand deaths just then.

෴

She was furious when he slammed the door and left. She pounded on the windows and screamed at the top of her lungs, but no one came. She could see the chauffeur standing beside the limo, but he didn't even act like he heard her.

The damn thing is sound proof! She fumed over what had happened and wondered why Nicho hadn't come to her defense instead of pushing her away. *How could he have done this to me? Hadn't he kept me away from all of those other men? Prevented them from even touching me? So why had he turned on me now? Why had he turned cold like I mean nothing to him? Was it true? Had I just been a job? Was that what he'd been trying to tell me all along? Was that true and I just hadn't wanted to see it? How could I have been so stupid?*

Adrenaline raced through her veins.

I will get even with them, starting with this damn bozo who bought me. I will make his life hell! He will be sorry he bought me! Damn him! Damn them all!

That was where she was, crouched in the corner of the seat when the limo door opened. She sprang at him with everything she had, clawing and flaying her arms, as hard and as fast as she could.

He had backed out and slammed the door. She saw him walk over to the chauffeur and they spoke for a minute. The door opened and she was ready to jump again, but it was the driver standing there, then strong arms grabbed her from behind and held her down. The chauffeur held her legs tight so she couldn't kick. She felt a sharp jab in her arm and she drifted into nothingness.

Damn himmm…

∽∾∽

Brad covered Darcey with a light blanket and instructed the chauffeur to head to the airport. He had called ahead and scheduled ORCA's private jet to be ready for takeoff as soon as they arrived.

He pushed Darcey's hair out of her face, letting his thumb brush gently across her cheek as his hand slid down her neck. She was safe now. He picked up her hand and gently kissed the palm, then let his head fall back on the headrest. Still holding her hand, he closed his eyes.

"She's safe, she's safe," he repeated to himself, as he drifted off into a light sleep, her hand still gently held in his.

The forty-five minute ride to the airport had been all too short. Exhausted, Brad felt like he had just closed his eyes when the limo pulled up alongside the ORCA jet. The pilot signaled Brad they were ready for takeoff when everything was on board. Brad nodded and carried Darcey's unconscious, blanket-draped body onto the plane. He buckled her in and adjusted the blanket, making sure she was covered chin to toe. The pilot pulled up the stairs and locked the door.

When they were in the air, Brad called Lilly to see where

things stood. Even though they had their differences, he trusted her completely and had left her in charge of the dome while he had gone to locate and then collect Darcey. She could be trusted to do what was needed.

"Yes, everything is on schedule and it looks like we will finish on time," she said. "The virus didn't do any lasting damage. Ty and his guys are keeping a close eye on everything, to make sure no one tries to do anything else."

"Any word on the investigation as to who was behind this?"

"No, there has not been anything new about who might be behind the sabotage besides Armando. However, corporate still continues the behind-the-scenes internal investigation into the matter."

He thanked her, hung up, and looked over at Darcey. She was still out and he prayed she would stay that way until they reached the dome. She'd been traumatized enough by the ordeal of the auction and then the scene with Nicho. No, Brad thought as he gently caressed her cheek. *Please let her sleep.* But knew that was doubtful. At least one more or maybe two more shots would be needed before they reached Lima.

Transportation would be waiting at the airport to take them directly to the dock when they landed. Brad had already arranged for one of the living quarters to be ready for Darcey when they arrived.

⌘

The plane landed smoothly. Brad, cradling Darcey's limp body in his arms, carried her to the transport. The short trip to the dock found the sub's captain ready and waiting for them. Gently, Brad draped Darcey's unconscious body over his shoulder as he started down the sub's ladder. Reaching the bottom, he swung her around and carried her to the waiting bunk the captain had prepared for her. The sucking sound of the airlock sealing signaled the start of the sub's descent to the ocean's depths and the dome.

Brad squatted beside the bunk for several minutes, his eyes feasting on the beautiful image before him. He ached to feel her body next to his and to feel her lips on his. But first, he had to punish Santiago for what Santiago had stolen from her—her memory. A dark cloud of anger hung over him as he stood up and stalked out of the room.

Linking his laptop into ORCA's database, Brad accessed the files he had complied on Carlos Santiago. Quickly reviewing them, Brad noted Carlos's home was in El Carmen, El Salvador, although, other notations in the file from Interpol, stated Santiago seldom visited his residence there. Seemed he spend most of his time cruising the world, trolling for women.

The two men working for Santiago—Quin Alvarez, and Ricardo Perez—Brad had not been able to pinpoint their homes. However, he imagined that wherever Santiago might be, Alvarez and Perez would not be far away.

There was not much more information on them. From what he read, neither one had been associated with Santiago longer than two years. Their work history before that was sketchy. Neither one had been in trouble with the authorities, but both were on Interpol's Trafficking Watch List along with Santiago.

As soon as Brad had Darcey squared away in the dome, he would call Vargas to see if he had any current information on Santiago.

oↄꙅↄ

Two and a half hours later, the sub reached its destination and rose up inside the dome's sub bay. The chief of the sub bay helped Brad to load an unconscious Darcey into a shuttle. "Good luck, sir," the chief said, smiling, as he watched Brad start up the incline with his precious cargo.

There had been much speculation in the dome about the time of the arrival of Brad and his lady. There was even a rumor floating around that the guys in Operations had a pool going.

The sub-chief had notified Lilly, per her request, that Brad had arrived. She dropped what she was doing and went straight to Brad's quarters. Lilly wanted to be the first to welcome him back. In her mind, the sub-chief was nothing.

Brad saw her as he pulled up in front of his quarters.

"Welcome back, sir," Lilly gushed as much as she was capable of. "It is excellent to have you back. How is Señorita Callahan?"

Lilly could care less how the woman was, but Brad seemed to, so she would play along that she was concerned, too, as long as it did not interfere with her plans.

Brad gently lifted Darcey out of the shuttle, carried her into his bedroom, and laid her on his bed. Brushing a stray strand of hair away off her cheek, he let relief flood his body. It was over. She was home. He turned and walked out of the room, standing briefly at the door, letting his eyes soak up the image before him, then quietly shut the door behind him.

Lilly had observed the little scene from the door and felt her face twist into a scowling mask that immediately vanished, replaced by a warm smile, which greeted Brad when he turned around.

"I'm going to call Luis to see if he can help me find Santiago. Then I'm going after him," he told Lilly. "I don't know how long that will take, so I'm asking if you will look after Darcey until I get back, please."

"Yes, I will be glad to look after her. What am I to tell her when she asks questions?" she asked as bitterness seeped into her heart.

Yes, I will look after her, she thought *if she does not interfere with my plans. I am on track now, and do not want anything to derail my well-laid plans. Maybe I can dump her off on someone else, if she becomes a problem,* she decided.

"Just answer all her questions as best you can. She has no memory of who she is, so just show her around and introduce her to Ty and the boys. Her clothes should be down on the next sub. I didn't take the time to bring them down now. Just make her comfortable and try to keep her happy. I believe she likes reading, so see what we have here and send some down from up top, too." Brad reached for his phone. "Thanks, Lilly," he called, over his shoulder walking on into the living room.

Lilly followed, a scowl replaced the smile as soon as Brad's back was turned.

Keep her happy? I am not her babysitter, but I will send her the whole damn library if it keeps her out of my hair, Lilly grumbled to herself.

She turned and glared at the closed bedroom door before following Brad into the living room.

"Luis, Brad here. We're here, and now, I'm going after Santiago. I need your help in finding him. Do you have any information on his location?" Brad asked, falling into his favorite overstuffed chair and throwing his leg over the arm.

He casually waved goodbye to Lilly as she left.

"Well, right now, I do not know," Vargas said thoughtfully. "When I talked to him last week, I told him to never call me again. Give me a few hours to talk to some people and I will have an address for you. I will call you shortly." Vargas was smiling to himself as he hung up the phone. If anyone could locate Carlos, it would be Nicho. "Nicho, Luis here. I have a job for you. I need you to find out where Carlos is. I do not want you to pick him up. I just need to know where he is and what he is doing."

"How soon do you need to know? I am a little busy at the moment," Nicho said.

Vargas chuckled as he heard a woman's laugh in the background. "Well, if you can let me know within the hour, that would suffice." He laughed and hung up.

Nicho sat there staring at the phone. "Damn! I still have a week left on my holiday," he grumbled. "Leave it to Vargas to ruin it." Mumbling to himself, Nicho called his friend who had his finger on the pulse of everything that might be going on in Santiago's world. "Nicho here," he said, as the person on the other end answered. "I need a location on Carlos Santiago and what he is up to, and I need it within the hour. Call me back at this number."

Nicho hung up and poured another drink, leering at the woman lying on the bed. She wasn't Saleem, but for now, she filled his needs. Comparing every woman to Saleem only made the pain of losing her worse.

Pulling her lower lip between her teeth, the woman gave Nicho her best "I've got something for you, baby" look and slid sexily off the bed. She ambled over to Nicho and slipped onto his lap, planting a big kiss on his smirking mouth. He barely got his glass set on the table before she would have knocked it out of his hand.

Nicho was having trouble concentrating on the woman. Vargas had intruded on his holiday with business, and it peaked his curiosity why Vargas would want to find Santiago. He thought that was over and done with weeks ago. With difficulty, he tried to drag his mind back to the woman contorting on his lap. He guessed the holiday was over when business could keep his mind off a little recreational sex.

The phone rang and Nicho unwound himself from the woman to answer it, dumping her unceremoniously onto the floor.

"I have the location you wanted. He is in Lima with his two buddies. Could not find out what they were up to, though," Nicho's friend told him.

"Thanks."

Nicho called Vargas. "They are in Lima. All three are there. I can be back tomorrow if you need me to do anything," he told Vargas, watching as the woman righted herself and sexily crawled across the floor to him.

She worked her hand up the inside of his leg and to his crotch. Caressing the hardening core of his crotch, her eyes danced as she watched Nicho's eyes close and his mouth open. A small gasp of desire escaped before he could stop himself.

"No, you do not need to come back early. Finish you holiday. You deserve it." Vargas laughed heartily and hung up.

Nicho watched as the woman continued the gentle massage, her tongue running across her lower lip. Groaning, he reached down and pulled her up, his desire for her obvious. Scooping her up, he tossed her on the bed, falling on top of her.

Vargas and the job were just distant echoes now.

⁊⁊⁊

As soon as he hung up from talking with Nicho, Vargas placed a call to Angelo, one of his elite squad members he had sent to Lima to check on some of his ladies.

Vargas asked him to find out where Carlos was and what he was doing. Angelo said he would have the information for him in the morning.

Afterward, Vargas placed a call to Brad and told him to sit tight. He would have the information he wanted in the morning Morocco time.

Brad walked into the bedroom and watched Darcey's rhythmic breathing. She looked beautiful and peaceful. But, considering her state of mind when he knocked her out, he had better prepare himself for an onslaught when she woke up.

He desperately wanted to lie down beside her and cradle her in his arms, but he couldn't risk sending her into a panic. She'd had enough stress to last a lifetime. Picking up the blanket, he spread it across her. Gently caressing her cheek, he ran his thumb across her soft lips, remembering the taste of her. He turned off the light and closed the door. He would sleep on the couch.

To be continued…

About the Author

Madge Gressley lives in Missouri with her granddaughter and three dogs (Pixie, Lily, and Milo). An award-winning visual artist for over thirty years, she decided to trade her paintbrush and canvas for paper and pen—in this case, computer and keyboard—and started her writing career in 2013. She works from home where she squeezes her writing in between jobs for her graphic design business and letting the dogs in and out—a full-time job in itself.

Gressley is an accomplished, award-winning visual artist. She is a Signature Member of the Missouri Watercolor Society and Best of Missouri Hands Juried Artist. The scope of her artistic talent covers a wide range of media, including acrylic, oil, watercolor, clay, and graphic design. Her work is proudly displayed in the collections of numerous corporate and private collections throughout the United States, Great Britain, and China.

She is also co-owner and graphic designer for Art & Graphic Innovations, LLC, a Missouri based graphic design firm, and owner of MEG Originals Fine Art.

Follow Madge on Twitter: https://twitter.com/mgressley1
Facebook: https://www.facebook.com/groups/1460702867501390/
https://www.facebook.com/MadgeHGressleyArtistAuthor/
Blog: http://mhgressley.com/
Website: http://www.meg-originals.com

www.ingramcontent.com/pod-product-compliance
Lightning Source LLC
Chambersburg PA
CBHW060953120726
47910CB00002B/618